EAST OF WIMBLEDON

Nigel Williams was born in Cheshire in 1948, educated at Highgate School and Oriel College, Oxford, and is married with three children. He is the author of TV and stage plays, and several novels.

NIGEL WILLIAMS

East of Wimbledon

faber and faber

LONDON · BOSTON

First published in 1993
by Faber and Faber Limited
3 Queen Square London WC1N 3AU
This paperback edition first published in 1994

Printed in England by Clays Ltd, St Ives plc

© Nigel Williams, 1993

Nigel Williams is hereby identified as author of this work
in accordance with Section 77 of the Copyright,
Designs and Patents Act 1988

A CIP record for this book is
available from the British Library

ISBN 0-571-17151-6

For Suzan

'I shall have you hanged,' said a cruel and ignorant King to Nasrudin, 'if you do not prove that you have deep faith and wise perceptions such as have been attributed to you.' Nasrudin at once said that he could see a golden bird in the sky and demons within the earth. 'But how can you do this?' the King asked. 'Fear,' said the Mullah, 'is all you need.'

from 'The Subtleties of Mullah Nasrudi',
in *The Sufis*, by Idries Shah
(The Octagon Press, 1964)

PART ONE

'We teach here,' said Mr Malik, 'Islamic mathematics, Islamic physics and of course Islamic games – '

'What,' said Robert, feeling it was time for an intelligent question, 'are Islamic games?'

Mr Malik gave a broad wink. 'Islamic games,' he said, 'are when Pakistan wins the Test Match.'

He spread his hands generously. 'You, of course, among your other duties, will be teaching Islamic English literature.'

Robert nodded keenly. His floppy, blond hair fell forward over his eyes, and he raked it back with what he hoped was boyish eagerness. He should really have had a haircut. 'In that context,' he said, 'do you see Islamic English literature as being literature by English, or Welsh or Scottish Muslims?'

They both looked at each other in consternation. Perhaps, like him, Mr Malik was unable to think of a single Muslim writer who fitted that description.

'Or,' went on Robert, struggling somewhat, 'do you see it as work that has a Muslim dimension? Such as . . . *Paradise Lost* for example.'

What was the Muslim dimension in *Paradise Lost*? Robert became aware that the room had suddenly become very hot.

'Or,' he went on swiftly, 'simply English literature viewed from a Muslim perspective?'

'You will view English literature from a Muslim perspective,' said Malik with a broad, affable grin, 'because you are a Muslim!'

'I am,' said Robert – 'I am indeed!'

He kept forgetting he was a Muslim. If he was going to last any time at all at the Islamic Independent Boys' Day School

Wimbledon, he was going to have to keep a pretty close grip on that fact.

He had decided to pass himself off as a Muslim shortly before his twenty-fourth birthday. His father had waved a copy of the *Wimbledon Guardian* at him as Robert was being dragged out of the front door by the dog. 'Could be something worthy of you in there,' he had said, prodding at the Situations Vacant column. And, out there on the Common, on a bench facing a murky pond, Robert had read:

ARE YOU A BROADMINDED TEACHER OF THE MUSLIM FAITH? ARE YOU YOUNG, THRUSTING AND KEEN TO GET AHEAD, WITH GOOD INTER-PERSONAL SKILLS? ARE YOU UNDER FIFTY-FIVE WITH A CLEAN DRIVING LICENCE? WE WANT YOU FOR A NEW AND EXCITING ALL-MUSLIM VENTURE IN THE WIMBLEDON AREA.

It was the word 'broadminded' that had caught his eye. It suggested, for some reason, that the job might lead to encounters with naked women. There was certainly something breezily sensual about the man now facing him across the desk.

He seemed pleased to see Robert too. There was no hint of prejudice in his eyes. Robert had feared the headmaster might be a sinister character of the type given to chaining people to radiators in downtown Beirut. He had stopped watching the news shortly after the hostage crisis. In fact, these days he found that, by lying on his bed with the curtains closed and deliberately emptying his mind, he was able to forget most of the unpleasant world events that had troubled him for the first twenty-four years of his life. He was no longer quite sure, for instance, who was the current leader of the Labour Party. With serious mental effort he was hoping to achieve the same state with respect to the president of the United States, the names of the countries of central Europe and almost every geopolitical incident not located within a five-mile radius of Wimbledon Park Road.

Mr Malik grinned, got up from his desk and crossed to a large map of the world on the wall next to the window. Ruffik or

Raffik, or whatever his name was, had been taping it to the wall when Robert came in for the interview. Already one corner had come adrift. North-West Canada lolled crazily out into the room. Timber forests brushed lazily against the deserts of Saudi Arabia, as the August breeze sidled in from Wimbledon Village.

'All of the world,' said Mr Malik, jabbing his finger in the vague direction of America, 'will soon be Muslim.'

'I hope so,' said Robert, knitting his brows with what he hoped was a typical convert's expression, 'I hope so!'

Mr Malik stepped smartly to his left and looked down at the green lawn that stretched between the Islamic Independent Boys' Day School and the High Street. Beyond the wrought-iron gates, flanked by two dwarf cypresses, girls in summer dresses, their legs and shoulders bare, walked homewards, calling and laughing to each other. Mr Malik gave them a tolerant smile.

'Muslim ideas and Muslim thinking are making great strides everywhere. Even in Wimbledon. Look at yourself, for example!'

'Indeed!' said Robert.

He hoped they weren't going to get into a detailed discussion of how he had seen the light, or whatever it was you saw when you converted to Islam. If the headmaster asked him which mosque he went to, he had already decided to say that he always visited the nearest one to hand. *What does one need*, he heard himself say, *except a prayer mat and a compass?*

'Were your parents Muslim?' said Malik.

Robert blinked rapidly and said, 'Our family has been Muslim for as long as any of us can remember.'

'Since the Crusades!' said Malik.

They both laughed a lot at this. But the headmaster of the Islamic Independent Boys' Day School then leaned back in his chair, folded his arms and gave Robert a slow, shrewd glance.

'My grandfather converted during the Second World War,' said Robert. 'He served in the desert, and I think that had a profound effect on him. He was involved with the Camel Corps, I believe.'

Malik was nodding slowly. He had a big, well-sculptured

nose. Tucked under it was an elegant moustache. But his eyes were his most notable feature. They flickered on and off in his face like dark lanterns, expressing now amusement, now scepticism, but mostly a resigned acceptance of human weakness.

'You were brought up as a Muslim?'

'No, no,' said Robert hastily, 'My . . . er, father was a . . .'

Malik was looking at him steadily.

'A Hindu!'

If the headmaster was surprised at the volatile nature of the Wilson family's religious convictions, he showed no sign of it. He got up and started to pace the threadbare carpet around his desk. 'Our boys,' he said, 'are sent to us because their parents wish them to become part of British society and yet to retain their Muslim identity.'

'I must say,' said Robert, with the unusual conviction that he was speaking the truth, 'that I don't really feel part of British society!'

Malik ignored this remark. He gave the impression of a man speaking to a large and potentially hostile crowd.

'Their parents,' he said, 'want them to be lawyers, accountants, businessmen, doctors. But they also want them to be brought up in a Muslim environment. By Muslims.' He gave Robert another shrewd, appraising glance. 'Such as yourself, for example!'

He should not have worn the sports jacket, thought Robert. Or the grey flannel trousers. He should probably not have come at all.

'Are you keen on games?' went on the headmaster in his fruitily accented English.

'Mustard!' said Robert. 'Keen as mustard!'

Mr Malik savoured this out-of-date colloquialism like a world-class wine-taster. He nodded slightly and then, backing towards the window, placed his left hand, knuckles outwards, over his ribs, and his right hand, palm up, to about head height. At first Robert thought he was going to be made to swear some Islamic oath. Then he realized he was supposed to get up from his chair. He did so.

'Let's look over the facilities,' said Mr Malik, rubbing his hands, briskly. 'As the brochure is not yet printed we can't look at the brochure, can we, old boy?'

Robert found he was laughing immoderately at this remark.

Malik opened the door and waved his hand, expansively, over to the right. 'Chemistry labs!' he said.

This sounded like something out of the *Arabian Nights* – a command for the chemistry labs to appear. It certainly bore no relation to the rather shabby stretch of corridor, leading to a narrow, circular staircase, towards which the headmaster was pointing.

'Impressive!' said Robert.

Malik's eyes narrowed. Robert wondered whether this might be taken for a satirical remark. Then he realized that the head-master was doing something natural to politicians or actors – putting on a face to match some titanic thought that probably did not exist.

'Yes,' said Mr Malik, looking off into the distance. 'Yes, it will be. I can see it. It will be! It will be . . .' He paused and allowed himself a smile ' . . . mustard!' Then he was off.

They walked, at some speed, towards the other end of the corridor. From there, a more impressive staircase – square, wooden, vaguely Jacobean in appearance – led down to a hall decorated with hanging carpets and peculiar bronze objects that looked a bit like cooking-utensils. It reminded Robert of an Afghan restaurant he had once visited.

Mr Malik did have something of the *maître d'* about him. As they clattered down the stairs, he waved his hand at the far wall. 'Praying area!' he said.

Robert had read something about this. Wasn't the general idea to line up against the wall and bang your head against it? Or was that Jews?

Why was he so appallingly ill-informed about the religion to which he was supposed to belong? How long would it be before Mr Malik rumbled him? Why had he even bothered to read the damned advertisement? He should have gone back to the video shop in Raynes Park. Maybe not. He thought of Mrs Jackson's face as she returned one of the staff's bootleg copies of *Let's Get Laid in LA*. He had given it to her in good faith. It had said *Fantasia* on the box. And by all accounts the children at Barney Jackson's eighth birthday party had enjoyed it a lot. He could go back to the Putney Leisure Centre for God's sake! Some people had spoken highly of his skills as a lifeguard. No one had actually *died* in the accident. Or the Wimbledon Odeon!

He shuddered as he thought of the Wimbledon Odeon.

Malik walked along the hall, opening doors and flinging them back against the wall of hanging carpets. He barked back over his shoulder at Robert. 'Large airy classrooms for the senior boys,' he said. 'Slightly smaller rooms for the slightly smaller boys. And here – ' He came to the last door in the hall – 'a very, *very* small area that will be used to accommodate the very, very small boys during their early weeks at the Islamic Boys' Day Independent School, Wimbledon.'

He didn't seem entirely clear about the title. Was it the Islamic Boys' Day Independent School Wimbledon, or was it the Islamic Day Boys' Independent School Wimbledon? They would need to have made their minds up by the time they got the notepaper.

So far, Robert had seen no sign of notepaper.

He peered in at the last room. It was the size of a generously proportioned cupboard, with a narrow skylight in the top left-hand corner of the far wall.

'This,' said Malik in the tones of a man who was about to lock him in and leave him there, 'will be your room.'

'It's lovely,' said Robert.

'That which Allah has in store is far better than any merchandise or muniment. Allah is the most Munificient Giver!'

This was obviously a quotation of some kind. Whatever Allah was dishing out, he clearly wasn't sending a fortune in the direction of the Islamic Day Boys' Independent Wimbledon School.

Even so, the place was clearly not without funds. The school occupied a fairly large eighteenth-century house which, although its walls bulged crazily and its ceilings were pregnant with age, had a grandeur about it that suggested some old-established colonial concern. How many pupils would there be?

Robert bowed his head and tried to look like a Muslim. Mr Malik looked at him with concerned curiosity. 'Do you wish to use the facilities?' he said.

'I'm fine, thank you, Headmaster,' said Robert. Should he, he wondered, have worn a hat? A turban of some kind?

'Over there,' said Malik, gesturing towards a door on the other side of the hall, 'are the kitchens.' All Robert could see was a large porcelain sink, lying upside down in the corner of the room. It did not seem to be connected to anything.

Mr Malik waved airily at the front door. 'Language laboratories,' he said. 'Information technology – or "IT" as it is known. This is the 1990s for God's sake, Wilson!'

He said this in tones that suggested that Robert had just proposed some alternative date. *Am I looking too combative?* thought Robert as he followed the headmaster out into the rear gardens of the Wimbledon Islamic Day Boys' . . . He really must try and remember the correct word order. Did he want this job or not? The Boys' Islamic Day . . .

'Playing-fields!' boomed Mr Malik. He threw both his arms wide and closed his eyes. He was obviously seeing playing-fields. Robert saw a large, shabby lawn, bounded by a high wall. There was an apple-tree in the far left-hand corner, and, next to it, a dilapidated climbing-frame.

'We have put the gymnasium in the orchard,' said Malik, 'and hope our boys will acquire healthy bodies in healthy minds. Tell the truth, Wilson, and shame the Devil!'

Robert tried to stop himself from twitching. He did not succeed.

'As for you sinners who deny the truth,' said the headmaster, peering closely at his prospective employee, 'you shall eat the fruit of the Zaqqum tree and fill your bellies with it. You shall drink boiling water; yet you shall drink it as the thirsty camel drinks!'

'Indeed,' said Robert.

It was time, he felt, to ask a few keen and thrusting questions.

9

Interview them, old lad, he heard his father's voice say. *Make the terms yourself. Be tough, Bobbo. You're too soft on people!*

'Where,' he heard himself saying in slightly querulous tones, 'is the staffroom?'

Malik gestured to a battered wooden shed about halfway down the garden. 'The staffroom,' he said smoothly, 'is located in the Additional Science Block Complex. Science and technology are vital, Wilson. Crucial!'

The door to the Additional Science Block Complex opened, and a small, wizened man in dungarees appeared. Robert recognized him as the man who had been taping the map of the world to the wall earlier. He addressed Malik in a language that could have been Arabic, Punjabi or, indeed, Swahili. He sounded annoyed about something. Malik shrugged, grinned, and, as they turned to go back into the house, said, 'Talk English, for God's sake! We are in bloody England. Don't come on like an illiterate wog! Please!'

The man in the dungarees narrowed his eyes. He did not look as if he knew any English. What, Robert wondered, was his role in the Wimbledon Islamic Boys' Day School? Groundsman? Janitor?

'Rafiq will be giving classes in macroeconomics,' said Malik, 'and he will also be dealing with engineering. He can make *anything*. He is one of my oldest friends. Even though he is from the University of Birmingham. You are an Oxford man, of course.'

'Indeed,' said Robert.

Robert had been to Oxford. He had been there for the day in 1987. It had seemed a nice place.

'I read classics,' he said, trying to remember whether that was what he had said in the application, 'and I was lucky enough to get a first-class degree.'

This seemed to go down quite well.

Robert had noticed quite early in life that people tended to believe what you told them. Even people who were professionally suspicious – lawyers, policemen and certain kinds of teacher – were never suspicious about the right things. The only difficulty

10

was remembering what you had said about yourself, and to whom. Only the other day a neighbour had asked him how the viola recitals were going, and there was an elderly man in the village who still insisted in talking to him in Polish.

'Oh God, yes,' said Mr Malik with some enthusiasm, 'the classics! Virgil. Homer. Horace. Harriet Beecher Stowe. Longfellow.'

He was heading back towards the school. Just to the right of the back door Robert noticed four or five battered wooden desks, piled crazily on top of one another. Malik waved at them. He seemed to feel that they spoke for themselves. As they went back into the hall, he said, 'Do you have a blue?'

A blue what? thought Robert.

Malik's eyes narrowed.

Robert considered a moment, then said swiftly, 'Cricket. Rugby football.'

'Well, Wilson,' said Mr Malik, 'we will take up references, of course. But I think we may well find ourselves working together at the beginning of the first term. I like the cut of your jib!'

'Well, Mr Malik,' said Robert, 'I like the cut of *your* jib!'

'Yes indeed,' said the headmaster – 'it is not a bad jib!'

He went, with some solemnity, to a cupboard next to the door leading to the smallest of the classrooms. 'You will work here,' he said – 'with the very small boys.' From one of the shelves he took a small, leatherbound volume. With some ceremony he handed it to Robert. 'You will have a copy of this, of course,' he said, 'but I offer it as a gift. I will be in touch as regards our terms of employment.'

He stared deep into Robert's eyes.

'Payment is on a cash basis,' he said. 'I like you, Wilson. I want to work with you!'

He put his hand on Robert's arm and pushed his face so close that their noses were almost touching. 'I think you have a good attitude!' he said throatily.

Then he went to the door, flung it open and sent Robert out into the glare of the August afternoon.

It was not until he was at the door of the Frog and Ferret that

Robert looked at his present. It was an edition of the Koran, translated by N. J. Dawood. Slipping it under his jacket, he walked up to the bar and ordered a large whisky.

2

He had got it out and was looking at it furtively when Mr Malik walked in and glared fiercely around. Robert shrank behind a pillar, and, to his relief, the headmaster did not appear to have seen him. He watched, as the headmaster strode up to the bar, tapped it imperiously with the edge of a fifty-pence piece, and said, in a loud, clear voice, 'A pint of Perrier water, if you please!'

The barman unwound himself from his stool and walked over to his customer. He muttered something, and Malik, addressing his reply to the whole pub, said, 'A pint. A bottle. Whatever. I am parched!'

Robert drained his whisky and shrank down into his chair. As soon as Malik turned back to the bar, he would make a run for it. Did he have a peppermint about his person?

No.

Malik gave no sign of turning back to the bar. He had the same, grand proprietorial attitude to the Frog and Ferret as he did to the Wimbledon Islamic Day Boys' Independent School. 'My mouth,' he said fruitily to the assembled company, 'is as dry as a camel's arse!'

No one seemed very interested in this. Robert recognized Vera 'Got All the Things There' Loomis over in the corner, smacking her lips over a glass of Guinness. Over by the window was Norbert Coveney, the brother of the man who had died in the Rush poisoning case three years ago. He did not seem pleased to see Mr Malik. The barman poured two bottles of Perrier into a pint glass, with almost offensive slowness.

Malik eyed him hungrily and then, with a theatrical flourish, turned back to the almost deserted pub. 'Give a poor wog a drink, for Christ's sake!'

The inmates of the Frog and Ferret did not respond to this. Although, thought Robert, from the look of them they would not have been much impressed had Malik yanked out his chopper and laid it on the bar as a testament of his good faith. Standing by the door with a pint of porter in his hand was Lewis Wansell, the downwardly mobile dentist, popularly known as 'Die Screaming in Southfields'. 'They work all hours,' he was saying, to no one in particular. 'They come here and they work all hours. What chance do we have?'

The headmaster turned his back on the company, applied his lips to the edge of the glass, and sucked up his mineral water.

Robert rose and started to tiptoe towards the door. 'Hey,' said a voice behind him, 'you forgot your book!'

Mr Malik turned round just as Robert got to his table. Robert, wondering whether it was a punishable offence to bring the Koran on to licensed premises – let alone leave it there – scooped up the volume and walked towards his new headmaster. He ducked his head as he did this, widened his eyes, and flung open his arms. This was intended to convey surprise, delight and a dash of Muslim fellow-feeling. As it was, he felt, he gave the impression of having designs on Mr Malik.

'We meet again,' he said.

Mr Malik did not smile. He nodded briefly. 'Indeed.'

Robert held the Koran up to his face when he got within breathing distance. The sweet, heavy smell of the whisky climbed back up his nostrils.

'I'm always leaving this in pubs,' he said, waving the sacred book, rather feebly.

This was not what he had meant to say at all.

'I mean,' he went on desperately, 'quite often, in the past . . . I . . . er . . . have left it in pubs. In the hope that people will . . . er . . . pick it up and . . . read it. Rather like the Bible.'

'Do people leave the Bible in pubs?' said Mr Malik, in tones of some surprise.

'They leave it in hotels,' said Robert – 'the Gideons leave it in hotel bedrooms. And I shouldn't be surprised if they left it in

14

pubs. Or even carried it round and sold it. Like the Salvation Army magazine.'

The headmaster was looking at him oddly. Why, having made a mistake, was he busy elaborating on it? Then Mr Malik said, 'Have a drink, Wilson, for God's sake. We are friends, for God's sake. Have a pint, my dear man! Have a pint of beer!'

This offer surprised Robert considerably. As far as he was aware, this was not the kind of thing devout Muslims were supposed to say to each other. Perhaps it was a trap.

'Just a Perrier for me,' he said, rather primly.

Malik winked broadly at him. 'Righteousness,' he said, 'does not consist in whether you face towards the East or the West. I myself am having a bottle of Special Brew.'

Robert coughed. If this was a trap, it was a carefully prepared one. Once you had said you were a Muslim, could they do what they liked with you? Was it a case of one sip of Young's Special and there you were – being stoned to death in the High Street?

'Just the water please, Headmaster,' he said. Mr Malik gave a broad and unexpected smile. It gave him the appearance, briefly, of a baby who has just completed a successful belch. *'Headmaster!'* he said. 'That is what I am!'

He snapped his fingers. The barman gave him a contemptuous look and ambled off in the other direction. A small, leathery-faced man was waving a five-pound note at him from the other end of the bar.

'They serve the regulars first . . .' said Robert.

'They serve the white chaps first,' said Mr Malik – 'and who can blame them?'

The barman finished serving the leathery-faced man. He gave Mr Malik a measured stare. He looked at the headmaster as if he was an item he was trying to price for a jumble sale. After a while he walked back towards them.

'A Special Brew, a Perrier water and a large Scotch for my friend,' said Mr Malik.

Robert gulped.

'Isn't that what you were drinking, old boy?' said Malik.

'I was . . .'

15

How did he know this? Had he made a special study of infidels' drinking habits?

The headmaster was looking up at the mirror above the bar. Robert followed the direction of his gaze. He found himself looking at the reflection of a man in a shabby blue suit, who was peering into the pub from the street. Apart from the fact that he had chosen not to wear a tea towel on his head, he bore a sensationally close resemblance to Yasser Arafat. Behind him, in a slightly less shabby blue suit, was a man who looked like a more or less exact replica of Saddam Hussein. Both men had two or three days' growth of stubble on them, and both were wearing dark glasses. This could explain why they seemed to be having trouble making out what was going on in the interior of the Frog and Ferret.

Both men seemed to be hobbling slightly. Perhaps, thought Robert, as they pressed their noses to the glass, they had been involved in some industrial accident. They looked as if they had been working together, for years, on the same, grim production line.

Their effect on Mr Malik was profound. He looked like a man who has just opened a packet of cornflakes and been greeted by a Gaboon viper. Ignoring the barman, he reached out for Robert and squeezed his forearm. Without turning his head, he said, grimly, 'Well, the Wimbledon Dharjees are upon us.' He carefully knitted a crease into his forehead. 'And not, I fear, the best type of Dharjee!'

Robert wondered whether the two men were brothers and this was their surname. Wasn't a dharjee something you ate, like a bhajji or a samosa?

Mr Malik started to move away along the bar, keeping his face, as far as possible, away from the visitors.

'Hey!' called the barman.

'Gentlemen's lavatory,' hissed Malik. And before anyone had time to question him further he was gone, moving with surprising speed for a man of his size.

Just as he left, the two men opened the door and started to hobble their way towards the centre of the room. It was only

16

now that Robert was able to see what was making them limp: both were wearing odd shoes. Robert's first thought was that this might reflect some kind of financial crisis in the immigrant community in Wimbledon. But then he noticed that each of them, on his right foot, was wearing what looked like a slipper. Not only that. As they moved into the pub they both stopped from time to time and wriggled their right feet anxiously. Did they suffer from some form of verruca, some ghastly mange that affected only the toes of the right feet?

When they reached the bar, the man without the tea towel on his head pushed up his glasses and peered round. He had small watery eyes. With his glasses on his forehead you got to see more of his nose. Yasser Arafat, Robert decided, was better-looking.

'Can I get you anything, gents?'

Yasser Arafat sneered. The barman sneered back. Then both men came over to where Robert was standing.

'A beer? A glass of wine?'

Both men ignored the offer of service. This was more or less the reverse of the usual situation in the pub. The barman screwed up his face into a tight ball. With a shock, Robert realized he was trying to smile.

'A soft drink of some kind?'

Saddam Hussein leaned his elbows on the bar and, looking sideways at Robert, said, 'I see you know the man called Malik. The big man. We know his business. He teaches here in Wimbledon.'

His appearance and delivery gave the impression that he had got this information from some oasis a few hundred miles south of Agadir. It suggested, too, that he was not looking for the headmaster of the Wimbledon Islamic Boys' Day Independent School in order to offer him a low-interest mortgage or a new kind of double glazing.

Robert decided to reply cautiously. 'Is he,' he said, 'a friend of yours?'

This seemed to amuse Yasser Arafat. 'Malik,' he said crisply, 'is a slug and a blasphemer!'

His friend leaned his head over his shoulder and cleared his throat loudly. The barman's mouth dropped a notch and he started to ask, in hostile tones, whether both men breezed into their own living-rooms without buying a drink.

'He is,' said his companion, 'excrement.'

This seemed a little harsh to Robert. There was, he had to admit, something not entirely trustworthy about the headmaster, but to call him 'excrement' was, surely, to overstate the case.

'He is,' said the man without a tea towel on his head, 'the vomit of a dog!'

For a moment Robert thought Saddam Hussein was going to spit on the floor. But his eye had been taken by the book, now lying on the counter of the bar. He looked at it suspiciously. 'What is this?' he said.

Robert coughed. 'It's the . . . er . . . Koran.'

They did not seem impressed. Perhaps he had not pronounced the word correctly.

'I haven't actually . . . er . . . read it yet,' he went on, brightly, 'but I intend to in the very near future.'

He had rather hoped that the book might provide a talking-point. But, if anything, its presence seemed to intensify the men's suspicion of him. He did not feel it prudent to tell them that he had just embraced the Muslim faith, partly because he was not sure that they *were* Muslims and partly because he was afraid they might ask him what he was doing with a large whisky and a bottle of Special Brew. Robert's voice died away.

'This is the Koran?' said the man who looked like Yasser Arafat.

'It is indeed!' These men, Robert decided, could not possibly be Muslims. Muslims would, surely, have felt the need to express some enthusiasm at finding an English punter leafing through it. 'And from everything I hear it's quite a book. It's had enormous . . . er . . . influence . . .'

It was fairly obvious that he was telling them nothing new. In fact they were looking at Robert, as people tended to do, as if he had some satirical intent.

The man without a tea towel on his head reached forward and touched the book with his index finger. He withdrew it very quickly, as if the volume carried some electrical charge. 'I have learned this book by heart,' he said.

'Good Lord,' said Robert, 'why did you do that?'

This was obviously the wrong thing to say.

'He carries it in his heart,' replied the second man, 'and he speaks its truth to all who will listen. To those who will not listen he does not speak.'

'Very sensible,' said Robert.

'He cuts them as he would slit the throat of a chicken.'

'Fair enough,' said Robert, 'fair enough!'

Malik seemed to be spending a long time in the lavatory.

The barman seemed now almost pathetically anxious to please the new arrivals. He was rubbing his hands and smirking. It was clear to Robert that the best way of getting service out of him was to look as if you were about to gob on the floor. He seemed to be trying, not at all successfully, to attract their attention.

'This is what one day will be done to Malik and those he serves!' said Saddam Hussein. 'He will be dragged in the dust and he will be pierced with knives. This will happen to those who serve him also.'

Perhaps, thought Robert, these men were from the Merton Education Authority. There was a clattering sound from out by the gentlemen's lavatory.

'You know him?' said the man without a tea towel on his head.

'I'm afraid I don't. Not *know* exactly . . .' said Robert.

'I think you do,' said Saddam Hussein. 'I think you will be a teacher at the Islamic School. I think you are Wilson. I think you live in Wimbledon Park Road. I think you are a hypocrite Muslim!'

News certainly travelled fast, thought Robert. He had only sent the application in on Monday. How could they possibly know these things?

'We have read your application,' went on Saddam, 'and we

know about your sports abilities. But we do not think you write like a true believer!'

'It will be a school for pigs and blasphemers,' went on his friend, 'and all who teach in it will die.'

'We are all going to die,' said Robert, as cheerfully as he could.

'Tell your friend,' said Saddam Hussein, 'that we are watching him. And we will watch you also.'

'OK,' said Robert.

'And tell him,' the man went on, 'that we have something that will make him and his friends ashamed to face the daylight. Something that, when our people read it, will make him and his friends crawl through the dung!'

Robert tried to keep very still. The man's face was now pressed closely into his. He smelt sweet and musky. *I should probably investigate alternative ways of making a living as soon as possible*, thought Robert.

'When the time comes,' the man was saying, 'we shall distribute this among our people. They will read and understand. And then, when the time of his Occultation is over, the Imam will come to us.'

The man who should have had the tea towel on his head was rummaging in his jacket pocket. It occurred to Robert that he might be looking for a gun.

Eventually the man pulled out a small parcel and set it on the bar, a few inches from Robert's copy of the Koran. He looked into Robert's eyes. 'When you see Malik, give him this box. Let him read and understand that he will die. And that all who serve him will die. And that the staff and pupils of the Wimbledon Islamic Independent Boys' Day School will burn in hell-fire when the day comes. And we know the day, my friend! It is coming!'

Robert was about to protest, once again, that he had only just met Mr Malik. But these men seemed worryingly well informed about aspects of his life about which even he was vague.

The first man made a complex, guttural sound and pushed

the box towards him. Robert picked it up. It was wrapped in green paper.

'If I see him,' he said, 'I'll do that.'

The man grabbed him hard by the wrist. He was breathing hard. 'You will see the Imam, but the Imam will not see you. Because, as it is written, hypocrite Wilson, the Imam sees not as we do! This, too, tells you you will be consumed in the fires of hell that do not cease!'

'I'm sure,' said Robert. 'I'm sure!'

Everyone will burn in hell-fire when the day comes, he reflected, as he walked out into the glare of the street, but the day, for Jew, Christian and Muslim, has been a hell of a long time coming.

3

When he got home, he found his parents making a cassoulet. This was slightly better than finding them making love, or in the middle of an argument. They did all these things with a great deal of noise and enthusiasm.

'What have you been up to today, Bobkins?' said his father.

Robert stared out of the window at the featureless lawn. Badger, the family's lurcher, was sitting in the middle of it, staring hungrily at passing flies.

'I got a job,' he said.

His father looked at his mother. They smirked at each other. Mr and Mrs Wilson were always convinced, each time their son took a new job, that this one would, in Mrs Wilson's phrase, 'lead to something.' She was, in a sense, right. She had been positive that Renzo's the Delicatessen was going to lead to something, although she could not have predicted that the 'something' was going to be the loss of Mr Renzo's thumb in the slicing-machine. She had been positive that Bearman and Studde, the estate agents, were going to lead to something, and, although Mr Bearman's suicide was not quite what she had had in mind, there was no doubt that Robert's presence in the firm had, in Mr Bearman's own words, 'changed it, changed it utterly!' Disaster had a way of following him. That was why for the last nine months he had stayed indoors as much as possible.

They beamed at him now from across the kitchen.

'What . . . er . . . is the job, exactly?' said his father.

Robert looked back at him cautiously. Both his mother and father encouraged him to use their Christian names, but calling them Norman and Sylvia had never helped him to feel more intimate with them. Nor had it helped to quell the guilt he felt every time he saw their eager little eyes brighten at the sight of their only son. He knew he was nothing to be proud of – why didn't they?

'I'm going to be a teacher,' he said.

'Great stuff!' said Mr Wilson senior, as he chopped a red onion into a frying-pan. 'I'd give my right arm to be able to teach. They do *such* an important job! And they're not really appreciated, are they?'

'You would be a marvellous teacher, Robert,' said his mother, 'and it's marvellous they've seen that without asking for all those stupid qualifications!'

'Qualifications!' said Mr Wilson senior, shaking the frying-pan violently. 'Who needs 'em?'

Norman Wilson, as he was fond of reminding people, had no qualifications. This could have been why the accountants for whom he had worked for twenty years had, early last year, asked him to leave. He did not seem worried about not having a job. 'I've got the redundo, old son,' he used to say, 'and now I can get on with my writing.' No one in the family knew what he was writing, apart from the occasional cheque.

Robert's mother walked swiftly towards the fridge. For a moment he thought she was going to grab it by the handle and throw it over her left shoulder, judo style, but at the last moment she veered off to the left and, grabbing a tin of haricot beans, trotted towards the door that led to the garden. Out on the lawn, Badger reared up, his face wild with excitement.

'No, no, no!' screamed Mr and Mrs Wilson, in perfect synchronization. 'Go away! Go away! Go away! Bad dog!'

Badger sat down again. He looked depressed.

'What will you teach, exactly?' said Robert's mother.

'English,' said Robert, 'Greek. That kind of thing.'

'Do you know any Greek?' said his father.

His mother was coming back, now, towards the sink. On the way she had acquired a corkscrew and a bag of potatoes. She threw the potatoes, viciously, on to the worktop. Out on the patio a small breeze stirred her geraniums.

'I picked up a bit,' said Robert, 'when I worked at the kebab place.'

They both seemed impressed by this.

'What kind of school is it?' said his mother.

Robert wondered how much to tell them. He decided that they were not quite ready for the Wimbledon Boys' Islamic Independent Day School. He would break it to them gently over the next few months.

'Oh,' he said, 'it's for boys. Small boys. Not big ones, as far as I can make out. And it's new. I'm getting in on the ground floor.'

His father pulled hard at the cutlery drawer. The handle came away, easily and smoothly. The drawer stayed where it was.

'Who built this kitchen?' said Mr Wilson senior. Nobody answered this question. With a sigh, Robert's father placed the handle in another drawer, picked up a carving-knife and began to attempt to lever the drawer open. This activity seemed to calm him.

'That girl of yours is waiting for you in your bedroom.' He turned to his only son and gave a suggestive wink. 'I wish I had young girls waiting for me in my bedroom!' he said, squatting on his haunches in front of the drawer and driving the knife in deeper. There was a splintering sound from inside the kitchen unit.

Robert's mother looked at him, a dreamy expression on her face. 'It seems only yesterday,' she said, 'that you and Maisie and Philip Chung and that Schnitzler boy were working for your GCEs. In this very kitchen!'

Philip Chung and the Schnitzler boy had, of course, managed to get some GCEs. Philip Chung and the Schnitzler boy had moved away from Wimbledon. As had the Borrage brothers, Susie Parsons, Linda Haddock and Janet Fitzpierce who did it with anybody. Only he and Maisie were left. Was it really eight years since he had left Cranborne School?

As he clumped up to his room, he thought about Maisie.

Of all the projects he had started, none had been more enthusiastically taken up by his mother and father than Maisie.

24

The daughter of local advertising man, Marco Pierrepoint, she was thought by many people in Wimbledon to be beautiful. There were those who said she was too plump. Gary Brisket, the music scholar, who had gone to Cambridge and never come back, always maintained that 'she had the biggest jacksie in SW19,' but, like many other boys in the neighbourhood, he had walked out with her for a while, and, when she told him she was in love with someone else, had cried, briefly, behind the pavilion at Cranborne School.

She was always falling in love. If not with people, then with things. One week she would be a vegetarian, the next a passionate student of the French troubadours. For months last year she had visited a gym in Putney every day, announcing her intention of 'building up my pectoral muscles'. She had only just stopped in time, thought Robert, as he peered at her through a crack in the bedroom door – her breasts were already the size of Rugby balls.

We're like brother and sister, Bobkins. That was what she always said, however much his mother winked, nodded and leered every time Maisie came to the house. If they were brother and sister, he said to himself, as he stood there on the landing, taking in that smell she had of pepper and vanilla and lily of the valley, he had been horribly close to incest for the last eight years. He stood for a moment outside his room, sniffing hard.

'Is that you, darling?' she said.

'Afraid so,' said Robert.

She had a flowery look about her too, he thought as he studied her through the crack in the door. He never really got the chance of a good look when he was in her presence. Maisie liked you to put in a great deal of work when talking to her; Robert was always too busy pulling funny faces or staring deep into her large, black eyes to appreciate what was on offer.

'Are you peering at me again?'

'Sorry.'

As he came into the room, Maisie rose and offered him her left cheek. Robert swooped in. As his lips made contact, her scent exploded in his nose.

'Mark's left me.'

'Oh *no!*'

'He has.'

She sat back on the bed and began to cry.

Robert wondered whether to put his arm round her shoulder. It seemed a rather forward thing to do. He had, after all, been in the room for over a minute. Physical contact with Maisie was usually limited to arrivals and departures. Perhaps he could embrace her and then rush out of the room muttering something about a previous engagement.

Her shoulders were heaving. Her large breasts shook under her crisp, white blouse. Robert put his hand carefully round the back of her head and landed it, as tactfully as possible, on her right shoulder. When it was clear she wasn't going to nut him or knee him in the groin, he gave the shoulder a little tug, and ten stone of Maisie fell against him, her long, black hair brushing against his face.

'I loved him so much . . .' she said.

'Yes,' said Robert – 'he was a really nice bloke.'

This didn't sound quite right somehow. Which one was Mark anyway?

Maisie started to laugh and groped for a handkerchief in her bag. 'He was a *bastard*, you *idiot*,' she said. 'He was a complete *sod!*'

'Why?'

Her voice had a note of genuine irritation as she said, 'Because he left me, stupid.'

Robert remembered Mark now.

'He was in the Air Force, wasn't he?'

Maisie was giving him a peculiar look.

'Or was it the Territorial Army?'

She started to laugh again. To try to prolong her mood, Robert took from his jacket pocket the parcel intended for Mr Malik.

'What's that?'

Maisie's eager, greedy eyes had begun to sparkle.

'Is it a present? Is it for me?'

26

'Of course,' said Robert. 'Of course it's for you.'

'Oh, Robert,' said Maisie, 'you are *sweet*!'

Robert wondered whether to take his hand off her shoulder. He did not trust himself to do so. The area between armpit and thigh, smelling as it did of soap, perfume and clean linen, was not one where he felt able to sustain the fiction of a brotherly embrace.

'Can I open it?'

'Of course, darling.'

She gave a little squeak and grabbed the box.

Maisie was experienced at unwrapping presents. She crooked her index finger under the string and yanked hard. As the string broke, the green paper fell away and the two of them found they were looking at a beautifully inlaid box, about the size of a packet of Kleenex. It was decorated with whorls and loops in what looked like ivory, but the material of which it was made, though it felt like polished wood, was probably something more valuable.

'Oooh, it looks valuable!' said Maisie. 'Is it onyx or something? Is it a valuable box, Bobkins?'

'It is a very valuable box.'

He coughed nervously.

'And what's in it, Bobkins? Is it just the box, or is there a bracelet in it? Is there a lovely bracelet in it?'

Robert wiped his forehead. 'There might be,' he said in paternal tones. 'Let's see, shall we?'

There might, of course, given the nature of the man who had given it to him, be animal excrement in there . . . or a poisonous tarantula . . . or . . .

'It's precious stones!' gasped Maisie as she slid her long, polished nails between the lid and the case, trying to force it up. 'It's joolery! Say it's joolery, Bobkins!'

'It might,' said Robert, 'be jewellery.'

There were those in Wimbledon who said that Maisie was spoilt. Her father was always giving her things. When he had been made creative director of Swan & Jenkins, he had bought her a car. She had run it into a wall after two weeks and had never driven again. There were those who said that, now she was in her twenties, her father should stop addressing her as 'the sexiest little princess in Wimbledon Park Road'. It was widely agreed that she should not sit in Pierrepoint's lap quite so much. There were those who said that she had been given too much, too often, too young. But it was impossible not to give her things – her pleasure in them was so fierce and childish.

Suddenly the lid sprang up. They found themselves looking at a silver locket, face down, wreathed in the same designs as the cover of the box. Underneath it was a roll of paper. At first Robert thought this must be wrapping, but, as they leaned their heads into the box, he saw that it looked more like medieval vellum than anything else. It was covered with writing.

'Oooh,' squeaked Maisie, 'is that Arabic?'

'It is,' said Robert in an authoritative voice. 'That is actual Arabic writing.'

It certainly looked like the stuff you saw outside halal meat shops in the Shepherd's Bush Road. And if it wasn't, Maisie would not be likely to know. Her father had managed to find her a job in the rare-prints section of Sotheby's, but, although she had been there nearly a year, she still seemed invincibly ignorant about all forms of calligraphy.

'What does it say?' said Maisie, clearly under the illusion that the early stages of conversion gave one unusual facility with the language of the Koran.

'It says,' said Robert, trying to look as if he was familiar with the incomprehensible squiggles, 'that you are more beautiful than rubies and that the dawn is not equal to your eyes. And your breasts are like . . . er . . . sand-dunes.'

Maisie looked suspiciously from the manuscript to Robert. 'I'm not sure I like the sound of that. Is that all it says?'

'It's a poem by a well-known Arabic poet,' went on Robert.

'What's his name?'

'Hoj!' said Robert, after a long pause.

'I think I've heard of him,' said Maisie, as she reached for the locket and started to scratch her nails into its side. Maybe, thought Robert, there was something nasty in the locket.

'It's a love-poem. Written in the tenth century, and it compares the beloved to the stars in the sky and the . . . er . . . Zaqqum tree and says her thighs are like . . . pistons!'

'Did they have pistons in the tenth century?' said Maisie, who was having no luck in her attempts to open the locket.

Robert, who was now getting quite involved with Hoj's love-poetry, ignored her. He was about to give her the details of Hoj's brief and unsatisfactory life in and around Baghdad a thousand years ago, when she gave a quiet shriek. The locket had flown open to reveal a black-and-white photograph of a boy of about ten years old. He had a thin, sensitive face, with black hair brushed neatly in a parting, such as you saw above the faces of British children of the fifties. On his right cheek was a huge strawberry mark. He was wearing a neat white shirt and, rather oddly, considering the rest of his appearance, a pair of dark glasses.

Maisie did not seem to like him being in her locket.

'Who's he?' she said, accusingly. 'Did you get it in an antique shop?'

The simple thing would have been to answer 'Yes.' But Robert was unable to resist a more complex response.

'It's a traditional Arab gift,' he said. 'When you're fond of someone, you give them a picture of a little child.'

Maisie looked at him oddly. 'For luck, sort of thing . . .' she said.

'That's it,' said Robert.

'Like Joan the Wad the Cornish Pixie?'

'Exactly like Joan the Wad the Cornish Pixie!'

She was still not happy about this. Her voice was anxious as she said, 'And he's just . . . *any* child. He isn't someone you know, is he, Bobkins?'

'It's just a custom,' said Robert – 'like . . . kissing under the mistletoe.'

'Oh, you are sweet. I don't want to know *what* it is. I just want to know it's from you and it's because we're friends and that in spite of all your problems we love each other. How much was it?'

Robert winced slightly and put his fingers to his lips. Maisie flung both her arms round him and kissed him full on the mouth. She looked up into his eyes. 'Sometimes,' she said, 'I wish you weren't gay.'

Robert wondered whether this was the moment to tell her he wasn't. The only trouble with this would be explaining why he had said he was in the first place. He could not, for the life of him, remember why he had told Maisie he was a practising homosexual. Maybe he hadn't. Maybe it had been her idea.

Thinking about it now, as she sprawled across his pink duvet, her black hair in an artful pool beside her, he decided it was probably Maisie's idea. She had most of the ideas in their relationship. If you could call it a relationship.

'Is it still just casual sex?' she said – 'in parks and so on?'

Robert shook his head vigorously. 'I'm through with all that. I want a serious relationship now.'

Who with? her expression seemed to say. Her eyes narrowed slightly as she moved down the bed.

'This boy in the photograph . . .' she began, rather sharply.

'Absolutely not!' said Robert, primly. He just managed to suppress an urge to tell her that he went in for older men. Especially those involved in the outdoor life. *Lumberjacks*, he almost heard himself say – *anything with broad shoulders and hairy legs!*

A year or so ago, just after she had broken up with Guy Hamilton-Barley, he had planned a spectacular conversion to the opposite sex. They had had dinner in an Italian restaurant in Wimbledon Village, and Robert had told her he had been having erotic thoughts about women. She had replied, rather briskly, that although they looked like women they probably weren't.

There was another of those silences between them. Maisie put her head to one side and watched him carefully. She clearly expected him to say something interesting. 'I love Robert,' she would say to mutual friends – 'he's so *funny*!' Robert had never thought of himself as funny. When people laughed at things he said, which they quite often did, he usually took it as a personal insult.

What could he say to interest her?

'I'm thinking,' he said, eventually, 'of becoming a Muslim.'

She seemed to like this idea. 'I think that's wonderful, Bob-kins,' she said. 'I think that's absolutely wonderful. Will it involve travel?'

'I don't think so,' said Robert.

He was beginning to find this conversation oppressive. You would have thought she would have put up a bit more of a fight for Christian values. He got to his feet and went to the window. The German next door was mowing his lawn. Beyond him the Patersons were playing tennis against the Joneses. *Why couldn't they find another way to compete with each other?* thought Robert. *Like – who could jump off the highest building head first.* Over to the left, a huge plane-tree, dulled by the August heat, cast dappled shadows on his father's lawn. Badger was lying on his back doing complicated cycling movements with all four legs. As Robert watched, the dog righted himself, shot out his tongue to the left of his snout and chomped his jaws together smartly.

He had never planned on staying in Wimbledon. He had always thought, somehow, that, like his friends and contemporaries, he would go somewhere glamorous and far-away. York, say, or Brighton. He had applied, years ago, to a polytechnic in North Wales. They had not even replied to his letter. He was still here, eight years after leaving school, in the beautifully kept room with the pink duvet, the twenty or thirty paperbacks and all the loving tributes to his childhood. *'We're the lost generation!'* Martin Finkelstein, the clever boy from South Wimbledon, used to say. *'We're the children of the eighties! We have no hope!'* At least Finkelstein had gone on to get a scholarship to Cambridge. Maisie and Robert were people who had even managed to go missing from the lost generation.

He felt just as much a Muslim as he felt like any of the other things he occasionally owned up to being.

'There's a guy called Malik,' he said. 'He's sort of my spiritual mentor. I'd like you to meet him.'

It was only as he said this that Robert realized that he really did like Mr Malik. Almost more than anyone he had met in the last five years. Not that he had met many people in the last five years.

'I'd love to meet him,' said Maisie. 'Is he young?'

It occurred to Robert that he had absolutely no notion of Mr Malik's age. He could have been anything from twenty-five to fifty. Was this, perhaps, in part due to his religion?

'Is he Pakistani?' said Maisie. 'I adore Pakistanis! Is he like Imran Khan?'

'I'm not sure what he is,' said Robert. 'He's not English, that's for sure.'

Except that there was something quite incredibly English about Malik.

Maisie was peering at the manuscript. 'Read me a bit,' she said in the slightly bossy squawk she acquired whenever she was genuinely excited.

Robert screwed up his eyes and gestured to the first page. 'All that,' he said, 'is about your breasts. Or her breasts, rather – Hoj's woman's breasts.'

Maisie looked at the letters dubiously. She held the manuscript out in front of her at arm's length. 'I suppose,' she said, 'you have to hold it upside down or back to front in order to read it. They do write back to front, don't they?'

'They do,' said Robert crisply, anxious to get off the subject of Arabic, 'but I quite often read the Koran in English.'

Maisie's eyes flickered. She seemed impressed. 'You're really serious about this, aren't you?' she said.

'Very serious,' said Robert, whipping Mr Malik's Koran from his jacket pocket. 'I never go anywhere without a copy of this. Believe you me, it makes quite a read!'

Maisie shook her head in something like wonder. The most interesting thing about Robert, up to this moment, her face seemed to suggest, was his impression of John Major. But now . . .

Robert flicked through the Koran's pages. It looked pretty

menacing stuff, even viewed at high speed. It also seemed worryingly long.

'You're not reading it backwards!' cried Maisie, in an accusing voice, 'you're holding it the right way up!'

'It's in *English*!' said Robert.

Not that reading it upside down or back to front would, as far as Robert was concerned, have made much difference, as he riffled through snappy chapter headings like 'The Blood Clots', 'He Frowned', and one entitled simply 'Sad'. There seemed to be four pages devoted to the Greeks, and a useful subsection on 'Kneeling'. Once again he found himself wondering whether he had the necessary stamina to be a Muslim, even an imitation one.

As he put the book down, the doorbell rang. He heard his mother's steps in the hall and then heard her clear, confident voice call up the stairs.

'There's a man here with a package for you, darling!'

With a sense of foreboding he could not quite explain, Robert tiptoed out on to the landing. A small man in a motor-cyclist's helmet was waiting at the door, holding a large brown-paper parcel. The fact that he looked as if he came from the Middle East did not disturb Robert particularly. But he found, as the messenger came into the hall, that he was checking the state of the man's footwear carefully, and was absurdly relieved to discover that he was wearing the same kind of shoe on both feet.

4

'Robert's thinking of becoming a Muslim,' said Maisie, brightly, over the dinner table.

After a brief, horror-struck pause, his father said, 'That's terrific!'

'Yes,' said his mother with alarming speed, 'it is terrific! It's great! It's wonderful!'

'Yes,' said Maisie, 'isn't it?'

Robert's mother helped herself to cassoulet.

'What are you going to call yourself?'

'Ahmed,' said Robert.

'Are you allowed cassoulet?'

'I'm not sure,' said Robert – 'I'll have to check.'

He heaped two pork sausages on to his plate and added some beans, a hunk of bacon and three or four stewed tomatoes. His father was splashing wine into Maisie's glass. '*If I ever had a daughter*,' Mr Wilson used to say, '*I'd like her to be like Maisie!*' Badger approached the head of the Wilson family and gave him a deep and soulful look. Mr Wilson gave him a carrot.

Next to Robert on the table was a package. On the outside he read, in clear, firm capitals:

FROM THE ISLAMIC BOYS'
DAY INDEPENDENT WIMBLEDON SCHOOL.

Underneath this were a few Arabic letters and under them, in quotation marks, the words, LET US WORK TOGETHER. In the top right-hand corner of the parcel was a large, printed message, warning people that it contained valuable documents. Someone had sellotaped the package together and someone else had torn off the Selloptape. Inside were a few sheets of paper.

As his mother and father heaped cassoulet on to their plates, Robert took out the first sheet. This was headed simply:

BROCHURE

Under this he read:

Muslim values and Muslim tradition are everywhere in ferment. We read in many newspapers of the need for Muslim schools, but we have to ask *What kind of Muslim schools? Are they to be a narrow, sectarian enterprise that only succeeds in alienating an already alienated Muslim population from a country where, like any immigrant community, it wishes only to belong?*

Next to this, in capitals that could only be Mr Malik's, he read:

I.E. NO LOONIES NEED APPLY

Robert read on as Maisie forked food into her face. Robert's father was asking her whether her father was any better. Maisie was telling him, in a cheerful, brightly inflected voice, that Mr Pierrepoint was not expected to live beyond October or November. 'We rather hoped he'd be around for Christmas,' she was saying, 'but it looks as if not, I fear. Although that may be for the best. He *loathes* Christmas.'

Robert spilt a small amount of gravy over Mr Malik's next paragraph.

The Independent Boys' Day School (Wimbledon Islamic) will provide a fully comprehensive education in the background of a supportive and caring Muslim environment. Although the medium of instruction will be English, and skills for dealing with the UK will be taught (we all are aware, I feel sure, of the 'Old Boy' network) we orientate our classes around a fully comprehensive awareness of the need to achieve in UK terms and yet maintain a wholly authentic, if modern, Islamic identity.

35

Next to this, Malik had written:

> I.E. GET THE LITTLE BASTARDS SIX 'A' LEVELS
> AND A PLACE AT OXFORD AND CAMBRIDGE.

Robert's mother was telling Maisie that it was wonderful that she had such a sense of purpose in life. Sotheby's, she was saying, must be a wonderful place to be. 'You are surrounded, my dear,' she went on, 'by beautiful things!' She looked, mournfully, at the men in her family as she said this. 'Some young people,' she continued, looking at Robert, 'just seem to *drift*.' Robert kept his eyes on the brochure. Badger sidled up to him and placed his long head on Robert's left knee. Robert gave him a bean.

> English literature and the classics will be taught by Dr Robert Wilson of the University of Oxford, a 'Varsity' man who is also a practising Muslim and has adopted the name of Yusuf Khan.

Next to this Malik had written:

> HOW DOES THE NAME GRAB YOU? I THINK
> IT HITS THE RIGHT TONE BUT WE CAN
> CHANGE IT IF YOU PREFER.

> Alongside him will be 'Rafiq' Ali Shah of the University of Birmingham, who will teach macroeconomics, engineering and practical artwork, and a fully qualified, all-male teaching core of experienced Muslims.

Robert's father was peering over his shoulder. Robert adopted a Quasimodo-like stance, hugging his plate to his chest as he turned over the page.

Lightly glued to a thick sheet of cream woven paper were several black-and-white photographs, clearly lifted from the pages of magazines. There were pictures of classrooms and laboratories, and one of a large, well-equipped gymnasium. A tall Indian-looking boy was balancing on his hands, watched by a group of rather suspicious-looking men in white coats. A caption underneath read ST EDWARD'S SCHOOL, BOMBAY. At the bottom of the page was a photograph of an Olympic-size swimming-pool. Malik's text read as follows:

Classrooms and laboratories offer the student the chance to grow and learn, in a pleasant and relaxed environment, while our swimming-pool will enable those who wish to 'swim' to do so whenever they feel the need. But we will also be mindful of the need of boys to fulfil the five obligations placed on Muslims, including, of course, the daily prayers, which will be an integral part of school life. The school's own mosque – built with funds supplied by the National Bank of Kuwait – will supply this!

Robert turned over the page. He found he was looking at what looked like a full-colour reproduction of the Taj Mahal. Next to it, Malik had written:

ACTUAL LIFE-SIZE OF PREMISES. SERIOUSLY
THOUGH, BASIC FUNDING IS IN PLACE BUT
ALL IDEAS WELCOME.

Underneath the photograph he had proposed the following text:

Financial backing for the school has been made available by Mr Shah, a leading figure in the Wimbledon Dharjee community. Mr Shah is a prominent local businessman whose interests include the 'Sunnytime' newsagent's and confectioner's and a tandoori restaurant in Raynes Park.

There were no other photographs on this page. Instead there was a raggedly typed series of paragraphs, headed:

STAFF BIOGRAPHIES
MALIK, J. (BA OXON, FIRST-CLASS HONOURS IN FRENCH, ENGLISH AND MATHEMATICS)

Mr Malik's family are from Pakistan but he was brought up and educated in the UK at Eton and Oxford, where he founded his successful company CORPORATE PRODUCTS LTD, now trading as RECESSION BUSTERS. He is a member of the Diners Club.

There was a space underneath this next to which the headmaster had written DASHING PHOTO OF SELF HERE! Underneath this was the photo of himself that Robert had enclosed with his application. It made him look more than usually like a tapir.

YUSUF KHAN ('ROBERT WILSON', MA OXON, FIRST CLASS IN CLASSI-CAL LANGUAGES. RUGBY FOOTBALL AND CRICKET BLUE)

Yusuf went to Cranborne School, Wimbledon, and is a recent convert to Islam. He is twenty-four years old, a fine games player and a dedicated teacher of the young! He wrote to us, asking to be included in our venture as follows –

With a thrill of horror, Robert recognized a (slightly doctored) paragraph from his letter of application:

I am a practising Muslim, based in Wimbledon, who is keen to develop my interpersonal skills in relation to other Muslims. I have taught at several non-Muslim schools and am keen to work with others of my faith in a supportive and fully Islamic environment! Wilson is six feet two inches, fond of opera and married with six children.

Next to this Malik had written:

I HOPE YOU LIKE THE OPERA IDEA. AND ONE OF US HAS TO BE MAR-RIED. IT MIGHT AS WELL BE YOU! I WANT TO DO A MAILSHOT OF ALL PARENTS WITH ISLAMIC NAMES WHOSE CHILDREN FAILED TO GET IN TO CRANBORNE SCHOOL. URGENT WE TALK RE THIS. POSS CHANGE NAME OF SCHOOL? LOSE REFERENCE TO ISLAM? I AM ANXIOUS FOR A BROAD BASE, WILSON. YOUR VIEWS, PLEASE, SOONEST!

The final staff biography read:

'RAFIQ' ALI SHAH (MSC BIRM UNIV.)

'Rafiq' is a close personal friend of Mr Malik and has been

closely involved in the Foundation Trust for the Islamic Boys' Wimbledon Independent School. He is a talented and modern-thinking scientist, with a great flair for doing and making practical things, from furniture to jewellery! He will be taking the boys in all aspects of crafts and sciences. 'Rafiq' also hails from the Wimbledon Dharjees, a group distantly related to the Nizari Ismailis, whose full history is available in a pamphlet written by Mr Shah, our patron, entitled FROM BAGHDAD TO WIMBLEDON. A BRIEF HISTORY OF THE WIMBLEDON DHARJEES!

Mr Malik had not been sure about this last sentence. He had crossed it out and, next to it, written:

'BRIEF' IS SOMETHING OF AN UNDERSTATEMENT. THE BOOK IS TWO THOUSAND PAGES LONG AND NOT RECOMMENDED TO ANYONE OUT OF SOLITARY CONFINEMENT. REMIND ME TO 'CLUE YOU IN' ON THE WIMBLEDON DHARJEES!

Next to Rafiq's name he had written:

POSS NOT MENTION RAFIQ'S BACKGROUND HERE. CERTAINLY NO PIC-TURE OF THE UGLY BASTARD. WE DO NOT WANT LOONIES!

No, thought Robert grimly, they certainly did not want any more loonies. His mother had always told him that he had no grip on reality. He wondered what she would have to say about Mr Malik.

Someone had clearly opened the package after Mr Malik had finished with it. It wasn't just the broken seal that told him that: there were grimy fingermarks across the photographs that could not possible belong to neat, well-perfumed Mr Malik. Could this be something to do with the two men in the Frog and Ferret? They certainly had an unhealthy interest in and knowledge of Robert's involvement with the school, and they looked like men who would have few qualms about intercepting people's mail.

'Won't you get involved in fatwas and things?' Robert's mother was saying. 'They can get awfully steamed up can Muslims, can't they?'

Robert found he had started to sweat. He rearranged his face, rather primly, and said, 'People in the West are very ignorant about Islam.'

He certainly knew nothing about it whatsoever. Everyone at the table, he realized, was looking at him. People always seemed to want him to speak, and he tried to oblige in his usual manner – by saying the first thing that came into his head.

'It isn't just about going down to the mosque,' he went on, in a stern, authoritarian voice.

'What *is* it about?' said Maisie, her eyes shining.

People certainly sat up and listened when you told them you were a Muslim. It was a talking-point.

'Well,' said Robert weightily, 'as far as I can make out – and it's early days yet – it's about . . .'

What *was* it about? His father was looking at him in that eager, doggy way in which he looked for exam results, sports results, girl results and all the other results Robert had not, so far, been able to deliver.

'It's about . . .' he began again.

Perhaps if he waited long enough he would receive some kind of divine guidance on this essential point. It did not, however, seem to be forthcoming.

'It's about the fact that Allah is . . .' he groped for the right word – 'very important. He is absolutely crucial. He is a . . . well . . . er . . . God!'

His father nodded, keenly, anxious not to interrupt his son's flow. 'I think,' he said, 'that Al-Lah is the Arabic word for "God"!'

'Is that right?' said Robert, trying not to sound too surprised by this fact. 'Well, of course, I am rather new to it. You probably know as much as me. More, probably!'

Mr Wilson shook his head and gave a slightly superior smile. 'Muslim . . . Christian . . .' he said. 'What's the difference basically?'

This seemed to have brought them full circle. As Robert was not able to enlighten anyone on this point, he contented himself with a kind of shrug.

Mr Wilson, who was showing worrying signs of being well-informed about the Islamic world, went on, 'The thing Muslims are very hot on is the Koran. They look at it morning, noon and night. They can't get enough of it. It is to them the *crucial* book!'

Robert's mother clearly felt her son was being upstaged. She cleared her throat delicately, smoothed her greying hair, and looked at Robert, as she often did, as if he was a nervous dinner guest whom she was determined to encourage.

'What's the Koran *like*?' said his mother. 'And how did you get involved with it? Did someone give you a copy on a station or something? A sort of missionary? Or was it someone at the door?'

Robert paused. Then he said, 'I just . . . er . . . picked it up,' he said – 'in a bookshop. And found it . . . you know . . . unputdownable!'

He didn't think they looked ready to be told about the school. His mother was gulping air, rather fast, and patting down the back of her hair – something she did only when seriously concerned. And his father's attempt at bluff, common-man-style interest in his son's conversion could not conceal the rising panic in his eyes.

'You should read it,' said Robert.

He, too, should get around to reading it – preferably in the fairly near future.

'They chant it,' Mr Wilson senior was saying, 'from the top of those high buildings they have. Will you be doing that? Do they have any of them in Wimbledon?'

'Any what?' said Robert's mother, with a little sniff of disapproval as she rose from the table and started to clear away the plates.

'Any of the tall things Muslims shout from in the mornings,' said Mr Wilson. 'I doubt they have any of them in Wimbledon.'

'There are *masses* of Muslims in Wimbledon,' said Robert's mother, 'but I've never seen them shouting from high buildings. At any time of the day. There were hundreds of them at Cranborne, and they were all very well-behaved.'

She looked, darkly, at Robert. 'They did very well in exams,' she said, as she stacked the plates on the sideboard. Then she turned to the group at the table, and, putting a hand, rather theatrically, to her close-cropped hair, said, 'Shall we have coffee on the *terrasse* and look at the garden?'

She was always saying things like this. She was never happier than when moving guests around her house in the interests of gentility. No sooner had you got comfortable than she was urging you to take *digestifs* in the conservatory, or *biscuits* on the lawn, or *gâteaux* on the roof. She pirouetted, briefly, in the middle of the wooden floor and waved a hand towards the upper part of the house. *'En route, mes braves!'* she said.

Mrs Wilson would have been happier in Versailles than in Wimbledon Park Road. But she was making the best of it.

'Ça sera superbe, chérie!' said Mr Wilson, rising bravely to the challenge of her French. 'That was absolutely *delicious!'*

Her food was always delicious. Her judgements always sound. Her dress sense always impeccable.

How did people manage to be happily married? thought Robert, as they trooped up the stairs. What was the trick of it? A dedicated cultivation of a certain kind of insensitivity, presumably. Years and years and years of managing not to notice things that might annoy you.

The Wilsons' *terrasse* was a wrought-iron balcony, jutting out from the back of their corner house. It afforded a view not only of the garden but also of a large group of communal dustbins belonging to the flats that overlooked their house. It also, as Robert's father was fond of saying, offered an unlimited chance to enjoy the advantages of a burnt-out car, a large concrete shed with the words CHELSEA WANKERS written on it and the street that led away from all this, up the hill to a part of Wimbledon the Wilsons had never been able to afford. Not that it had stopped them dreaming – Mr Wilson had expected promotion right up until the moment he had been made redundant.

They had only just sat down when a car screeched round the corner, climbed on to the pavement, and stopped a matter of inches from a neighbour's garden wall. It was a silver Mercedes, about the size of a small swimming-pool, but its bodywork was badly rusted, and the engine sounded as if it was trying to absorb a few kilos of iron filings. It roared ambitiously, then died. The driver's door opened to reveal the headmaster of the Wimbledon Islamic Independent Day School (Boys).

He looked anxious. He almost ran towards the Wilsons' house, then stopped, with a theatrical flourish, just short of it and, shading his eyes with his hand, looked up at the balcony.

'Wilson!' he said, in deep, urgent tones. 'Wilson! You must come! You must come now, Wilson! Urgent school business! Wilson!'

Robert found he was getting to his feet. Maisie, for some reason, was doing the same. She moved to the iron railing at the edge of the balcony and peered down at Mr Malik like a keen student of aquatic life who has just spotted a new species of tropical fish.

'Bring your wife, Wilson,' said Mr Malik, 'and also your children if necessary. But come! I beseech you! I beg and implore you! Come!'

Mr Malik was stretching out his arms. He looked like a man about to fish out a small guitar and continue this conversation to musical accompaniment.

Robert's father and mother were both, in different ways, narrowing the distance between chin and neck, a gesture that, like tortoises, they often used when threatened. His father was making rapid, worried clicking noises at the back of his throat as he too rose and moved – in a racially tolerant manner – towards the edge of the balcony.

'Is he . . . one of . . . *them*?' whispered Mrs Wilson, with the kind of clarity actors affect when playing a deathbed scene to a large theatre.

Robert, as he made his way down to Mr Malik's car, followed by Maisie, did not attempt to answer the question. He would have described Mr Malik, to almost anyone, without being quite sure why he was doing so, as '*one of us*'.

43

5

Mr Malik beamed at Maisie, and rubbed his hands together briskly. 'You have a beautiful wife, Wilson!' he said.

'Oh, we're not married,' said Maisie, swiftly. 'I'm just a very, very old friend of his. Are you Robert's spiritual mentor? You see Robert needs help, because he's –'

Before she had the chance to say anything more about their sex life, Robert grabbed her arm and steered her towards the car.

'What's the problem, Headmaster?'

'We are going to collect a pupil!' said Malik.

This, Robert felt, was somewhat alarming news. It was, after all, the middle of August. He had assumed, from the deserted look of the school, that, like every other educational establishment in England, they were on holiday. Perhaps, he thought, as he and Maisie got into the back seat, the Islamic school year was different.

'We have to go to them if they won't come to us, Wilson,' said Mr Malik, who was watching Maisie with some interest. 'We have to get out there and pitch!'

Robert felt nervous. For some reason he did not like the idea of Mr Malik being so close to his territory. And he liked even less the fact that his employer seemed prepared to adopt Maisie. He found himself wondering where the headmaster might live. Did he, perhaps, live above the school? He gave the impression of a man who had simply appeared in the middle of Wimbledon, like a djinn in a fairy story.

'Who is he?' hissed Maisie. 'Is he a mullah?'

'I don't think so,' whispered Robert, in reply – 'or if he is he keeps very quiet about it!'

It was also, thought Robert, a bit late in the day to be starting lessons. Perhaps the Islamic Wimbledon Boys' Day Independent School was going to be working a night shift.

Maisie turned to Robert. 'I think he's *sweet*!' she shrieked quietly.

Malik ignored the remark, but put one large, well-manicured hand up to his hair. The back of his tropical suit, Robert noted, was powdered with dandruff.

'Are we going to pick all the children up ourselves,' said Robert, 'or will some of them get to school by public transport?'

'A school,' said the headmaster, giving him a curious glance, 'can develop in various ways. The majority of the boys will obviously arrive under their own steam – although, Wilson, I have to say that at this particular point in time we do not have any boys!'

He gave a rather mad laugh as they drove, at some speed, up Wimbledon Park Road towards the Village. To their right was the All England Lawn Tennis and Croquet Club. As they passed its steel gates Robert felt the usual surprise that such a monument should be there at all. Although its windows caught the sun, and behind the barbed-wire-crested wall you could see the military green of its oval stands, it had the air of some sinister scientific research establishment – a place designed for something darker than tennis.

'Although the school is not fully operational,' said Mr Malik, 'we will collect this boy now.'

He turned round and looked Maisie full in the face, as he accelerated towards an oncoming lorry.

'His parents wish us to "hang on" to him until we are ready to go. He has fallen under harmful influences and needs the support of a typically stable "UK" background. He can stay with you, Wilson!'

This seemed a slightly unusual way of proceeding. Robert had never heard of a school in which pupils were acquired on a door-to-door basis. But, of course, education, like so much else these days, was a business.

'He is a very intelligent boy,' said the headmaster, as if in answer to Robert's unvoiced doubts, 'which is why I want to get my hands on him at double-quick speed. I think I am going to give him a scholarship.'

'Oooh!' said Maisie, who seemed to have no problems adapting to the curious pace of life in the Boys' Wimbledon Independent Day Islamic School. 'What in?'

They had somehow survived the lorry. They were now headed, at about fifty miles an hour, for someone's front garden. Malik bashed the horn two or three times, took his hands off the wheel, and waved his arms expressively. He braked hard, and the car hit the kerb and bucked across the road like an angry horse.

'Oh,' he said, 'physics, Greek, Latin, French. That sort of thing. A general scholarship. He is a first-class boy.'

'How did you find him?' said Robert. 'Did you advertise?'

Malik laughed in an open, friendly manner. He rapped on the horn as if to emphasize his good humour.

'Precisely, Wilson!' he said. 'I advertised. I put an advert in *Exchange and Mart*!'

He seemed to find this thought very amusing. When he had reasserted control over the Mercedes, he said, in a suddenly sober voice, 'Actually, Wilson, that is not at all a bad idea.'

He paused, as if considering something.

'I must tell you something, my dear Wilson,' he went on, 'about the extraordinary history and traditions of our Wimbledon Dharjees. I am sure you have seen them about the place.'

'I'm afraid,' said Robert, 'I haven't.'

'They are a very fine bunch of chaps,' said Mr Malik thoughtfully – 'not unlike the Bombay Khojas. But of course based in Wimbledon as opposed to Bombay. They are distantly connected to the Nizari Ismailis, of whom I am sure you have heard.'

Robert tried to look as if he had heard of at least some of the people Malik had mentioned.

'But,' went on the headmaster, 'there are bad eggs amongst them, as there are everywhere. Strange secrets and stories from the dawn of the Islamic era!'

Robert nodded.

'That,' said Malik, 'is all you really need to know. Some of the Dharjees are first-class chaps and others are really awful ticks. I will tell you which ones are which.'

When they reached Wimbledon Village Malik drove north, towards the large houses that face the Common. About half a mile further on, he turned right through a pair of huge iron gates. As they came in to the front drive, the gates closed, silently, behind them. Something made Robert look up at the window above the front door.

A young man was wagging his finger at an elderly woman in a white headscarf. He looked as if he was telling her off about something. She cowered away from him as if he was about to strike her.

'That's the bloody woman!' said Mr Malik. 'Been filling the boy's head with a lot of absolute rot!'

These were obviously Dharjees to be avoided. Assuming they were Dharjees and not Khojas or Ismailis. Whatever any of these things might be.

'Do you know the parents?' said Robert.

'Very well,' said Malik. 'They are professional acquaintances. We play golf together when we can get the chance.'

The front door of the house opened and two men in dark-grey suits came out. One of them looked more like a well-tanned version of the Duke of Edinburgh than a man from the Indian subcontinent; in profile, Robert decided, he would look well on a postage stamp. He half expected him to call for polo ponies. His companion was a small, round, jolly-looking character. The taller of the two called, in aristocratic English tones, 'My dear Malik! This is so kind!'

They walked towards him, in almost perfect step.

'This is *frightfully* good of you, Malik,' went on the tall man, 'and I am so sorry to bother you with our troubles!'

'There are lunatics, my dear Shah,' said Malik darkly, 'everywhere.'

'My dear, there are,' said the tall man. 'And the sooner we can get the boy lodged away from our people the sooner it will die down.'

He beamed at Robert. 'We are delighted to have an Oxford man on board,' he said. 'You must have been up at the same time as the Crown Prince of Dhaypur!'

'I think I remember him,' said Robert cautiously. He was aware that this must be Mr Shah, the school's principal backer. It was important to make a good impression.

'We always called him "Lunchtime Porker"!' said Mr Shah.

Mr Malik laughed, and it seemed wise to do the same.

'There were quite a lot of us Muslims up at Oxford,' said Robert, 'and we all used to hang out together. Go to the same clubs and . . . er . . . listen to the same sort of music.'

They were looking at him oddly. Why had he opened his mouth?

The tall man's demeanour would not have been out of place at Greyfriars Public School. There was a peculiarly English reserve about it. But Mr Shah's friend was obviously more in touch with his emotions. In the manner of a man who had been waiting to do this for some time, he suddenly seized the headmaster, lifted him clear of the ground, and rocked him backwards and forwards. Robert could see Malik's neatly shod feet pedalling wildly as his new friend hoisted him up higher and higher. Perhaps he was going to put him over his shoulder and burp him.

'Wilson,' said the headmaster, 'this is Mr Shah, our benefactor, and another member of the Wimbledon Dharjee community, Mr Khan. Mr Khan is here on business.'

The second man put the headmaster down and grinned. 'I am a vastly inferior variety of Dharjee,' he said, 'and I am honoured to meet you, Wilson! Mr Shah, I fear, will have nothing to do with my proposals! You are welcome at my restaurant at any time of the day or night. Except on Wednesdays.' Mr Shah was looking vaguely discomforted. Mr Khan, right arm forward, marched towards Robert.

To Robert's relief, the man did not look as if he was about to give him anything less formal than a handshake.

'Should I cover my head with something?' hissed Maisie.

'Why?' said Robert. 'I think you look very nice.'

48

Maisie looked impatient. 'I'm a woman,' she said, 'and I've got bare arms and a bare head!'

She said this as if trying to excite him in some way. Before he had the chance to find out any more about this, she had backed away towards the car, opened the back door, and started to grovel around on the seat.

If she was looking for something to cover her head, she was out of luck. As far as Robert could remember, all there was on the back seat was a damp chamois leather. The thought of Maisie appearing with this perched on her head made him twitch uncontrollably.

Neither Malik nor Mr Shah nor Mr Khan seemed very bothered about this. Mr Khan, the restaurant-owner, seemed to have decided that a handshake wasn't enough. He was clearly anxious to get stuck into Robert in a more serious way.

'Oh, Wilson, my dear chap,' he was saying, in a tone of voice that made Robert feel like a jelly at a children's tea party – 'Oh, Wilson, Wilson, Wilson! You will be friends with a poor restaurateur, won't you?'

He leaped into Robert's arms and got to work on his hindquarters, watched with some embarrassment by the Duke of Edinburgh look-alike.

'Are you . . . er . . . Dharjees?' said Robert through a mouthful of Mr Khan's jacket. Both men laughed uproariously at this. Robert made a mental note to find out more about this particular Islamic sect. It was hard to connect the two men in the pub with these two rather jolly creatures.

'Where is my teacher?' came a small voice down to Robert's left.

Robert looked down and saw a boy of about ten years old. He had neatly brushed black hair, a dark-blue jersey and baggy grey shorts of the kind worn by boys at an English public school. He was standing very straight and very still.

There was something strikingly familiar about him. Robert felt sure he had seen him somewhere before. That, surely, wasn't possible. He knew very few adults and hardly any children. Had he, perhaps, seen this boy on television? Perhaps he was a prince of some kind. What had Malik said: 'fallen under harmful influences'?

'Hello there!' said Robert, in a jolly, yet formal, voice. He was trying to sound like a schoolmaster (on his application he had claimed four years' service at a fictional prep school called The Grove) but he had not yet managed to acquire the manner. He sounded, he thought, like a paedophile. To make things worse, he discovered he had put his hand on the boy's shoulder.

'Are we going to have all Dharjees, or will there be any normal Muslims?' he asked, to fill the awkward silence.

Mr Malik and Mr Shah gave him tolerant, slightly weary, smiles.

'Normal Muslims!' said the school's benefactor, in an amused tone. 'I think we are *fairly* normal Muslims, don't you, Malik? I think it is you that is the "weirdo"!'

'Wilson,' said his headmaster, 'is a comparatively recent recruit.'

Mr Shah nodded in a kindly manner. 'What made you convert to Islam?' he said, in the studied, neutral tones of someone asking someone else about their children.

'Er . . .' Robert looked wildly about him. 'I was desperate!' he said eventually.

Mr Shah took his hand. 'These are desperate times, Wilson,' he said – 'desperate, desperate times. A spirit walks the land, and it is an ugly, intolerant spirit, and many of us are frightened – frightened unto death!'

'I am desperate,' said Robert, looking over towards the Common. (Had he seen a glimpse of one of the men in the pub, there, among the birch-trees about a hundred yards away from them?) 'I am absolutely desperate. I am thinking of going to Mecca.'

All three men nodded slowly. They seemed sympathetic to the idea. Robert tried to remember where Mecca was. He was going to have to bone up on this kind of fact if he was going to be able to hold his own in this section of the Wimbledon beau monde.

'We are talking fifty a week for the boy,' said the restaurant-owner. 'He eats anything apart from cheese.'

Robert nodded and tried not to look confused. He had not thought that the school fees would be so reasonable. Perhaps there was a special offer on. Perhaps they were going to wait for the school to become fashionable and then treble the prices. Anything was possible at the Independent Islamic Wimbledon Boys' Day School.

'He is called Hasan,' said Mr Shah, 'after a great ruler of the Ismailis!'

He knelt to the little boy's level and put his hands on the lad's shoulders. He patted his face.

'Hasan I Sabah,' he said, 'and Hasan the Second. On his name be peace!'

Then he embraced the child. 'You are Hasan of our house!' he said, in a low, gentle voice. 'Go with Wilson.'

Robert looked down at the little boy. He was still standing absolutely still. His thin shoulders, his delicate wrists and his finely drawn neck gave him a lost air. Something about him made Robert's heart lurch. The boy turned his head, and Robert caught sight of a huge strawberry mark on his right cheek. Now he remembered where he had seen him before. The hair, the features, even the slightly desperate, pleading stance of the shoulders, were those of the boy in the photograph in the locket that he had given to Maisie only that afternoon.

It wasn't only this, though, that chilled him suddenly, made him feel, for reasons he could not have explained, unaccountably nervous. The little boy was oblivious to the sun, and the blue sky, and the terraces of thick, green leaves on the chestnuts that faced the house. He was not wearing glasses, as he had been doing in the photograph, and now Robert was able to see that his big, pale pupils were jammed uselessly in the porcelain of his eyes, staring endlessly at nothing.

6

Perhaps, thought Robert, as they climbed back into the car with
Hasan, he had simply failed to notice an adjective in Malik's
prospectus. Perhaps he was going to work in the Wimbledon
Independent *Blind* Islamic Boys' Day School. Or – this seemed
rather more likely – Malik was having to take what he could get.
His manner to Mr Shah had been positively servile.

'Don't you want to wave goodbye to your dad?' Robert asked
his new pupil.

'Mr Shah is not my "dad",' said the little boy, in a curiously
precise voice. 'I am an orphan. I am brought up among his
servants. I think I speak for his servants. For all the poor of the
earth!'

The headmaster cut across them. 'My dear Hasan,' he said,
with more edge than Robert had seen him use before, 'you have
been listening to that nurse of yours!'

'I can't help listening to her, Mr Malik,' said Hasan, 'because
she talks to me.'

The little boy sat, quite still, between Maisie and Robert. One
frail hand rested on Maisie's knee. She seemed confused by
him. She had not found anything to cover her head or her arms,
but Mr Malik seemed to find this situation quite satisfactory. In
fact, as he studied her in the driving-mirror, Robert could have
sworn the headmaster was licking his lips.

Robert patted Hasan on the knee. He felt the need to say
something reassuring.

'Well,' he said, with slightly forced cheerfulness, 'we are all in
the hands of Allah!'

The little boy wrinkled up his face. Maybe the Dharjees were
such a specialized variety of Muslim that they had not yet

caught up with Allah. Someone would certainly need to tell him before he started at the Boys' Wimbledon Day Independent Islamic School. Or possibly, once again, Robert had slipped up on pronunciation.

'I presume,' he said cautiously, as they started down the hill, 'that the majority of the pupils will be . . . you know . . . your basic . . . Muslim.'

Mr Malik grinned. He seemed to find this line of approach immensely amusing. 'Who knows?' he said.

'Well,' said Robert, 'there can't be much demand for . . . er . . . Islamic games among non-Muslims!'

Malik grinned again. 'Who knows?' he said.

Here he winked at Maisie.

'They're very fatalistic,' she hissed. 'It may not be the will of Allah that you get any Muslim pupils. You may get coachloads of Unitarians or people who really wanted to get into the Royal College of Music. But you can't do anything about it. It's fate!'

Malik nodded vigorously. 'Your wife is right,' he said. 'What is willed is willed. We simply have to do our best. In fact, some Islamic theorists think it makes bugger all difference anyway.'

The car leaped round a corner, scraped a lamppost and bounced sideways down towards Robert's house. There was, thought Robert, a lot to be said for a religion that relieved you of all responsibility for your destiny. Especially when you were being driven by Mr Malik.

'I could eat a cake,' said Hasan, in a small, thoughtful voice, 'with jam on it.'

No one offered to respond to this remark.

Robert leaned forward across the passenger seat. 'Tell me, Headmaster,' he said. 'Those men in dark glasses in the pub – '

Malik did not seem keen on this line of conversation. 'My dear Wilson,' he said, 'don't even think about them. If they come up to you in the street, cut them dead. They are NOSP, if you take my meaning. Not Our Sort of People!'

He caught Maisie's eye in the driving-mirror and gave her a broad wink. 'My dear girl,' he said, before Robert could finish his sentence, 'are you also of the Muslim faith?'

'It seems,' said Maisie breathlessly, 'a very attractive option.'

Malik grinned. 'It is,' he said. 'It is an attractive option. It is, I would say, very *user-friendly*!'

Maisie nodded. 'Yes,' she said. 'It has a rugged, masculine feel to it!'

Malik's hand went up to his neatly combed hair. He patted it into place with a small smile. 'It is not,' he said, 'a religion for softies!'

'I'm amazed Bobkins sort of embraced it,' said Maisie, 'because you see he is a practising – '

'Catholic!' said Robert. 'I mean I *was* a practising Catholic!'

'Catholics, Buddhists, Muslims – you Wilsons have got the lot, I would say, my dear boy,' said the headmaster as he jammed on the brakes and the Mercedes jerked to a halt outside Robert's house.

Hasan jumped off the back seat like a puppet on a string. He made a small, whooping noise. As far as Robert could tell he had enjoyed the experience.

Malik leaned his arm across the passenger seat and looked into the back with intense frankness. 'I want you to look after Hasan, Wilson,' he said, 'because Hasan is a very, very important little boy. I do not want you to let him out of your sight. Do you understand?'

Robert gulped. 'He will be staying with . . . er . . . me?' he heard himself say.

'That is correct, Wilson,' said the headmaster. 'There are people who are trying to . . . get to him, if you take my meaning.'

Perhaps, thought Robert, other schools were trying to snaffle him. Scholarship boys were obviously a valuable commodity. The boy quietly sat between Robert and Maisie. He was not very large. They could put him in the back kitchen with the dog.

'Right, Headmaster,' said Robert.

'And,' said Malik, 'even when you are in the house, watch him carefully.'

Robert looked apprehensively at Hasan. Was he, perhaps,

liable to violent fits of temper? Could he have a serious incontinence problem?

'Look,' said the headmaster, 'I am sure I am worrying about nothing. I've simply seen something I probably did not see. But, for the first few days anyway . . . keep him away from windows.'

'On religious grounds?' said Robert. Perhaps Dharjees were against windows.

'Absolutely,' said Malik. 'Absolutely. On religious grounds. And if anyone comes asking for him at the door, or comes up to you in the street and expresses an interest, you haven't seen him. Right?'

'Right!' said Robert.

'Especially,' went on the headmaster, 'those gentlemen in the pub.'

'With the peculiar shoes,' said Robert.

Mr Malik wrinkled his brows and gave Robert one of those swift, shrewd glances that hinted at a complex, subtle person behind the actor's manner. 'You noticed that, did you?' he said. 'There is probably no significance in it. After all, my friend, we are the other side of August the eighth!' And with this inexplicable remark Mr Malik leaped from the car, opened their door, and, like a chauffeur, bowed them out on to the street.

Robert trudged up the steps to the front door, after Maisie and Hasan. Mr Malik got back into the car. Robert turned back towards him but, before he had a chance to say anything, the headmaster had driven off towards Southfields.

There was quite a lot that Robert wanted to ask. Had they acquired this pupil by entirely legal means? Where were the other pupils going to come from? What was so dodgy about August the eighth? And what was the problem with windows as far as Muslims were concerned? Were they, perhaps, unclean?

Robert added one more biggie to that list as he turned back to Maisie and the little boy. How was he going to explain away the arrival of a ten-year-old blind Muslim boy in his parents' house? Not to mention the fact that Hasan seemed to be looking for house-guest status for an unspecified period of time. Mr and

Mrs Wilson were almost irritatingly tolerant people. They had been kind when Robert had failed all of his GCEs apart from woodwork. They had not minded when he failed to pass his driving-test or, indeed, when he failed to show any aptitude for anything apart from walking round Wimbledon Common with Badger. But on this occasion he might well have gone too far.

'Isn't he *sweet*?' said Maisie.

'Will you give me some tea?' said the little boy. 'And a cake with jam on it?'

Robert looked down at his new charge and felt as if he was falling through space.

The boy took his hand and pressed it to his face. 'You are a kind man,' said Hasan. 'I can hear it in your voice. I can tell a great deal from people's voices.'

'What can you tell from mine?' said Maisie.

The little boy paused. 'You are a very wise woman,' he said. 'You are very strong and clever and brave.'

Clearly Hasan's voice test was not an infallible guide to a stranger's personality. Or maybe he just said this to all the girls. But there was something impressive about him. He could have been very clever, or very well born, or very, very lucky. Or, possibly, simply *look* as if he might have been any of these things. But there was something about him . . .

As usual, Robert had forgotten his key, and, as usual in the Wilson house, no one was answering the door. Somewhere deep inside the family home, Robert heard his father shout, 'I'm on the lavatory!'

'*I'm* on the lavatory!' came his mother's voice, making its normal, easy transition from gentility to an almost bestial direct- ness of approach. 'They'll have to wait!'

'It might be someone interesting!' yelled his father.

Whatever he was doing in the lavatory didn't sound very demanding.

'Surely you've finished by now!' yelled his mother. Over the years, the two men in the Wilson family had made so many inroads into her natural delicacy that now, at nearly fifty, she would sometimes seem to parody maleness, to flaunt it at its

56

possessors, in an attempt at that last, desperate act of criticism – sarcasm.

'Get your arse on down there,' she yelled – 'only make sure you wipe it first!'

Robert heard his father guffaw. They still had the capacity to amuse each other, even if they left him stone cold.

Before this conversation could become any more specific, Robert leaned on the bell, hard.

'I'm coming!' yelled his father. 'Hold your horses!'

Hasan, his head and shoulders still eerily still, was smiling in a benign manner at the letter-box. He continued to hold Robert's hand tightly. Robert tried to look natural, and failed.

'He's coming!' said Hasan, 'I hear him!'

There was a clumping sound from within the house. The door opened, and Robert found himself, once again, looking at his father. He took in the long, shaggy hair, the wire glasses, the beaky nose and the slightly anxious expression. Mr Wilson senior always looked as if he had just remembered that he had forgotten something. This was, indeed, quite often the case.

It was possible, he thought to himself, that his father would never work again. In which case he, Robert, would be the only earner in the household. He would have to try to do this new job in a thorough and conscientious manner. He would be a *good* teacher. He would be the inspiration of a whole new generation of British Muslims. He saw himself, sitting cross-legged in a stone courtyard, surrounded by eager little children from the Third World, dressed, like him, in long, white robes. Did Muslims sit cross-legged? Or was that the followers of the Maharishi Yogi or whatever his name was?

'Hello there!' said Mr Wilson to Hasan. 'And how are *you*?'

He was talking as if to an old friend – a manner he quite often affected with complete strangers. Behind him, Mrs Wilson had appeared. She was bobbing up and down beside his left shoulder, jabbing her finger towards Hasan.

'Who is *he*?'

This question was voiced silently, with a great deal of lip and teeth work. She could have been presenting a programme for deaf people. Robert did not answer her.

'Is he one of *them*?'

Robert nodded.

Mrs Wilson looked determinedly saucy. She clearly hoped that social life in Wimbledon Park was going to look up now that her only son had become a Muslim. *Let them all come*, her expression seemed to say. *Baggy trousers, prayer-mats – wheel 'em in!* She pranced out of the front door. 'Welcome to our house,' she said to Hasan, in the low, solemn voice she used in the Wimbledon Players. 'Welcome! And peace be on you and on your house!' She bowed low as she said this, and walked backwards into the hall.

Behind the kitchen door, Badger was making small, high-pitched noises from the back of his throat.

Robert took one last, despairing look back at the street as he followed his mother inside. There was a man standing in the shadow of one of the plane-trees opposite. He was wearing a shabby-looking leather jacket, jeans and a check shirt. Although he was of Middle Eastern appearance, at first Robert took him for a punk, because his jacket was ripped at the back. It looked as if it had been torn in the interests of fashion. And, although it was hard to judge at this distance, there was definitely something suspicious about the man's shoes.

Mrs Wilson did not seem unduly alarmed at the prospect of having acquired a paying guest. As they went into the front room, she announced her intention of giving Hasan her husband's office upstairs. 'You never do anything in it anyway,' she said in a cheerful voice, 'and at least he won't notice the wallpaper. It's amazing the way he gets about, isn't it? For a blind person, he's very quick on his feet!'

She made no attempt to modify her voice. Perhaps she had decided that Hasan was deaf as well as blind.

'Where's he from?' said Robert's father, clearly feeling, like his wife, that the little boy was not up to responding to direct questions.

'Bangladesh,' said Robert, aware that his parents liked defi-
nite answers.

Hasan walked into the sofa, fell on to it, and curled up like a
cat. He smiled to himself. He seemed pleased to be in the
Wilson house. 'The time of my Occultation is not yet come!' he
said.

Robert thought this was probably good news. He thought of
asking the little boy when he thought his Occultation might
be. They might need to get in special clothing, or warn the
neighbours.

Hasan, as if sensing Robert's curiosity said, 'I must not speak
of these things. It is forbidden to speak of them!'

Maisie, standing over by the bookcase, next to Mr Wilson
senior's collection of country-and-western records, wore a
solemn, almost religious, expression. 'They're very strict are
Muslims,' she said, in the kind of voice that suggested she
wouldn't mind them being a bit strict with her. She cast her eyes
down to the floor. 'Especially towards women!' she added.

Robert looked at her and at Hasan. It was obvious that the
Independent Boys' Day Islamic School Wimbledon was going to
change his life in more ways than he could anticipate.

He went over to the window and looked out at the street. The
man in the ripped jacket was still there, although he was no
longer watching the house. Now he was able to take a good long
look at him, Robert could see that there was something strange
about his shoes. One of them was a normal black leather boot.
The other was a slipper-like creation of vaguely Eastern design.
As he stood there, looking up the street, the man lifted it from
the pavement and rubbed it against his leg, as if his foot was
infected with some curious itch. Then he looked back at the
Wilson house and stared, insolently, in at the blank suburban
windows.

PART TWO

7

There had been difficulties with local planning officials. There had been opposition from local residents. Herbert Henry, the taxi-driver, had told customers in the Frog and Ferret that its effect on house prices would be catastrophic. 'Would you like to live next door to a Muslim school,' he said, 'considering what they get up to?' When asked *what* they got up to, he had muttered darkly that he knew a thing or two about Muslims and ordered drinks all round. His son Alf, the skinhead, had said that he would personally strangle any Muslim he found messing with his wife, adding that if Tehran was such a great place why didn't the bastards go back there?

Henry Farr, the solicitor from Maple Drive, who could be *so* funny when he chose, had said, in his comic colonel voice, that 'Johnny Muslim can be quite a tricky customer!'

But, somehow or other, Mr Malik's school was in business. He opened, five weeks behind schedule, in mid-October. It had been, as the headmaster pointed out to Robert, a desperate scramble to get any of the punters in at all. A mole working inside Cranborne School had supplied them with a mailing-list of all Muslim parents whose children had been rejected by 'This is a Christian Country' Gyles, the Junior School headmaster, and Robert and Maisie had been through the telephone directory, picking out anyone with a Muslim-sounding name. Apart from a few Sikhs and a very irritable Hindu from East Sheen, most of the targeted persons seemed quite pleased to be asked.

Teachers had been more difficult. 'There are not many people in Wimbledon who have your qualifications,' Mr Malik had said to Robert in the pub. This was not surprising. Since his appointment, Robert had awarded himself a degree from Yale, an honorary doctorate from Edinburgh University, two novels and a successful season with the Chicago Bears football team.

They had interviewed a man from Bombay who claimed to have a degree in physics but turned out to be a defrocked dentist, and they had nearly offered a job to a man from Sri Lanka who seemed to know everything about the school apart from the fact that it was supposed to be for Muslims. He turned out to have escaped from an open prison in Dorking. Finally they had hired an almost completely monosyllabic man from the University of West Cameroun called Dr Ahmed Ali. All he had said at the interview, apart from 'I completely agree with you' and 'You are absolutely right, Headmaster!' was 'Let's get this show on the road!'

'He's a dry stick, Wilson,' said Mr Malik, 'but he is 100 per cent loyal. And I am looking for 100 per cent loyalty. Everything else can go hang!'

Dr Ali was to teach maths, chemistry, philosophy, geography and world events. He was, presumably, at this very moment, teaching one or some or all of these things in the large, airy classroom he occupied next to Robert's. As usual, no sound whatsoever came from his room.

Robert was not teaching. He was in the state – now, after two months of the autumn term, agonizingly familiar to him – of being about to teach. *At any moment*, he told himself, *I will find myself up on my legs, waving my arms around in the air and giving.* His mother was always telling him that it was important for techers to give, although what they were supposed to give she did not say. What did the little bastards want?

He sat at his desk and looked at his class. They looked back at him. 'Right,' he said, threateningly, 'I am going to call the register.'

Mahmud put up his hand. 'Please, sir,' he said, 'I want to go to the toilet.'

Robert sighed. 'Right,' he said, even more threateningly. 'Does anyone else want to go to the toilet?'

No one moved. Fifteen small faces, in various shades of brown, studied him impassively.

'*A Muslim should enter the lavatory with his left foot first, saying, "Bismillah Allahumma Inni a'udhu Bika min al-Khubthi wa al-Khaba'ith" (In the name of Allah, Allah in You I take refuge from all evils).*'

'I know what'll happen,' said Robert. 'Mahmud will go to the toilet and then you'll all want to go. You'll all rush out after him, won't you? I want you all to think very hard about whether you *really* want to go to the toilet.'

The pupils of the reception class at the Independent Wimbledon Day Islamic Boys' School did not enter the lavatory with their left feet first. They ran at it, screaming, in large numbers. Like children everywhere, they seemed to find lavatories hilarious.

Robert had read the chapter on lavatories in *Morals and Manners in Islam* by Dr Marwan Ibrahim Al-Kaysi of the University of Yarmouk. It was tough stuff, and here, as in so many departments, the Independent Boys' Islamic Day Wimbledon School was falling short of Dr Al-Kaysi's, admittedly high, standards.

Morals and Manners in Islam was the only book on the subject he had been able to find in Wimbledon Public Library. Apart from Mr Malik, it was Robert's only real guide to his assumed religion. But was it right? Was Al-Kaysi on the money? He certainly seemed to strike few chords with Class 1.

'If you really, *really* want to go,' Robert went on, 'then now is the time. There will be no other chance for the rest of the lesson. From now on in it's do-it-in-your-pants time.'

His class laughed. They liked him. And Robert, in some moods, found the company of boys under ten both soothing and stimulating.

Sheikh, a small, pale boy of about seven, leaned forward in his desk. 'Is this number ones and number twos, sir?' he said – 'or is there any flexibility on that?'

Sheikh was going to do well. His father described himself as a lawyer, although, like most of the parents and many of the staff of the Wimbledon Islamic Independent School (Boys' Day), Robert suspected he was not being entirely open about his status.

'We must all pull together in the various departments!' Mr Malik had told Robert, Rafiq and Dr Ali at their first staff meeting. 'We are going for maximum expansion. You are in on the ground floor of something very, very exciting!'

It was true they had kitchens now. And once, through the open door of his classroom, Robert had seen Dr Ali using a Bunsen burner. But there was still an alarmingly improvisatory air about Mr Malik's school. Rafiq, for example, who had not changed out of the grubby overalls that he had been wearing on the day of Robert's interview, seemed to spend most of his time painting the walls of his classroom. And the headmaster had a disconcerting habit of offering jobs to people he met at dinner parties. A man called Harris had been offered a shadowy role as Exterior Liaison Officer, and Mr Malik was always talking of 'finding something' for Maisie.

Maisie, in her turn, was always hanging around the school. She had bought her own copy of the Koran and was to be seen reading it on her way to work in the morning. She was on page 124 and pronounced it 'riveting'.

It was two weeks away from Christmas. Outside, in the street, there were Christmas trees and coloured lights in the windows of the shops. People pushed along the pavements of Wimbledon Village, grey faces stung into crimson by the wind, and, on the Common, the last scraps of last year's leaves bowled crazily through the defeated grass. A winter's day in the 1990s.

Or, alternatively, a winter's day in the 1380s. That was the period according to the Islamic calendar. In here it was the 1380s.

Or was it? Robert had not quite mastered the Islamic calendar. But, since no one he had met in Wimbledon Islamic circles seemed to use it, it did not prevent him from holding his head up in the staffroom. It was something to do with the year of the Prophet's birth, or the year in which he had gone to or come from Mecca or Medina, but Robert could never remember which.

He really must get hold of another book. *The Bluffer's Guide to Islam* – that was the kind of thing he needed.

The class were looking at him. They were silent, rapt. They viewed Robert as an exotic form of entertainment. Mafouz, a tiny, pale, Egyptian boy, had said to him a week or so ago, 'Sir – I am not allowed television. But you are better than television!'

He must use this moment to demonstrate his familiarity with Islamic law. 'Now,' he said, pacing in front of the blackboard, 'if you do go to the toilet, and if you do a number two – '

The class laughed. Robert continued: ' – which hand do you use to wipe your behind?'

This, he thought, was pretty basic stuff. It was there, clearly set out in Dr Marwan Ibrahim Al-Kaysi's indispensable guide to how to get ahead in the Islamic world. And here they were, nearly twenty-odd children, gaping back at him as if he had just asked them to run through the periodic table.

'Sir,' said Sheikh, 'you don't use your hand. You use paper.'

This went down very well with Class 1. They rocked on their heels. Robert, mindful of Dr Al-Kaysi's injunction to Muslims on page 139 – '*A Muslim should avoid: 1. Being nervous, highly strung or liable to sudden anger and 2. Bad relations with others*' – smiled benignly back at them.

'You use your *left* hand!' he said, slowly and clearly, in the tones of one who knew a thing or two about Islamic *adab*.

'Ergh!' said Sheikh. 'I won't shake hands with you then!'

What did their parents teach them? Did they even attend the mosque on a regular basis? And, if so, which one? It wasn't a question Robert felt he could ask. Anyway, the mosque was one of the many subjects he felt it safest to avoid until he had plucked up the courage to go into one.

When the school had started, Robert had expected tobacconist's sons, monolingual Turks, or youths with swarthy faces and hooked noses, clad in sheets. But, as Mr Malik kept reminding him, this was not the target audience of the school. They were after upwardly mobile Muslims. Perhaps because they were the only people able to afford the fees.

The children Robert was attempting to teach were, although they didn't know it, the latest recruits to the mysterious section of English society known as the lower upper middle class. They were the sons of dentists, ambitious businessmen and fairly successful academics. The vast majority of them had tried, and failed for one reason or another, to get into one or other of the local preparatory schools. Their parents were sending them to the Wimbledon Islamic Day Independent Boys' School because they wanted them to grow up English.

The only truly exotic one among them was Hasan. He sat, as usual, at the back of the class, his little shoulders eerily still, his face tilted to one side, as if drawing warmth from some invisible light-source. He never spoke to the other boys, and they never spoke to him. At the end of each day, as he had done since the beginning of the autumn, Robert took him home, where Mr and Mrs Wilson petted him, fed him, and put him to sleep in the spare bedroom as if he were their own son.

'Let me remind you,' said Robert, 'of one of the *hadiths* of the Prophet. Who knows what a *hadith* is?'

No one knew. Not even Mafouz or Sheikh. *No wonder the Islamic world is in such a mess*, thought Robert angrily, *they don't even know what a* hadith *is. Where have they been all this time?* Or (he did not like this thought) were they winding him up? Were they all pretending to be ignorant in order to trap him into making some punishable blunder?

It was possible they didn't know. They spent so much time in Zap Zone at Streatham, scampering about in clouds of dry ice, zapping each other with laser guns, so many hours watching *Neighbours* or running up and down shopping-malls, playing Super Nintendo, they had probably not had time to go anywhere near a mosque or get their heads round the basics of Islamic education. Ayatollah Khomeini, he thought grimly, had a point. He wouldn't let the Iranian people watch *Neighbours*. He knew where such behaviour leads.

'A *hadith*,' said Sheikh eventually, 'is a saying of the Prophet.'

'Good, Sheikh,' said Robert. 'Good!'

Sheikh was an important man to have on your side.

They knew, all right. They were just not telling him. With the uncanny prescience of children, they had divined that he was a fake. They had gone home and told their parents. Mr Mafouz, a big, jolly man who worked for a travel agent, was compiling a dossier on him. He would send it to Baghdad or Cairo, and, within minutes, men even more serious than the two in the Frog and Ferret would be on their way to Wimbledon with automatic rifles.

One of the men from the pub (the Yasser Arafat look-alike) was also working for the school. Mr Malik had given him a job as a janitor. 'Aziz is a shifty fellow,' Mr Malik had said, 'and he is on no account to be allowed near Hasan. But he is first class with the mop and broom. He cleans as he sweeps as he shines!'

Aziz spent most of his time skulking about the corridors, snarling at people or banging his pail loudly immediately before and immediately after daily prayers. 'He is that kind of Dharjee,' the head had said, when Robert asked him about this. 'What more can one say?' And he added, as he laid his finger to the side of his nose, 'It is not advisable to discuss religious questions with him!'

Robert was not about to do so. His principal endeavour was to stay off the subject of Islam except when alone with the children. But Mr Malik was always bringing up the subject. He seemed fascinated by the details of Robert's conversion. Robert had been vague about them on an embarrassing number of occasions.

It might be simpler, in the end, to actually *become* a Muslim. Was it, wondered Robert, something one could do by post?

'A *hadith* is a saying of the Prophet. A man called Bukhari went around after Muhammad died and spent sixteen years compiling his collection. He talked to over a *thousand sheikhs* in Mesopotamia and – '

Where else? All this information, derived as it was from chance remarks of Mr Malik's, threatened to slip away from his memory even as he was talking. Robert put a lot into the delivery of the speech. He tried to make it sound fresh and exciting. He spoke slowly and clearly and smiled a lot. But Class 1 looked back at him listlessly.

'Well,' Robert went on, aware that he had lost his audience, 'someone called Abu Quata . . . Abu . . . Anyway, someone called Abu told Bukha . . .'

Was it Bukhari or Bukharin? Robert groped for a familar name.

'Anyway *Muhammad* said to this chap that when you go to the toilet you shouldn't wipe your bum with your right hand.'

They were bored. He thought he was on safe ground with lavatories, but they were bored. The only thing they wanted to hear was that the Prophet had said that everyone could go to Zap Zone and stay there for the rest of their natural lives. Robert thought of the day he had taken Class 1 to Zap Zone, and shuddered.

He went to the far side of the classroom. He climbed on one side of the desks, stood on tiptoe, and, forcing up the skylight, eased his head through into the icy December wind. The class, used to his eccentricities, waited patiently.

Robert looked across at the High Street. There was the man standing near the gates of the school. It was Aziz the janitor's friend from the pub. The one who looked like Saddam Hussein. He was always hanging around near the entrance of the school. Sometimes the two of them could be seen muttering together in the playground.

Robert peered back at Hasan. All this was something to do with the manuscript. Why else had Hasan's picture been put with it? But what else where they after? And why had Hasan been entrusted to him?

He was getting paranoid. This had to stop. No one was after him. He was pretending to be a Muslim. He was indulging in a little harmless deceit. That was all.

As he stood there, a woman, heavily swathed in black drapes, turned into the driveway of the school and started towards the front door. It wasn't until she got within a few yards of him that he realized it was Maisie. Robert looked back at his class. They were watching his legs with polite interest.

'What are you doing in that?' said Robert. 'You look as if you've climbed into a bin-liner, Maisie.'

'The name,' said Maisie, 'is Ai'sha.'

She held up her right hand, and brandished what looked like a Batman mask on a stick. 'You shouldn't really be looking at my eyes,' she said.

'I don't see how we can avoid that,' said Robert, 'unless you use some kind of periscope.'

'Don't be stupid, Bobkins,' said Maisie. 'You must stop being stupid. We must be friends now. We are Muslims.'

'We' are Muslims! Uh?

'The Muslim,' said Maisie, in a complacent tone of voice, 'is the brother of any other Muslim. He should not oppress or surrender him.'

Robert recognized this quotation – it was one of which Malik was particularly fond. The headmaster had a large store of quotations designed to show what a nice, easygoing bloke Muhammad was. He did not dwell on the hyena spotted in blood that Abraham was going to throw into hell on the Day of Resurrection, or on the necessity of chopping male infidels into small pieces.

'When,' said Robert querulously, snatching a glance back at Class 1 as he spoke, 'did you become a Muslim?'

'This afternoon,' said Maisie. 'It's as easy as falling off a log.'

'Something you'll be doing rather a lot of,' said Robert, 'if you insist on wearing those ridiculous clothes.'

How did one become a Muslim? It wasn't really a question he could ask at this stage. But, however you did it, Maisie was clearly keen on doing the job properly.

'Mr Malik's converted me!' said Maisie.

Robert had still not been able to discover the headmaster's first name, although on occasions Malik had asked to be addressed as Abdul, while making it clear that this was not his name. Apparently – he told Robert – anyone at his school who was not 100 per cent white had been referred to as 'Abdul.' Mr Malik had been brought up in Cheltenham and had attended a public school, although he was never precise about which one.

'How has he done that?'

'He sort of lays his hands on you,' said Maisie – 'it's extraordinary!'

Robert did not like the sound of this. He looked back, briefly, at his class, resolving to have a word with the headmaster as soon as possible. Saddam Hussein, on the other side of the street, lifted his right leg and scratched his toes against his left calf. He was, like Aziz the janitor, definitely wearing one shoe and one slipper. Robert started to withdraw his head.

'I'm going to come and work at the school,' said Maisie. 'I've given up Sotheby's.'

'What are you going to do?'

Maisie smirked. 'I'm not going to *teach*, obviously. I'm a woman. I'm not capable of teaching. I shall probably do something humble, like work in the kitchens making Islamic school meals.'

This was not wholly bad news. The food at the Boys' Day Islamic Independent Wimbledon School was unspeakable. It was cooked by a woman, or something that looked like a woman but could have been a giant panda. She was reputed to be a relative of Mr Malik.

'Anyway,' she went on, more urgently, 'I need to talk to you. I've found out something rather alarming.'

Robert looked across the street. Saddam Hussein was still scratching his right foot. What was with these guys' feet?

'It's about that bit of paper you gave me. With the locket with the photo of Hasan in it.'

'What about it?'

Maisie looked sulky. Robert looked back into the class. He could just see Hasan, sitting, as usual, quite still, his hands resting lightly on the desk in front of him. He realized, suddenly, he didn't want to know who or what the little boy was. He simply wanted him to go on sitting there.

'You told a fib, Bobkins. It isn't about Hoj or Hoj's woman's breasts. It's about something rather disturbing!'

The man was now working his right foot out of its slipper. Why was he doing this? The temperature outside was down to nearly zero.

'What?'

From the class there were the beginnings of whispering. Soon the whispering would become talking, and soon the talking would become shouting. After the shouting would come screaming, biting, dancing in circles, waving the arms and legs and many other things not recommended by Dr Marwan Ibrahim Al-Kaysi as truly Islamic behaviour.

'I'll tell you when I see you. But it's rather worrying. It's all to do with some people called the Assassins!'

With these words, Maisie snapped her mask up to her face and went up to the front door. Over on the other side of the High Street, Saddam Hussein had straightened up. In his right hand he was holding his slipper. He waved it, mockingly, at Robert. Somewhere inside the building the bell went for break.

Robert drew his head back inside the classroom and, taking a deep breath, climbed down from his desk.

8

Robert climbed the stairs to the staffroom. They had moved in from the garden during a cold spell in November. On the landing, looking out over the High Street, Aziz, wearing new brown overalls bought for him by the headmaster, seemed to be waving to his friend. When he heard Robert, he scuttled away down the corridor. His right foot, Robert noted, was half in and half out of his slipper. From below came the sound of small boys damaging furniture. Break, as always at the school, was unsupervised. 'We all need a break,' Mr Malik used to say – 'including the staff!'

Two open wooden crates, piled high with computer keyboards, were stacked against the wall outside the headmaster's study. They were labelled MALIK. BIRMINGHAM. THIS WAY UP. Robert knew their presence would not be explained. They would be taken away one day, like the seven hundred cans of dogfood, or the fifty television sets, and never seen again. There were no signs of monitors or printers. Mr Malik seemed to specialize in bits of things. One week there had been fifty fridge doors outside his office, another week forty or fifty bicycle frames, although Robert had not so far caught sight of a single chain, tyre, wheel or handlebar.

Robert stopped and put his ear to the headmaster's door. When he wasn't teaching, Malik was usually on the phone, and you could hear him through the wall. Often he seemed to be selling things. This week it was cars.

'Listen,' Robert could hear him say, his voice booming in the barely furnished room, 'I can let you have the Cortina for *nothing*. I am serious. It will cost you absolutely nothing at all. And it is a car with a great deal of character!'

Then the headmaster laughed. He was always laughing. It was, in Robert's experience, a sign that things were not going well.

Robert then went up to the staffroom door and listened. There was, as usual, no sound from within. With a familiar feeling of dread, he pushed the door open.

Rafiq was over by the window, reading a technical magazine. He turned to Robert, gave him the thumbs-up sign, and returned to the study of a complicated diagram. The science and engineering master was always amiable. His sign language was, on the whole, positive. But Robert could have wished the man would get some false teeth.

Opposite him, sitting well down in his chair, staring hard at the carpet, was Dr Ali. Dr Ali had not spoken to anyone since he had got the job. There were times when Robert wondered whether he was capable of speech. Robert had once put his ear to the door during one of his colleagues' classes and had been able to hear nothing from Class 2 but an eery silence. In Dr Ali's right hand was a book entitled *Basic Mathematics for Schools*. It was not one of the textbooks supplied by Mr Malik from the Lo-Price Bargain Bookstore, Clapham. It looked about thirty or forty years old. Perhaps the man had picked it up in West Cameroun.

'When are the next prayers?' said Robert in a cheerful, optimistic voice.

Both men looked at him closely. Neither attempted an answer to this question.

'I lose count,' went on Robert, 'but I've got the feeling we're due for another bout of banging the forehead on the carpet.'

He knew, as he said this, that it was not a good thing to say. But the more he repeated the simple daily rituals of Muslim belief, the more he felt the urge to adopt a brusque, English attitude to them. It was as if he was frightened they might lay a claim on him. As if he might actually *be* a Muslim, in spite of himself.

'I can't wait,' he went on, aware that – as usual – he was

75

making things much worse. 'You've no idea how much it means to me to be part of all this.'

Still no one spoke.

Sometimes, during the ritual prayer, now he had got over the early stages of wondering when to get on the floor, when to rise, and exactly how to get the fingers up to the earlobes, he found himself begging to be excused any significance in his actions. This happened, for some reason, when he was close to Dr Ali.

'A good Muslim,' said Dr Ali, 'should pray five times a day. I do not think we do this.'

Robert was so surprised to hear the mathematics master speak, he found his mouth was hanging open like a fish's. What Dr Ali said was certainly true. Although they had started, at the beginning of term, to pray five times a day, it was already down to two sessions. And Mr Malik, who generally led the school, adopted such a histrionic attitude that it was often difficult to tell whether he was praising God or auditioning for him.

Next door, the headmaster was on another call. 'I have had sight of the manuscript,' Mr Malik was saying. 'Wilson gave it to the girl. It is a sign that they are serious.'

It sounded as if whoever was on the line did not agree.

'My dear Shah,' said the headmaster, 'this is stuff from the dawn of time. It won't go away . . . any more than . . . Robin Hood or King Arthur will go away. They will try anything to get to Hasan!'

His voice dropped. Robert leaned back in his chair so that his ear was touching the wall.

'We must hold our nerve,' Malik was saying, 'and have some-one look at the damn manuscript. They won't move until nearer the time, anyway. Now Wilson must –'

His voice dropped even lower. Robert gave up the attempt to eavesdrop. When he looked up, he realized that Dr Ali was looking at him.

'Have we met before, Yusuf?'

'Oh,' said Robert, weakly, 'I don't think so.'

Dr Ali did not take his eyes off his face. 'Were you ever,' he went on, 'at the University of West Cameroun?'

'Oh no,' said Robert, 'I've never been out of Wimbledon!'

He was beginning to find Dr Ali's conversation even more disconcerting than his silence. In order to escape the gaze of the doctor's large, black eyes, he studied the rather grubby lapels of his suit. He concentrated upon the doctor's neat, white shirt, his thin, anxious neck and his general air of having just surfaced from some particularly nasty branch of the Inland Revenue. Perhaps he wasn't going to talk any more.

'Things are going on at this school,' went on Dr Ali, in a whisper, 'of which it is difficult for a good Muslim to approve.'

'Really?' said Robert. His voice, he thought, sounded curiously squeaky.

Dr Ali kept his eyes on Robert's face. He drew up his bony index finger, stood it to attention next to his aquiline nose, and wagged it furiously. 'We shall assemble the sinners!' he said. 'Their eyes will become dim with terror and they shall murmur among themselves, "You have stayed away but ten days!" '

'Indeed!' said Robert. He spotted at once the no-nonsense tones of the Koran, and, as always when The Book was being quoted, kept his eyes on his chest and tried to look like a man willing to leap off his chair on to all fours, ready for total prostration at any moment.

'Hell lies before them,' went on Dr Ali, in conversational tones. 'They shall drink stinking water; they will sip, but scarcely swallow. Death will assail them from every side, yet they shall not die. A dreadful torment awaits them.'

He hadn't yet said who 'they' were, but Robert had a fairly good idea that some of them might well be unemployed young men pretending to be Muslims in order to worm their way into jobs that should have been occupied by the Faithful.

Dr Ali looked over his shoulder. Rafiq seemed occupied with his magazine. The next remark was hissed directly into Robert's ear, and Robert felt his neck lightly sprayed with saliva. 'Trust nobody,' Ali said. 'Do not trust Malik. Malik is vile with the knowledge of his vileness. He crawls on the ground like a snake. He is loathsome, and spotted.'

This did not seem a helpful thing to say about one's headmaster. Had Mr Malik known quite what he was taking on when he hired Dr Ali?

'I am trying to get through to the Islamic Foundation,' went on Ali, 'to warn them of what is going on here. Of the laxness. Of the vileness. But since my revelation they do not listen to me.'

'When did you have your revelation?' said Robert.

'I had one this morning,' said Dr Ali. 'But I have them all the time. I have never spoken of them before to anyone here.'

This would explain why the good doctor had got in here. Mr Malik had been at pains to exclude what he continued to call 'the loonies' – that is to say, anyone whose attitude to the practice of his faith was, in the headmaster's opinion, excessively enthusiastic. 'Islam,' he was constantly telling Robert, 'is not a faith that pries into a person's soul. We have never really had an Inquisition, never really persecuted people for their beliefs. We have always recognized the danger of self-appointed visionaries.' Somehow or other Dr Ali would seem to have slipped through the net. Robert decided to try and find out a little more about him.

'When did you have your . . . first . . . er . . . revelation?' he asked in a low voice.

'At the Business Efficiency Exhibition at Olympia,' said Dr Ali. 'A vast pillar of fire rose up through the floor and decimated the display of the Nugahiro Corporation's new range of lap-top computers!'

'Did anyone else see it,' said Robert, 'or was it just you?' He leaned forward and spoke quietly. Rafiq was studying his magazine with the kind of intense concentration often assumed by those who are listening to other people's conversations. 'It could have been industrial espionage!'

Ali ignored this remark. 'I have seen it subsequently,' he went on. 'I have seen it come down from the sky with a noise like thunder, and I have seen within it the bodies of those who were Too Late!'

'At Olympia?' said Robert weakly.

'I have seen it in Wimbledon,' said Dr Ali. 'It has been lowered over my head many times, and then, as I have reached up to smite it, it has passed before me and consumed many people. I have also heard the sound of mocking laughter.'

'Is that right?' said Robert.

He wondered whether Dr Ali had confided this fact to Class 2. It could explain the terrified silence that reigned every time they were locked up alone with him. He had better get to the headmaster and warn him.

But, now that the mathematics master had decided to trust him, he seemed unwilling to let Robert go. He grasped his sleeve urgently. 'I must talk to you during the nature walk,' he went on, 'and tell you what is going on here.'

He indicated Rafiq with a brief nod of the head. 'What is his game?' he whispered.

'He teaches engineering and design,' said Robert.

Next door, Mr Malik was back to talking about cars. 'It has done forty thousand miles,' he was saying. 'It has forty thousand on the clock, and that is how many miles it has done. Take it or leave it. It has a new engine. It has rust protection. It is a beautiful car, I swear to you.'

Robert got up and, muttering something about marking, made as if to leave. To his consternation, Dr Ali started to follow him. When they got to the door Robert looked over his shoulder at Rafiq, but the engineering master was still deep in his magazine.

'Tell me,' said Ali, 'why do they bring their filth before us and spread it on the ground like raiment?'

'I don't know,' said Robert slowly. 'I haven't actually –'

Dr Ali smirked in triumph. 'The Dharjees will be consumed in eternal hell-fire,' he said, 'and out of their loins will come many-headed creatures. They will be torn limb from limb and cast into a lake of serpents!'

There seemed little point in continuing this conversation.

Robert was far more interested in finding out where they stood on footwear, but this was clearly not an area that interested Ali.

'I must get on with Sheikh's essay,' said Robert – 'it's twenty pages long!'

Dr Ali gave a sniff of disapproval and, falling once again into his customary silence, slouched back to his chair. He did not, as usual, read or stare out of the window or make tea or do any of the things Robert assumed one usually caught teachers doing in off-duty moments. He sat, slumped back, chin on chest, staring down at the intricate patterns of the carpet, in a seemingly unbreakable silence.

Robert went next door to the headmaster's study and tapped at it nervously. Inside he could hear Malik's voice. The headmaster sounded tense. 'You are welcome to come and inspect us any time you like,' he was saying. 'Come and have a look over the gymnasium. Have lunch in the canteen. Sit in on one of my lessons. I am an Oxford graduate. You may learn something.'

Robert opened the door. Mr Malik waved him in. As Robert closed the door behind him, the headmaster put his hand over the telephone. 'Spies,' he mouthed. 'Government spies!' This meant he was on the line to the local education authority.

Beckoning Robert to a seat, he continued to talk into the mouthpiece about the school, about its playing-fields, its concert hall and several other items that, so far at any rate, existed only in his imagination. He seemed to be making some impression on the person at the other end of the phone.

Robert looked round the headmaster's study. It was decorated with photographs of his relatives. Mr Malik had relatives everywhere. He had aunts in Bombay and brothers in Edinburgh, cousins in North Africa and sisters-in-law in Australia. The only place they did not appear to have penetrated was Wimbledon – which was perhaps as well, since it left Mr Malik as the sole source of information on the Malik family history. This left him an enormous amount of scope for demonstrating the kind of narrative energy that most English fiction-writers would have given a great deal to acquire.

'My mother,' he would sometimes say, 'was an Englishwoman called Perkins. She married my father for sex. Purely for sex. And he was never quite sure why he had married her at all.'

His mother wasn't always called Perkins. She wasn't always an Englishwoman either, although more often than not the headmaster gave one of his parents British nationality. Not that it mattered. Mr Malik, Robert reflected, as he sat watching the headmaster discuss the school's proposal to take boarders, build an indoor tennis-court and a hard playing-area and organize a Community Service scheme, was a creature of his own imagination. He needed far more than the normal ration of two parents, each with only one identity apiece.

'We'll do that,' Malik was saying. 'We'll have a pint! We will! Absolutely, my dear boy! We will!'

He put the phone down. He looked at Robert. He did not smile. When he spoke, his voice was trembling. 'You have deceived me, Wilson!' he said. 'Why have you deceived me?'

Suddenly, to Robert's consternation, the headmaster burst into tears. This was not what he had expected him to do. The headmaster of Cranborne School had made it his business, during Robert's nine years in the place, to make sure that other people did the crying.

Unsure of what to do, Robert started round the desk. He had a strong urge to put his arms round the man, and indeed was about to do so, when Malik thrust him away, sobbing.

'Don't touch me! Ai'sha has told me about your proclivities!'

Robert backed away towards his chair, trying to work out whether this was the deception to which the headmaster was referring. Even if he had been a screaming queen, he thought, it wasn't something he was bound to mention on the application form for a boy's public school. What did the man expect?

'What proclivities?' said Robert, who was not entirely sure what the word meant.

Malik raised a tear-stained face towards him. 'What you do in your spare time, Wilson,' he said, 'is absolutely your affair. There is, I am glad to say, no direct allusion to the activities in which you engage in the Koran or in the Hadith of the Prophet, although from what I know of the blessed Muhammad – may

God rest him and grant him peace – it is not something of which he would approve. He was a man's man, Wilson.'

Robert coughed. 'I want to stress, Headmaster,' he said, 'that . . . er . . . the . . . proclivities referred to were . . . er . . . a phase!'

Why was he so incapable of truth that he wasn't able to deny something that was patently false? Perhaps because denial seemed such a crude affair, and truth so lamentably one-dimensional.

'I am through it, Headmaster,' he said, 'and out the other side.'

This, somehow, did not seem quite enough.

'It is an unspeakable thing,' went on Robert. 'It is the loneliest thing in the world to wake up in the middle of the night and realize you are one of . . . *them*!'

Mr Malik seemed to find the lack of political correctness in this remark reassuring. He held out his hand to his junior master and composed his face into a solemn expression of trust. 'Very well, Wilson,' he said. 'And now, I beg you, I beseech you, to reassure me that you are not also one of those unspeakables of which I think we both know the name only too well.'

Robert could not think what he meant by this. What else was he supposed to have been up to? Cross-dressing, perhaps? Where did Islam stand on that one? He tried to recall some of Marwan Ibrahim Al-Kaysi's dos and donts. *'It is indecent for a Muslim to look at his private parts and his excretion.'* Was that it? He was always looking at his private parts. Or had Maisie invented even more ghastly crimes for him. *'Dogs are not allowed in the dwellings.'* Maybe she had accused him of doing appalling things with Badger.

'What do you . . . think I . . . er . . . might be, Headmaster?' said Robert.

Malik looked puzzled by this remark. 'Why, Wilson,' he said – 'a *Twenty-fourther*, of course. What did you think I meant?'

This, thought Robert, had a definitely sexual ring to it. Was it some ghastly anal version of *soixante-neuf*?

'A Twenty-fourther,' went on Mr Malik, 'like that damned

Aziz and his friend! A group that threatens to split the Wimbledon Dharjees *right down the middle*! That endangers the security of this school, Wilson!'

'Do you mean,' said Robert, 'those people who wear peculiar shoes on their right feet?'

The head seemed amused by Robert's obvious ignorance of the subject. 'They do indeed wear "peculiar shoes", my dear Wilson! They do indeed! And you know why?'

'I'm afraid I haven't a clue,' said Robert.

Mr Malik leaned forward. The muscles in his neck were quivering. Robert could not remember seeing him as disturbed as this. *'So as they can whip them off at a moment's notice!'* he hissed. *'So as they can get their damned toes out and waggle them at people!'*

Robert's expression had obviously convinced him of his innocence.

'The Prophet said, "Don't walk with only one shoe. Either go barefoot or wear shoes on both feet." '

'Did he?' said Robert brightly. Muhammad had certainly covered the ground as far as etiquette was concerned. It was, in a way, rather restful to have a series of instructions covering almost every area of one's life.

'Long ago,' continued the headmaster, 'before the Dharjees came to Wimbledon, they shared a common history with the Ismailis. The Nizari Ismailis. Are these people familiar to you? They are an old, old sect in Islam.'

He grabbed Robert's arm and squeezed it. 'They are after Hasan!' he said. 'They won't move yet, but when they do . . . watch out! You must watch him every minute of every day! And when we come near to the time of his Occultation you must never let him out of your sight.'

'When is that?' said Robert. 'Is it in the school holidays?'

Mr Malik laughed wildly. 'My dear Wilson,' he said, 'all you need to know is that it is not yet come. But it will. There are secrets of the Nizari Ismailis that are never spoken of – never spoken of! Like the Golden Calf of the Druze, my friend, they are a real and living mystery!'

But, before Robert had the chance to ask him about the

Golden Calf of the Druze, or what a Nizari Ismaili might be, or how many of either group might be lurking around Wimbledon, the bell sounded for the end of break, and, below them, in the Great Hall, he heard the sounds of the whole school assembling for nature, recreation and Islamic dancing.

Malik strode towards his study door, flung it open, and turned to Robert with a firm, manly smile. 'We will discuss this later,' he said, 'and we will think of a way to build trust between us. I like you, Wilson. I worked with you on the brochure. I want there to be trust between us. I want to feel that I have entrusted Hasan to a gentleman. You understand my meaning?'

Without waiting for an answer to this, he turned on his heel and went down to his waiting pupils.

It was not difficult to see how he had converted Maisie. After a few minutes with Mr Malik, Robert himself quite often felt like making the frighteningly short journey from doubt to belief. Islam, as the headmaster was always reminding him, meant *surrender*. Maybe he should surrender. Waggling his arms and legs in preparation for Islamic dancing, Robert started down the stairs after Rafiq and Dr Ali. *If things get too complicated*, he told himself, not for the first time in the last few months, *I can always make a run for it*.

9

Mr Malik was very fond of nature. He used it, freely, in argument. 'Look at the birds!' he would say. 'Look at the frogs! Are not they an example to us? We hang around shuffling our feet and making phone calls and they just *get on with it*!'

Whenever he had the chance he got the whole school out on to the Common. When they weren't running across it, cheered on by the headmaster, they were snipping bits off it and bringing them back to school to put in jars. Once Malik had cut down a small tree, dragged it across the grass, and cut it up in the back garden, with the help of two large boys in the third year. Flora Strachan, the ecology-conscious pensioner, had chased after him, waving a copy of her pamphlet *An Uncommon Common* and threatening to report him to the police.

'*If you kill a wall gecko at a single blow, a hundred merits will be credited to your account. To kill it with two blows is less meritorious!*' Malik would say, grabbing Robert's sleeve as he did so. 'Do you know who said that?' And Robert, who was by now learning the basic rule that if anybody said anything interesting it was probably Muhammad, would ask if by any chance it just happened to be a saying of the Prophet, to which the headmaster would reply, his eyes shining, 'That's it! That's it! What a man! He covers everything! Cats! Dogs! *Wall geckos*!' And, rocking with laughter, he would clasp Robert to him – something, thought Class 1's form master, as he joined the throng in the hall, the headmaster would probably not be doing a lot of in future.

'In a line, boys!' Mr Malik was calling. 'In a line! Let us show them that the Wimbledon Independent Boys' Day Islamic

School is the best behaved, the best organized and the best equipped in Wimbledon!'

Mahmud and Sheikh were on the floor. Mahmud was trying to strangle Sheikh. Sheikh was trying to jab a pencil in Mahmud's eyes. Mr Malik beamed at them in a fatherly manner. 'Nature,' he beamed. 'This too is an aspect of nature. It is natural for young men to try and kill each other. Absolutely natural!' So saying, he aimed a kick at Sheikh's ribs and lifted Mahmud clear of the ground by his collar, flinging him into the stew of boys gathered around the window that overlooked the front garden.

Through the doors at the back, from the kitchen area, came Maisie. She started, very cautiously, towards the assembled school. For a moment Robert thought she might have had her feet bound, and then he realized that her problem was simply that her face-mask was now so in line with Islamic law that her field of vision was only about six inches to the left and right of her. She stopped, raised her head, and tracked it left and right, like a robot searching out its target. When she had located the headmaster she moved towards him.

Mr Malik, ignoring these manoeuvres, swept out towards the front door. Dr Ali, suddenly submissive, moved quickly in front of him and opened it. Rain and wind swirled in, scattering papers and banging the door to Class 2's room.

'I need to talk to you,' said Robert to Maisie, as the school filed out towards the Village.

'You can't,' hissed Maisie. 'I'm a woman!'

'That doesn't mean I can't talk to you, does it?'

As far as he could remember from Marwan Ibrahim Al-Kaysi, you were allowed to talk to women. There was a tricky thing called *the seminally defiled state*, and you had to make sure that when your old lady left the house she was doing so *for a specific purpose*, but on the whole even Marwan was pretty *laissez-faire* about a girl and a boy talking about subjects of mutual interest.

Maisie's conversation wasn't quite as much of a surprise as it should have been. And even her clothes, once you had got over the original shock, were part of a long tradition of home-made outfits dating back to her days at the Mother Theresa Convent, South Wimbledon. The see-through trouser suit she had designed herself had caused a sensation at Rachel Ansorge's party.

Islam was the first project they had shared since the Cranborne/Mother Theresa joint school production of *The Tempest* all those years ago. Perhaps that was why he was beginning to find her almost unbearably attractive. He had never, before, seriously thought that she would get beyond the occasional sisterly peck on the cheek, or allowing him the privilege of listening to her troubles. But since the school term had started they had spent hour after hour in intense, ill-informed conversations about who was who in seventh-century Medina. Robert merely had to drop a few *bon mots* from Marwan Ibrahim Al-Kaysi's handbook into the conversation and Maisie's eyes widened the way they did when you offered to take her out for a meal or when she was telling you how someone had told someone that she had a beautiful mouth.

Her costume made her more, rather than less, attractive to him. '*A Muslim woman's dress consists of three items – a shift, a veil and a cloak.*' So, according to Marwan anyway, underneath that long, black cloak was a shift. And underneath the shift . . . As the school filed across the High Street and up towards the Common, Robert found he was sweating. Was there anything underneath the shift? Assuming he did, one day, manage to get her into bed, what would happen after she had shimmied off the veil, let the cloak fall around her naked ankles, and then eased her white, sweet-smelling flesh out of the shift to reveal . . . What? What was ideologically correct Islamic underwear? Presumably an item so secret that they were even keeping it from Dr Al-Kaysi of the University of Yarmouk.

She was about ten yards behind him as the party splashed its way into the swampy grass. But every time he turned round to look at the black shape labouring after him he was confirmed in the suspicion that Islamic outfits were far sexier than boring old black-leather bras, split-crotch panties or steel suspenders. What must it be like for the lads in Riyadh or Tehran, watching

87

the women of their choice swoop around the supermarkets in twenty-five yards of black drapery? How did they cope? With each movement under the flowing garments, Robert imagined breasts, flecked with pink nipples, a pleasantly loose belly, white thighs grinding against each other. *Oh, my God*, he thought, *would that there were an Islamic garment for men, designed to conceal massive erections!* Ahead of them, a woman of about sixty in a blue tracksuit pawed the ground in the jogger's equivalent of neutral. Listing at about ten degrees off vertical, she seemed to be hoping that the grass of the Common would itself carry her forward, like a travelator. If something like that did not happen soon, Robert thought, she might well not have long to live.

'Are you all right, Yusuf?' said Dr Ali.

Robert looked down. Dr Ali was scurrying along beside him and from time to time glaring down the line of boys. Whenever he caught the eye of one of them, the boy would look away and allow his conversation to die. The maths master looked as if he was about to have another revelation.

'I'm . . . er . . . fine,' said Robert, desperately trying to work out how he might get close to Maisie, 'but I am . . . er . . . worried about the boys.'

In the distance he could see a group of dog-walkers. Dick Shakespeare, who did the gardening programme on television, was striding after his black labrador, Chesty. He was wearing green wellingtons and a flat cap, and round his neck was a huge silver whistle. 'Chesty!' he barked. 'Come away down there!'

Dick Shakespeare had a large repertoire of traditional sheepdog commands, picked up from videos of *One Man and His Dog*. He was always asking Chesty to lie down, and come away, and sometimes trying out weird commands all of his own. Chesty had been publicly ordered to 'lurk', to 'fold', to 'carry the juice' and, on one occasion, to 'walk away down there nicely'. The dog never paid any attention to any of these commands, but, like most dogs, carried on eating golf balls, smelling strangers' private parts, and looking immensely pleased with himself.

When things got really bad, Mr Shakespeare used the whistle. This, too, Chesty completely ignored.

Robert wondered whether the dog-walkers might provide cover.

'Hi there!' called Dick Shakespeare. He indicated the pupils of the Wimbledon Islamic Boys' Day Independent School, put the tips of all ten fingers together, and bowed, briefly. 'Three poppadams,' he said, 'and a little piece of mango chutney!'

Behind him was Marjorie Grey, in her green anorak, surrounded by Franks the poodle, Macintyre the elderly Border collie and Stroud the unstable Staffordshire terrier. Robert waved briefly, ducked, and looked for an alternative means of escape.

He would just have to walk, openly, away from the main body of the school, get downwind of Maisie, stalk her carefully, and, when they had reached the birch-trees on the other side of Cannizaro Road, creep up on her and leap out at her when she wasn't looking. It shouldn't be difficult. With a field of vision as limited as hers it was amazing that she could see anything at all.

Just at that moment, Mahmud started to shriek. The small boy had just caught sight of his cousin, who went to Cranborne School. Mahmud's cousin, clad in a pair of white shorts, was running, with a fat boy in glasses, towards the Wimbledon Islamic School. Robert thought he recognized the fat boy. Mr Malik and he had visited Cranborne in order to organize a chess match between the two schools. The fat boy had mated him in four moves.

'Chalky!' Mahmud screamed, 'I got *Monkey Island* off Sheikh, but this is better than *Monkey Island*! It's better than *Coconut Forgery*! You're a mercenary and you kill people with laser guns! It's really good!'

Ali's nose twitched. He looked like a man who smelt un-Islamic behaviour. Either that or he was about to sneeze. But, although the headmaster turned to frown at Mahmud, Robert didn't yet feel he had any justification for leaving the neat line of boys and tracking down Maisie.

'It will be interesting to see,' said Dr Ali, 'whether, during the month of Dhu'l-Hijja, our "friend" Malik offers a sacrifice.'

'It will,' said Robert.

'Our "friend" Malik,' said Dr Ali, 'is a passport Muslim, and that is all. He is *Sahib nisab*, I presume?'

'I would have thought so,' said Robert quickly – 'a man of his age.'

He looked about him desperately. Behind him, Rafiq, as always, was walking with Hasan. The little boy had his hand in the engineer's. From time to time Rafiq would gently prise his hand free and stroke the boy's hair, murmuring some soft endearment. Hasan was almost the only person to whom he spoke. Behind him a huge, dangerous-looking jogger in bright purple shorts thundered up and then, after a brief, explosive display of sweat and breath, was off into the quaking grass.

Robert became aware that the mathematics master was talking, once again, about sacrifice. 'A camel or she-camel,' he was saying, 'if chosen, should be more than five years old.'

Robert nodded vigorously. 'We only have a rabbit,' he found himself saying, 'but we kill that usually. That or the dog.'

Mahmud had broken away from the main crocodile and was engaged in earnest conversation with the small fat boy. The fat boy was holding out a pile of thin plastic diskettes. Mahmud, as far as Robert could make out, was offering the fat boy a ten-pound note for them. It was, thought Robert, probably the same ten-pound note that had been awarded to him by Mr Malik for his prizewinning essay 'My Snake'.

'I wonder,' said Robert idly, 'what the Prophet would have thought about computer games.'

'They are,' said Dr Ali, 'the work of the Devil.'

It was amazing, really, thought Robert, that Dr Ali allowed himself to be anywhere near a place as fundamentally un-Islamic as Wimbledon. Had he fallen out of an aircraft on its way from New York to Tripoli? Had he walked out of the Lebanese embassy one night and come down with an attack of amnesia? According to the headmaster, he had a degree from the University of Surrey. Before the maths master started on what to sacrifice when you couldn't lay your hands on a goat, or how to cope with Ramadan in a modern technological society, Robert, muttering something about the need for discipline, marched off towards Mahmud.

Out of the corner of his eye he could see Maisie, who was now about a hundred yards south of the rest of the school. Whether this was Islamic modesty was hard to tell – she could have got her shift stuck in a tree-trunk. Mahmud and his cousin were haggling over the price of a game called *Willy Beamish*. 'It is write-protected,' he heard Mahmud say. 'I only got it from Lewens for fifteen!'

Robert leaned over the little boy. 'If you do not return to the line now, Mahmud,' he said, 'I am going to cut off your knackers!'

Mahmud glanced briefly up at him, considered this proposition, and went back to negotiating the price of the computer game.

Robert looked back at the school. Mr Malik seemed now to have taken on board several other members of Cranborne School who were growing tired of cross-country running. He had arranged them, with his own boys, in a circle round a plane-tree and was giving an impromptu lecture on the classificatory work of Darwin to both notionally Muslim and notionally Christian pupils. *If only*, thought Robert, *I had had teachers like that*. There was something so constantly curious about the head-master of the Boys' Wimbledon Day Islamic Independent School that, after a while, you stopped wondering where, or indeed whether, he had acquired a degree in anything, and surrendered to that mellifluous, actorish voice.

He moved stealthily into the trees. As far as he could see, Maisie, who was now thoroughly disorientated, was headed for the pond in the centre of the Common. Occasionally she made brief, distressed movements of the head, rotated right, left and right again, but was unable to get the rest of the school in her sights. Back on the main road, Robert caught a glimpse of Aziz the janitor. He was still carrying his mop and broom and wearing his brown overalls. He looked as if he was about to start sweeping the Common.

As Robert watched, Aziz raised hs mop and started a kind of semaphore in the direction of the Windmill. He raised the bucket too, and shook it rhythmically, as if it was some kind of primitive musical instrument. Looking behind him, Robert saw that he was signalling to his friend from the Frog and Ferret, who was crouched in the long grass.

Perhaps they were going to go after Hasan now. Perhaps Mr Malik had got it wrong. Perhaps the time of his Occultation – whatever that might be – was almost upon them. It was something of a shock to him to realize how fond of the little boy he had become. He didn't want him to be Occultated. Whatever it might involve, Robert felt sure that Hasan was not ready for it.

He thought about Hasan at the swimming-baths. Hasan loved to stand in the shallow end, splashing his face and chest with the warm water, his face lifted to the lights in the roof. He thought about Hasan and the television, about the way the little boy placed his olive cheek next to the loudspeaker, caressing the wooden cabinet, while the Wilson family watched the evening news. And then, without caring what the headmaster might think, he ran after Maisie as fast as he could. She was now about a hundred yards away from him, apparently on a collision course with an Irish wolfhound belonging to Jake, 'The Man You Avoid on Dog Walks'.

He finally caught up with her about thirty yards away from the pond. In order not to alarm her unduly, he moved into a space about ten yards ahead of her, and started to walk backwards and forwards on a ten-degree arc in her direct line of vision. Finally she stopped, and from deep within the black bag that enveloped her there was a kind of squeak. 'Bobkins!' she said. 'What are you doing here?'

'I need to speak to you,' said Robert.

She started to make small, whimpering noises. She sounded, thought Robert, rather like Badger shortly before one opened a can of dog-food.

'It's about Hasan . . .' he said, glancing back towards Hasan and the rest of the school. Aziz the janitor was now headed for the trees from which Robert had just come. He seemed to be focusing his attention on the group that Mr Malik was teaching. 'And what you said this morning . . . about that manuscript I gave you. With the photo of Hasan in the locket. And you said something about assassins!'

'*The* Assassins,' said Maisie, in a slightly superior way, 'were a group from the fortress of Alamut. They were the servants of Hasan I Sabah, the Old Man of the Mountains. From this sect called the Nizari Ismailis. He sent them all over the Islamic world to kill his enemies.'

'As far as . . . er . . . Wimbledon?' said Robert tentatively.

Maisie laughed scornfully. 'All this happened about a thousand years ago,' she said. 'But there's something even weirder in that manuscript you gave me. I showed it to Mr Malik, and he said it was very strange *indeed*.'

'Why show it to Mr Malik? What's going on between you and Mr Malik?'

'Nothing, Bobkins,' said Maisie. 'He's just converting me, that's all. I thought you'd be pleased!'

'Well I'm not,' said Robert, 'and I want to know what you've found out about that manuscript I gave you!'

Feeling suddenly cold and miserable, Robert moved towards a bench at the edge of the pond. Ahead of him Cranborne School presented a Christian, redbrick face to the long sky above the Common.

'Where are you?' squawked Maisie.

'I don't know why you're wearing that ridiculous outfit,' said Robert, 'and I don't know why you're telling all these things to Malik and telling him about things I gave you as a present.'

Maisie snorted and, following the sound of his voice, traced him to the wooden bench. She sat next to him. A glum-looking man in wellingtons followed his dog round the circle of iron-grey water. Above them, seagulls mewed and wheeled in the December wind.

'It's nothing to do with you who I talk to,' said Maisie. 'Why shouldn't I show it to him, anyway? He's a Muslim. He knows about these things. You're gay, anyway.'

'I am not gay,' said Robert. 'I am a normal, healthy man with normal, healthy feelings!'

This was not strictly true, but it was certainly more true than saying that he was gay. The fact was that, now that Maisie was about as closely concealed from daylight as a roll of undeveloped film, his desire for her had passed the point where it was possible to conceal it. It was somehow easier to say these things to something that looked like a top-secret weapon in transit.

'I think about you all the time,' he went on. 'I think about your body. I want your body. I want to penetrate you.'

There was a kind of squeak from deep within the black bag.

'I lied about being gay,' went on Robert. 'I lie about everything. I'm incapable of the truth. But I want you. I dream about having you. I dream about your body and its – '

'Bobkins,' said Maisie, in tones that suggested that this was a not entirely unwelcome topic, 'this isn't getting us anywhere.'

Robert rather disagreed with this. He had never before been able to be quite so frank with anyone about his innermost feelings. Was it that, at last, he was learning to face up to himself? Or was it simply that she looked like a large, mobile bag of laundry?

'You've got an erection!' she said, accusingly.

This, thought Robert, was something of an optical achievement on her part. It had been touch and go whether she would get herself anywhere near, let alone actually *on*, the bench.

'I love you,' went on Robert, 'and I want to have sex with you, and – '

'Shut up, Bobkins!' said Maisie. 'I thought you wanted to know about Hasan. And about that manuscript you gave me.'

Mr Malik and the rest of the school had now disappeared. Robert could just make out a thin line of boys struggling through the trees at the edge of the horizon. Aziz's friend seemed to have gone too.

'Where did you get it?' said Maisie. 'In an antique shop?'

If he had told her the truth, she would not have believed him.

Anyway, the truth was – as usual – inelegant, implausible and hurtful. He didn't like to think he was the kind of person who took things from strangers in pubs and then passed them off as presents to girls he was supposed to love.

'That's right,' he said, trying to think of why Hasan's photograph might have been inside the locket. 'I think Hasan's parents must have sold it. Apparently they went through a very hard time recently. His father had a lot of money in BCCI.'

Maisie peered out at him suspiciously. 'You're lying, Bobkins, aren't you?' she said. 'You're telling a fib. I don't know why you tell fibs all the time. Mr Malik says he's always catching you out in fibs. I don't know why he likes you. I don't know why *I* like you. If I like you.'

There didn't seem much point in commenting on any of this. Robert leaned his chin on his hands and looked glumly across the winter grass. 'What's in this manuscript, anyway?' he said, finally.

Maisie's voice thrilled in his ear. Muffled by thick, black cloth, it had the quality of a woman speaking of a secret assignation. As she spoke, the drab, tussocky surface of the Common, the whirling grey clouds and the unstoppable north wind were replaced by walled gardens, the scent of flowers and a crescent moon in a dark sky.

'It's a prophecy, apparently,' said Maisie. 'It dates from hundreds of years ago. And it tells how a remarkable boy is going to come and save the world. And it describes him – in great detail!' Her voice sank to a thrilling whisper. 'And, Bobkins – he sounds just like Hasan. Exactly like him in every respect. Right down to the mark on his cheek and the fact that he's blind. Hasan is the Twenty-fourth Imam!'

10

Robert was not sure whether this was good or bad news. It sounded important, anyway. He didn't know much about Islam but he was aware that being an imam was a bit like being a Vice-President for Life. People tended to make way for you in bus queues when you were an imam. They quite often leaped about on national monuments screaming, ripping apart their black pyjamas, and generally behaving as if you were all of the Grateful Dead rolled into one.

Perhaps they should have been using better cutlery, thought Robert, or calling Hasan 'sir' and making sure he had the best chair. They certainly should not have been letting him curl up on the floor next to Badger. They certainly should not have allowed Badger to lick his ear.

'I suppose you know,' went on Maisie, in the tones of someone who has recently become an expert on something, 'that there is a split in the Muslim world.'

Robert had not known this. But, then, his entire stock of knowledge about Islam was derived from *Morals and Manners in Islam* by Dr Marwan Ibrahim Al-Kaysi. He really must get back to the library and see if it had any more books on the subject. There was the Koran of course. But, so far, at any rate, he had not been able to get beyond page 12. And, in those pages anyway, the book had said nothing about a split. It had rather given the impression that splits were not the done thing.

'Don't you read *newspapers*, Bobkins?' hissed Maisie.

Robert did not read newspapers. He had looked at one, years ago, but it had taken him three days to read it, carefully, from cover to cover, by which time he realized that, if he was going to do the thing at all conscientiously, he would never be abreast of current developments. He learned about world events rather as a Trobriand Islander might – from chance remarks and accidental contacts – and, from the little he had heard, he had not much desire to know more.

'There are Sonny and Cher Muslims, you see . . .'

She could not possibly be right about this, thought Robert.

'*Sunni* and *Shiah* – and they're sort of . . . deadly enemies.'

'How awful!'

He had got the impression, from Marwan Ibrahim Al-Kaysi and from Mr Malik, that Muslims were supposed to be nice to each other. What could they find to disagree about, anyway? Weren't they all supposed to stick together and clobber the opposition?

'The Shiah, for example, or at least the ones in Iran, believe that the Twelfth Imam – who disappeared in mysterious circumstances over a thousand years ago – is going to come back with a huge army and take over the world.'

This did not, to Robert, seem very likely. He could not, either, remember this fact being mentioned in the Koran. But, then, he had only read about twelve pages. He really *must* get on and finish it.

'What's all this got to do with Hasan?'

'The manuscript,' hissed Maisie, 'is from Iran. It dates from the twelfth century.'

Robert tried to marshal a few facts about twelfth-century Iran. They would not come.

'Mr Shah, who put up the money for the school, is a Wimbledon Dharjee. The Dharjees went from Iran to Bombay in the seventeenth century and came to Wimbledon in 1926, mainly to get away from Bombay but also, apparently, for the tennis.'

Why was she so well informed about Islamic history? Presumably Mr Malik had been giving her tutorials.

'But the Dharjees were once members of the Nizari Ismailis, who are themselves a breakaway sect of the Shiite Muslims. Like the Bombay Khojas.'

Robert wished people would not keep mentioning the Bombay Khojas. Just when you started to think you had finally got a grip on this thing they would throw in the Bombay Khojas and you were right back where you started. It was all very confusing. Just as he was beginning to adapt to the fact that there were Muslims – and that some of them were quite pleasant – it turned out that there were as many strains of Muslim as there were of the virus responsible for the common cold.

'Why did the Dharjees leave the Ismailis?' said Robert. 'Because they go around murdering people?'

'I think the Dharjees just sort of wandered off. It might have had something to do with tennis. The Ismailis are quite nice now. The Aga Khan is one of them,' said Maisie, as if this dispelled any doubts on the subject. 'He went to Harvard. He must be all right!'

Robert was not entirely sure about this. He had vaguely heard of Hasan I Sabah, the Old Man of the Mountains. And it was curiously unnerving to realize that the little boy staying in his parents' house should bear the same name. He looked over his shoulder towards where the school party had gone, but could see nothing but a flat field of windblown grass.

'Some of the Wimbledon Dharjees,' went on Maisie, 'have been waiting for the Twenty-fourth Imam. For hundreds of years. He's going to do something amazing, apparently. And this manuscript really makes it look like Hasan is the Twenty-fourth Imam! Its serious, Bobkins! It's not like us nipping down for a pint with the vicar!'

'I thought,' said Robert, grimly, 'that we were supposed to be Muslims.'

Maisie seemed surprised to recall this fact. She rocked backwards and forwards on the bench. 'Oh God,' she said – 'so we are.'

Robert did not like to remind her about the nature of her costume. She put her hand up to her veil and started to chew it through the material. He felt a stab of desire for her once again, but, this time, did not try to put it into words.

'It says, apparently,' she went on, 'that a blind boy with a mark on his face will "come out of the West". That's us, isn't it?

And he'll do all sorts of terrible things. Hasan is a sort of . . . magic child!'

She turned her head and looked Robert full in the face. Neither of them spoke for several minutes. Robert thought about Hasan: about the strange, powerful stillness he carried with him, about his high, precise voice and his exquisite fingers, laced together on the desk at the back of Class 1.

It was not, Robert decided, very sporting of the headmaster to park the Twenty-fourth Imam of the Wimbledon Dharjees on him. He appreciated the headmaster's affection for all things English, even including the Wilson family, but to spring the Islamic equivalent of the Messiah on them seemed a little unfair. No wonder men had been watching the house. When the time of Hasan's Occultation came, they would, presumably, be swarming up the drainpipes waving scimitars and carrying on like a thwarted group of reporters from the *Sun*.

'I think,' said Robert, trying to stop his voice climbing any higher, 'that we should find Hasan a properly Islamic home as soon as possible. And we should hand the manuscript in. To Lost Property or something. Or put it in a left-luggage compartment somewhere.'

'Suppose it's cursed!' wailed Maisie. 'Suppose it's one of those things that follows you round – like Tutankhamun's mummy.'

He had never confided any of his suspicions about being followed to Mr Malik. He would go and see him as soon as they got back to school and tell him everything that had happened since he had come to the school. He had the irrational feeling that Mr Malik would make it all right.

'We'll be all right,' said Robert, with a confidence he did not feel. 'We're Muslims.'

'We are,' wailed Maisie – 'we are. And we should not oppress or surrender each other. We should all stick together for Christ's sake!'

Robert nodded vigorously. He must try and look on the positive side as far as Maisie's conversion was concerned. At least now they had something in common. She was a Muslim and he was pretending to be one. That was a start, wasn't it?

'Does Mr Malik give . . . er . . . classes?' he said.

'Oh no,' said Maisie, 'we just talk. And he takes me to an Italian restaurant in Mitcham. La Paesana. He does my horoscope.'

Robert did not like the idea of Maisie and Malik *tête-à-tête*. The head was not, he was fairly sure, her type. But . . .

'I feel closer to you, Bobkins,' said Maisie. 'I feel we're both struggling. Are you struggling? You seem to me to be struggling. I like that in you.'

From under her cloak, Maisie took the scroll of paper that he had given her back in August. With it was the locket. She held both out, at arm's length, to Robert. 'There you are,' she said. 'I think you'd better have them back.'

Robert touched the manuscript nervously. 'Er . . .'

He didn't take it from her.

'What exactly does the Twenty-fourth Imam *do*?' he said.

'Oh,' said Maisie, her eyes wide and shining with newly acquired faith, 'apparently he hurls thunderbolts around and sort of dries up wells and does tremendous damage to buildings.'

Robert resolved to be more respectful to Hasan. Only last week he had told him to get out of the bath and described him as 'a little rat'. It was comforting to note, however, that, so far at any rate, the little blind boy had shown not much talent for destruction. The only thing he had so far managed to wreck was the Wilson family's CD player.

'It all happens,' Maisie said, 'after his Occultation. He's fine until the Occultation, and then . . . you know . . . he's dynamite! It's all in the paper you gave me.'

Resolving to pass them on to someone else as soon as possible, Robert took hold of both locket and manuscript and put them in his jacket pocket.

'Do you think you could ever . . . you know . . .'

'What?'

But it was hopeless. It wasn't simply that he seemed incapable of telling the truth: he couldn't begin to express any thought without it sounding false or grotesque. He would go and see the headmaster as soon as they got back. He had the absurd conviction that his new boss would look after him, somehow explain things and make them right. *'A Muslim is the brother of every other Muslim. He must not oppress or surrender him.'* Except he wasn't a Muslim, was he? Or was he?

As if in answer to his doubts, from out of the birch-trees came Mr Malik, at the head of a line of boys. He raised his right arm, pirouetted, and landed, like a ballet dancer, some yards ahead of himself, on his toes. He spun round with both arms extended, and started to shake his hands vigorously. After him, giggling furiously, came Sheikh and Mahmud. Behind them came the fat boy in glasses from Cranborne School. He too was waving his arms, then lifting a leg each in turn and shaking his feet at the leaden sky. Perhaps, thought Robert, he had been converted.

As Maisie, too, turned to watch, the whole school emerged into the vacant space of the Common, each one lifting now one arm, now the other, leaping and landing, shaking and pirouetting, and all of them, apart from Dr Ali, laughing wildly. This, to the wonder of anyone who happened to be passing, was Islamic dancing.

'Come, Wilson!' called the headmaster. 'Come! Dance! Dance!'

Stiffly, Robert got to his feet.

'My dear girl,' Malik called to Maisie, 'dance!'

This was not a possible option for Maisie. Making small noises of distress, she started to do a three-point turn, reversed – hard – into the side of the bench, and squawked loudly.

'Take off those ridiculous clothes,' called the headmaster, 'and dance!'

Maisie, from deep inside her black linen bag, was muttering about how it was all right for some people. The line of boys and masters – Hasan and Rafiq bringing up the rear – made its way through pools of water and patches of sodden black earth, across the cinder track leading up towards the Windmill, and to the chestnut-trees, now almost empty of leaves, that shadow the edge of Parkside. Hasan, holding tightly to Rafiq's hand, was laughing and thrashing his body like a swimmer in difficulties

Robert looked beyond the line of boys, but Aziz the janitor and his friend were gone. Maybe conditions were just too bad for a man forced to operate with only one shoe. Awkwardly, moving like a much older man, he made his way after Mr Malik. Behind him, puffing and blowing, came Maisie. As he walked through the wet grass, the locket and the thick scroll of paper banged at his chest, like an urgent warning. The words of the man in the pub came back to him, crowding out his thoughts, rising up to his face like a blush of shame: *'All who serve Malik will die. And the staff and pupils of the Wimbledon Independent Islamic Boys' Day School will burn in hell-fire when the day comes!'*

Maybe the day was coming. And sooner than he thought. With Maisie still keeping the regulation distance between the two of them, he almost ran after the headmaster, swinging his arms crazily and taking strides so long that a casual observer might have been forgiven for assuming that he, too, was practising the art of Islamic dancing.

11

Robert always had a free period after lunch. He was allowed this in return for taking detention, which usually involved sitting in an empty classroom with Mafouz and the Husayn twins. As Maisie and Mr Malik's relative were clearing away the destruction (the Huysan twins had been having a mashed-potato fight with school spoons), he made his way up to the headmaster's study.

Mr Malik usually had an hour off after lunch. No one knew quite what he did; sometimes the sounds of country-and-western music drifted out from his study, sometimes he emerged smelling strongly of alcohol, but mostly, judging from the titanic snores that shook the wall of the staffroom, he slept.

It was impossible to tell what he was doing this afternoon. No sound whatsoever came from behind the door. Robert knelt by the keyhole and fixed his eye to it. From Class 2, down below, came the noise of Dr Ali's mathematics class, twenty-five children chanting in unison:

> Eight eights are sixty-four,
> Nine eights are seventy-two,
> Ten eights are eighty,
> Eleven eights are eighty-eight,
> Twelve eights are –

There was an awful, horror-struck pause, followed by several conflicting opinions of what twelve eights might be, and, eventually, a wild scream from Dr Ali. *'Twelve eights are ninety-six! You hear me? Ninety-six!'* The mathematics master obviously intended to make up for his long silence during the earlier part of the term.

All Robert could see through the keyhole was the blur of Mr Malik's grey jacket, passing and repassing; he seemed to be running, now in one direction, now in another. After a while he went to the desk. Robert had a clear view of him there.

The headmaster pulled back the top right-hand drawer and took out a large, new-looking cricket bat. He gripped it hard with both hands and beat the air with it. Then he crouched over it and squared up to an imaginary ball. As he waited for delivery, he started to mutter to himself in what sounded like a Gloucestershire accent. 'Locke delivers it,' he said, in a slow drawl, 'Malik waiting his moment. Calm and steady as a rock, the Pakistan captain just waiting here for the ball to come . . .'

Suddenly his voice rose. '*And he plays it – smashes it through the covers straight for four! Oh this is remarkable!*'

At the same moment he made stabbing movements, at shoulder height, with the bat. They resembled no cricket stroke that Robert could remember. The headmaster looked as if he was fighting off a large insect that was homing in on his neck.

'*Malik has done it again! It's four runs! Oh, this is remarkable! Remarkable play by the Pakistan captain!*'

He gave one last poke with the bat and, throwing it to the ground, clasped both hands and raised them above his head.

Robert knocked, quite hard, at the woodwork. The headmaster started in guilty surprise. He straighted up and, in a deep, serious voice, called, 'A moment please!' Then he scooped up the bat, swept it back into the drawer, and composed himself at his chair. From his jacket pocket he took a small vanity mirror and adjusted his hair. When he was ready, he presented a three-quarter profile towards the door and said, 'Come!'

Robert came.

Mr Malik's mood of earlier in the day seemed to have evaporated. He appeared genuinely pleased to see his reception-class teacher. He rose from his chair and held out his hand, as if this was the first time the two of them had met.

'Wilson!' he said. 'Don't tell me! You want more money!'

This, as it happened, was perfectly true. But Robert did not feel able to say so. Instead he gave a weak smile and fingered the locket, through the cloth of his lapels.

Malik clasped his hands behind his back. He moved over to the window and looked out across rain-driven Wimbledon. In the distance, a police car wailed its way towards them up Wimbledon Hill.

'It must be difficult for you,' he said, 'surrounded by all these wogs. I imagine you are deeply confused. Bowing to the East and carrying on like lunatics. I expect you say to yourself, "*Send the bastards back to where they came from!*" '

'You mean – Cheltenham?' said Robert, unable to repress a smile.

The headmaster looked suddenly serious. 'I am not a very good Muslim,' he said, 'but I do my best.'

Something in his childhood had obviously prompted this remark. Indeed, Mr Malik took on the same, sad, soulful air whenever Cheltenham was mentioned. It can't have been easy to have been a good Muslim in Cheltenham, thought Robert. There was probably not a good supply of mosques available.

'You know about my mother, of course,' went on the headmaster, 'but what can you do if your father is called Malik and your mother is called Frobisher? There is no meeting of minds.'

'I thought,' said Robert boldly, 'she was called Perkins.'

Malik shrugged with infinite resignation. 'Frobisher . . . Perkins,' he said – 'what's the difference?'

Robert decided to come to the point. He took the locket and the manuscript out of his pocket and laid them on the desk in front of the headmaster.

Mr Malik did not seem pleased to see it again. He backed away. His hand went up to his collar and started to loosen his tie. He looked from the manuscript to Robert and back again. 'I knew you had obtained this and gave it to . . . er . . . Ai'sha, Wilson,' he said. 'How did you come by it?'

'Two men gave it to me,' said Robert, 'in the pub. The day I came for the job. Do you remember?'

Malik looked at him. He looked like a man trying to do a

complicated piece of mental arithmetic. 'Aziz our janitor . . . and . . . another man . . .'

'The ones with one shoe,' said Robert brightly. 'The Twenty-fourthers! You didn't seem very keen to meet them.'

The headmaster threw back his head and gave out the kind of laugh dished out by medieval jailers to boastful prisoners. 'Keen to meet them, Wilson! Keen to meet them! I hardly dare to think that such people exist! I flee from such people – and I advise you to do the same! They are dangerous lunatics! They are madmen! They are fanatics!'

'They told me to give it to you, Headmaster,' said Robert. 'But I didn't, I'm afraid.'

Malik did some more of the laugh. This time it was more the kind of mirth displayed by, say, Rommel, shortly after the battle of El Alamein. To say it was effortfully hollow would have been an understatement.

'Please don't apologize, my dear Wilson. If this should prove genuine, it is about as welcome as a High Court summons – another document I expect hourly unless the Bradford branch of the Inland Revenue adopts a more compassionate attitude to its clients.'

He looked down at the manuscript and locket and gave a little shudder. Below them, Dr Ali's boys were getting started on the ten times table. They didn't sound very convinced about it.

'Run from it, Wilson. You run as fast as you can away from it. Cower in the bowels of the earth from it, and pull the bedclothes over your head. You change your name and address and never tell a soul you saw it. You flee it, my dear boy.'

Robert looked down at the manuscript. 'And what does it do?' he said. 'Turn into a snake and slither after you?'

Malik practically ran at him and grabbed him by the lapels. 'Ha ha ha!' he said. 'Ha ha ha ha! Frightfully funny! What a laugh! Ho ho ho ho! How amusing!'

Robert did not know what to say to this. The headmaster went back to his chair and sank into it, with a groan. He put his head in his hands and rocked backwards and forward for some minutes.

'They can't be all that bad,' said Robert. 'I mean, Aziz seems OK . . . You obviously thought he was all right.'

'I wanted him where I could keep an eye on him,' said Mr Malik through his hands. 'I wanted to find out how many of these damned Twenty-fourthers there are about the place.'

Robert coughed. 'I keep thinking I'm seeing them,' he said. 'I can't take my eyes off people's footwear. They're everywhere. I'm surprised you haven't seen them. They're all over Wimbledon.'

Malik gave a shriek. 'Twenty-fourthers!' he yelled. 'All over Wimbledon! Why didn't you tell me?'

'I didn't know they were Twenty-fourthers,' said Robert. 'I just thought they were people wearing one shoe. I didn't know they were after Hasan. I haven't a clue what's going on really.'

Malik sat back in his chair and sighed. 'No,' he said, 'there is no reason why you should have a clue. We really haven't discussed these things, have we?'

He looked down at the manuscript. He picked it up with all the enthusiasm of a man finding a mail-order death-warrant on his mat.

'The Twenty-fourth Imam,' he said, 'has often been spoken of among the Wimbledon Dharjees. But there have never been writings about him. And this . . .' he tapped the manuscript and shuddered – 'points clearly to the little boy in your house. You have a great responsibility, Wilson. You must protect him. You must stand guard over him at all times.'

The headmaster did not make it clear whether this was because Hasan might, at any moment, start chucking thunderbolts around the place. Robert still felt some confusion about what Aziz and his friends might be expected to do around the time of the little boy's Occultation. Was it, he wondered, like a bar mitzvah? He had been to Martin Finkelstein's bar mitzvah and had been given a small white hat, which was still on his mantelpiece at home.

'Twenty-fourthers,' he said, 'are –'

'Are animals!' said Mr Malik. 'They are wild beasts! They are brutal, misguided thugs! And, I am afraid that, like the Mounties, they always get their man!'

Robert wondered, but did not ask aloud, who their man might be. He might have to do something more radical than simply leave this job. He might have to get some dark glasses and retire to a small island off the coast of north-west Scotland.

'This manuscript,' said the headmaster, 'must be examined carefully. We must put it in the hands of trained Islamic scholars and get them to run tests on it. They must carbon-date it and put it under the microscope, and we must examine Aziz carefully and get him to say where he found it. I assume he did not pick it up on Southfields Station!'

He looked up at Robert. 'You have indeed a grave responsibility, Wilson. I feel I do not know you. I feel I do not know all the secrets of your heart. I must look deep, deep into your soul and grow to trust you as a brother!'

Robert gulped. He tried, without much success, to look like a man who had a soul into which you could look.

The headmaster looked up from his desk and peered, searchingly, into Robert's eyes. 'Why did you become a Muslim?' he said.

This was the one question Robert had been hoping the headmaster would not ask him. He gulped again, but found he was unable to answer.

'We will fight them together,' said Malik, rising from his chair. 'You and I will fight them together. We are Muslim brothers, you and I. We have never talked of these things, Wilson. We must talk of them. The Muslim is the brother of every other Muslim. He must not oppress or surrender him.'

So saying, the headmaster flung his arms round Robert and squeezed him warmly. Robert, feeling rather like a tube of toothpaste, stood, quite passive, in Mr Malik's fierce embrace.

'I have not listened to *you*, Wilson,' went on the older man, still not slackening his embrace. 'I have talked only of my own concerns. It must have been hell for you. You are lost in a strange country, among a lot of incomprehensible wogs going on about Twenty-fourthers and God knows what, and you are probably scared stiff!'

Robert, his voice muffled by Mr Malik's right arm, said, 'I am. I'm terrified!'

Malik straightened up and broke away. 'I shall put Hasan in your trust,' he said, 'and I will inform Mr Shah that a first-class man is "on the job". We must get first-class information about what these damned Twenty-fourthers have planned. And as we approach the Occultation we must take extra care.'

Not, thought Robert, that there would be much anyone could do should the Twenty-fourth Imam decide to loon around SW19 behaving like a negative version of Superman.

'And I must hear your side of the story, Wilson. It is a basic principle of man management. You must share your feelings with us!'

At this moment the door opened and Rafiq came in. Robert could not have said why, but he had the strong impression that the engineering master, too, had been listening at the door. Rafiq did not speak but stood looking at his two colleagues, an enigmatic smile on his face.

Malik turned to him. 'Assemble the school,' said the head-master. 'A special assembly. I think it is time we listened to our new brother. We have closed our ears to his cries and left him in the shadows while we walked in the light.'

Rafiq said nothing. Down below, Dr Ali and his class had relapsed into silence. All Robert could hear was the wind, shouldering vainly against the windows of the headmaster's study.

'Wilson is going to talk to the whole school,' said Mr Malik. 'He is going to share his feelings with us.'

Unable to resist any longer, he flung himself back at Robert. He dug his fingers into his ribs, massaged his cheeks, and patted the back of his thighs as if they were unproved bread.

Robert, gasping for breath in his arms, wondered whether Mr Malik's request for him to give an account of himself was entirely motivated by concern for his staff. *He suspects*, he found himself thinking. *He's on to me!*

'He is going to tell us,' Malik went on, 'how he became one of us. He is going to confide the secrets of his heart to us. He is going to tell us how he came to be a Muslim.'

12

Mr Malik looked round at the assembled school. They were sitting cross-legged in what he liked to call the Great Hall. There were only ninety of them, but it was a tight squeeze. Boys were jammed together like rush-hour travellers on the Underground. Saddawi, known as 'The Boy with the Pointed Head', was only just in the room. He was peering in on the proceedings from the kitchen, while his best friend, Mafouz, had retreated to the stairs and was looking down, intently, on Mr Malik's elegantly coiffeured hair. Robert was standing a little behind him. As the headmaster gave the Husayn twins what he called 'the cork-screw' – an intense stare combined with a slow quiver of the nostrils – they slackened their hold on the new recruit to Class 1 – a Bosnian refugee whose name no one could pronounce.

'Today,' he said solemnly, 'Mr Wilson, or Yusuf Khan as he likes to be sometimes known, is going to tell us how and why he became a Muslim.'

He turned to Robert and extended a welcoming hand. *He knows*, thought Robert, *he knows. He is having fun at my expense.*

'It is no easy thing for a person like Wilson, whose family has had a complex religious history – his father, for example, was a . . . er . . . Buddhist – to ally himself with a religion whose roots lie far from Wimbledon.'

The boys gazed up at him in rapture. They must, thought Robert, have seen some strange things in their lives. Their parents had travelled thousands of miles, from all parts of the globe, to make a new home in quiet England, safe among the ashes of empire, only to have their children greeted by Mr Malik, a man more exotic than any schoolboy had a right to expect a teacher to be.

'Wilson, or Yusuf Khan, or whatever you like to call him, is, as you are all aware, a man of many talents. He is a complex individual, rich in fruit, with a good long "nose" and plenty of body. In short, someone who is, as it were, drinking well now and well worth laying down for the future.'

Robert patted his hair down and tried to formulate a few opening remarks. Conversions were often the result of a journey, weren't they? Where could he have been going? *I was on my way to West Wimbledon station, when* . . . When what?

'Wilson is white. He is Anglo-Saxon. He is, although this may seem incredible, the kind of man who used to rule the world!'

Robert coughed apologetically.

'And now he is *Muslim*. He is 100 per cent pure Muslim. He reads the Koran, he attends daily prayers, and occasionally, when there is a gap in the conversation, he babbles of going to Mecca. Can you imagine him there in his sports jacket, among the thousands of pilgrims?'

The boys laughed at this sally. Robert, who found he was sweating, started to try to recall some key phrases from Marwan Ibrahim Al-Kaysi. Could a case be made for the sports jacket being an Islamic garment?

'Things are changing, gentlemen!' said Malik, clasping his hands behind his back. 'The Church of England is no longer the only game in town. And Wilson here is, we might say, the future – the first sign that British society is going to throw off the shackles of racism and colonialism and produce something genuinely multicultural, like . . . er . . . him!'

Loud applause greeted this remark. The headmaster seemed sincere enough, but his manner was so perfectly poised between gravity and teasing that Robert's discomfort increased.

'Listen to him now as he tells us how and why he became a convert. Listen to his story, and profit by it. And afterwards we will take questions from the floor.'

Here Mr Malik stepped back with a flourish, and Robert found he was walking out in front of the whole school, his heart thumping, his mind a complete blank.

'I became a Muslim,' he said, 'at four-thirty on Wednesday the twenty-third of July. On Wimbledon Station.'

This, thought Robert, had the right ring to it. It sounded concrete, authentic.

'I had never, in my life, up to that point, met a Muslim. I had never even *seen* a Muslim – apart, of course, from on the television, and the ones I had seen there – I will be absolutely frank – did not seem a particularly inspiring bunch!'

Mr Malik seemed to like this. The headmaster smirked to himself, chuckled, and drew the edge of his right hand carefully along his moustache.

'Colonel Gaddafi, for example – an obvious loony if ever I saw one. Saddam Hussein, for example, and his Ba'ath Party – a man, I will be absolutely frank, I would probably cross the street to avoid.'

Sheikh was looking at him intently. The little boy's chin was cupped in his hands. He was wearing, as were all the boys, the school uniform designed by Mr Malik himself – grey jersey, grey trousers, black shoes, and bright green tie and socks. He must get off the subject of Saddam Hussein, thought Robert.

'Ayatollah Khomeini, for example,' he heard himself saying, 'was a complete . . .' He managed to head this sentence off its track just in time. ' . . . mullah. He was in every sense a man of the cloth. Whereas Yasser Arafat . . . er . . . for example – '

Here he caught sight of Aziz the janitor, who was standing at the back of the hall with his mop and bucket. He seemed to have decided that now was the right time to clean the Great Hall floor and was poking the mop head in among the boys' legs, muttering to himself.

' . . . who bears a close resemblance to our school janitor, Aziz – although, as far as I know, Aziz does not wander around with a tea towel on his head organizing terrorist attacks – Yasser Arafat – '

How had he got on to the subject of Yasser Arafat? Why had he got on to the subject of Yasser Arafat? How could he leave the subject of Yasser Arafat?

' . . . is the leader of the Palestinian Liberation Organization.'

This was safe ground. They couldn't be expected to argue with that. Islam, as far as he was aware, had no objections to a man stating the obvious.

'The Palestinian Liberation Organization was founded, after the Second World War, with the intention of liberating Palestine. As we all know.'

This was all right as far as it went. But Dr Ali was looking restless. His head snaked forward. Over his not entirely clean white collar you could see his Adam's apple thumping. Robert tried to concentrate on a spot just above the doctor's head. He fixed his mind on a rule his father had given him for public speaking: *Get a vague plan and then say anything that comes into your head*. But no words would come. What they wanted to hear was why he had become a Muslim. And he simply could not think of anything that might have made him become a Muslim.

'I can hardly believe,' he found himself saying, 'that someone like me could have become an . . . er . . . Muslim. Because quite a lot of Islam is, frankly to me . . . er . . . well gobbledy-gook!'

Dr Ali, his chin in his hands, was staring at Robert. His lips seemed to be mouthing something, but Robert could not make out what it was. He looked as if he was reciting some charm to ward off evil spirits.

'Take the Koran, for example,' went on Robert. 'Take it. You know? Get it out and take a close look at it. I have to say that from my point of view – and this is only my point of view – it is *not* a page-turner. It just isn't. It is obviously a very popular book and, according to my edition, has sold millions of copies worldwide – as has Enid Blyton, for example – but . . .'

This was the wrong direction. He must get off the subject of the Koran. And why was he mentioning Enid Blyton? He must get off the subject of anything controversial. But every single thing to do with being a Muslim seemed quite incredibly controversial. Why had he become a Muslim? Why hadn't he become a Sikh or a Hasidic Jew?

'Why,' he went on, 'didn't I become a Sikh or a Hasidic Jew? I mean, it is possible that their . . . er . . . holy books are a less tough read than the . . . er . . . Koran.'

Dr Ali had put both his index fingers in his ears and was rocking backwards and forwards in his chair. He looked like an airline passenger who has just been told that all four engines on his 747 have just failed.

'Take,' went on Robert, 'the chapter called "The Bee". For the first four or five pages there is absolutely no mention of a bee. In fact it seems to talk about almost every kind of animal there is *apart* from the bee, and, for someone like myself, a total newcomer to Islam, this is, I have to say in all honesty, deeply confusing. I mean, you know, why not call it "The Ant"? Or "The Porcupine"? Or "The Frog"? You know?'

Some boys in the front row laughed. Dr Ali increased the rocking movement until the point where his forward movement was critical. Suddenly the mathematics master was on his feet. He was pointing at Robert and yelling something that sounded like Arabic but turned out to be very emotional English. 'I cannot listen to this!' yelled Dr Ali. 'I cannot allow this to continue!'

Mr Malik turned sharply to his second master. 'Wilson is simply expressing the doubts and fears of a new – '

But Dr Ali did not listen. He raised his right hand and threw a quivering index finger in Robert's direction. 'This man,' he said, 'is a blasphemer and a hypocrite! I have been watching him for some weeks, and I accuse him publicly – before the whole school!'

Robert started to shake. 'I don't think – ' he began.

'Did you or did you not read this book to the reception class?' yelled Ali. He produced from under his jacket a small paperback book which he waved in the air, furiously. 'A book, gentlemen, which will make you physically ill should you even catch sight of it in Waterstones! A book which has as its hero – as its *hero* – '

He held the book out between finger and thumb as if it contained some dangerous virus which at any moment could threaten the whole school.

. . . a *pig!* A pig is the hero of this book! *The Sheep-Pig*, by Dick King-Smith! *And this is not all!'*

Mr Malik, too, was on his feet, waving his arms. 'My dear Ali,' he was saying, 'our religion forbids us to eat pigs. It doesn't prohibit us from talking about them. May I remind you that –'

Robert had read *The Sheep-Pig* to Class 1. He had, on rainy afternoons, read quite a lot of books about pigs to them.

'The Tale of Pigling Bland,' Dr Ali was yelling, 'by the woman Potter! *Horace: the Story of a Pig*, by Jane DuCane Smith. *Pigs Ahoy!*, by Hans Wilhelm. *Pig Time*, by Duncan Fowler and Norman Bates. *Don't Forget the Bacon!*, by Pat Hutchins. The man is obsessed with pigs!'

It was true that Robert had always liked pigs. But no one in Class 1 had seemed unduly disturbed by his account of them, even if the Husayn twins had said that pigs were 'boring' and had asked if they could bring in the novelization of *Terminator Two*.

Dr Ali was now incoherent with rage. He looked, thought Robert, like something out of one of his own visions. Whirling round on his toes, he kept stabbing towards his fellow member of staff with his long, bony fingers. But it wasn't until Robert thought he recognized a familiar English word that he leaned across to the headmaster to check if he had heard it correctly.

'I think,' said Mr Malik, cheerfully, 'he is sentencing you to death.' He dropped his voice to a confidential whisper. 'Apparently,' he went on, 'he does this quite a lot. I have been researching into his background, and apparently he is a member of an organizaation known as the British Mission for Islamic Purity. We must endeavour to rise above, Wilson. Rise above!'

But the mathematics master, now dribbling freely, his face contorted with hatred, continued to dance from foot to foot, watched impassively by the ninety or so young British citizens of the Wimbledon Islamic Day School (Independent Boys').

Mr Malik put his arm round Robert and continued to watch this display with apparent unconcern. He beamed again as Ali, practically choking on his own saliva, fell forward into a group of pupils.

He was practically laughing out loud as Ali reached critical mass. Foaming at the mouth, the maths master, now on his knees, raised both hands above his head and shook them violently. He was screeching, sobbing and wailing with the aplomb of a professional mourner and it wasn't always easy to understand what he was saying. But the gist of it seemed to be that there should be an early, and preferably unpleasant, end to the miserable life of the blasphemer and pig-fancier, Wilson.

PART THREE

13

Islamic time seemed to pass more quickly. Christmas had only just gone, and now the mornings were bright. On longer evenings the sound of wood against leather could be heard in the garden behind the large house.

'You'll be late, darling,' called Mrs Wilson. 'You don't want to be late, do you? It's Sports Day!'

Robert did, actually, quite want to be late. He had never found it easy to get up in the morning, and being under sentence of death did not make the prospect of a new day any more enticing.

Outside, April had come to Wimbledon. A blackbird was singing, carelessly, in the trees behind the house. A breeze stirred the curtains. On the chest of drawers in the corner of the room was Malik's newsletter: SPRING NEWS FROM THE ISLAMIC SCHOOL WIMBLEDON.

> *Admissions are up by 30 per cent and we are ahead of budget. The profit-sharing scheme is coming on line in June and we are already planning a follow-up to our successful Islamic Quiz Evening on March 12th. Well done, Mr Mafouz – we hope you enjoy the tickets for Les Miserables! Plans for the swimming-pool continue apace!*

The swimming-pool was something of a disappointment. Rafiq had dug a twelve-foot hole at the bottom of the garden, and then, in the grip of one of his periodic fits of depression, had abandoned it to the spring rain.

'You can do nothing with Rafiq during Ramadan,' Mr Malik had said. 'He just lies on his bed and thinks about having his end away!'

But, for the first time in his life, Robert felt part of a success. Every day a new parent would appear in Mr Malik's office. And, so it was rumoured, 'This is a Christian Country' Gyles, of Cranborne Junior School, had privately denounced the head-master's operation as being 'a bucket shop'. The inspector of schools had, however, described the operation as 'offering an entirely new slant on the core curriculum'. They even had locks on the lavatory doors.

Islam had offered him a lot. Among the things it had offered him was Maisie. If it had not been for their long, soul-searching conversations about the Koran and the life of the Prophet, he would probably not, now, be sleeping with her. Next to him, she snored lightly. As he got out of bed, she moved. The top of her thigh just cleared the duvet. He gulped.

She was still convinced he was homosexual. They had been having sexual intercourse about three times a day, every day, for the last six weeks, but Maisie still maintained that Robert was faking it. His orgasms seemed to him to be perfectly genuine, but once Maisie had an idea in her head it proved difficult to shift. There were still moments when he worried about her attitude. Might Malik be something to do with it? Did Malik still suspect him of not being quite the full shilling as far as heterosexuality was concerned? Such ideas were hard to dispel.

At the mere thought of the word *shift* his penis leaped doggily to attention. *Islamic underwear!* he crooned to himself, as he groped for his grey jersey. *It takes so long to get off!* Her clothes, lying across the back of the bedroom chair, spread out in a black line towards the door. There was enough material there, thought Robert, reaching for his green tie, to shroud a fair-sized glasshouse in darkness. You could climb in there with her and still have room to conduct Beethoven's Fifth Symphony. Her garments were so large and flowing that a man could have pleasured her while she was waiting at a bus-stop and no one would have been any the wiser.

'We'll be late, darling!' he called, lightly. 'Darling!' She let him talk dirty whenever he felt like it!

She had been living with the Wilsons for nearly three months.

Maisie's father had died just after Christmas. He had been briefly but sincerely mourned. Her mother had surprised everyone by dying just as they were recovering from her husband's death. She was helped into the gardens of paradise by a number 33 bus, which had reversed over her while trying to execute a three-point turn outside the Polka Theatre, but some people still claimed that her death was, in part anyway, due to a broken heart. 'If she'd been herself,' Maisie wailed to Robert, 'she'd have looked.'

Maisie had been more affected by her mother's death than most people thought possible. She had always referred to her as 'the old bat', or occasionally as 'that hard bitch'. Mr and Mrs Wilson had been very sympathetic.

Maisie had moved out of her parents' house and come to stay at the Wilsons' shortly after her mother's funeral, a multi-denominational affair dominated by the headmaster of the Wimbledon Independent Islamic Boys' School (Day). Mr Malik's speech – described by one of Maisie's mother's oldest friends as 'a masterpiece of bad taste' – had dwelt, at great length, on the sexual prospects awaiting the Faithful in heaven. Maisie was no longer on speaking terms with any of her family ever since her stepbrother's son had asked her where she had parked the camel and when she was going to be circumcised.

Robert struggled into his green socks. Mr Malik had insisted the staff also appear in uniform since early February, although Robert suspected this was only because he had a deal with the shop that supplied the ties and the socks. He had come to quite like the outfit. *I will die with my boots on! It can't be worse than Ramadan!*

He shuddered slightly as he thought about Ramadan. Dr Ali had been particularly active during Ramadan. He kept leaping into the darkroom, created for the Photographic Society on the first floor, and claiming that he had heard the sound of munching.

It was surprising, really, that the only person in the school whom Dr Ali had sentenced to death should be Robert. Close examination of the man's conversation suggested that no one in the Western world was safe. There was quite a lot of his conversation. Like the woman in the fairy story, once Ali started talking he did not stop.

There were, as far as Robert could tell, no other members of the British Mission for Islamic Purity, the organization the doctor claimed to represent. Ali had an aunt in Southfields, but, he told the headmaster, she was doomed to everlasting hell-fire. The man was, as Dr Malik had pointed out to Robert, a fundamentalist's fundamentalist. 'As far as he is concerned,' said the headmaster one evening in the Frog and Ferret, 'there is Allah, there is Muhammad, and then there is him. What can you do with such people?'

Ali, it turned out, had been sentencing people to death for years. He had sentenced the owner of a garden centre in Morden to death when the man refused to take his Access card. He had sentenced the entire General Synod of the Church of England to death. He had sentenced over fifteen hundred journalists to death, including all of the staff of *The London Programme*. He had terrifyingly conservative views on the ordination of women.

The encouraging thing was that all the people he had sentenced were, so far at any rate, in good health. Some of them, as far as Robert could tell, were completely unaware that Dr Ahmed Ali had officially decreed they were no longer worthy to share the planet with him. Some of them seemed to have positively enjoyed the experience. One of them – the owner of a mobile whelk stall in South Wimbledon – had told the doctor that he could sentence him to death until he was blue in the face and that he, personally, could not give a flying fuck. This was more or less the view of the headmaster.

'By all means sentence Wilson to death,' Mr Malik had said. 'By all means. I think we should all start sentencing each other to death. It clears the air. Let's "go for it". Sentence me to death if it makes you feel better.'

Mr Malik's tolerance was limitless. 'I may have tried to keep the loonies out,' he said, 'but once they are in, they are in!' The more eccentrically his maths master behaved, the more Malik was prepared to defend him. At half-term, Ali had offered ten pounds to any of 'the proud Muslim people of South-West London' who would be prepared to finish off Robert Wilson, but, even though he had raised this sum to twelve pounds fifty, there were, so far at any rate, no takers.

Robert's real worry was that he could not understand what it was that had caused offence. If he had been able to understand that, he might at least have been able to formulate a coherent apology. It couldn't have simply been his reading *The Sheep-Pig* to Class 1. Maybe the doctor had some inside information on him. Anyway, if he opened his mouth again, he thought glumly as he started downstairs to breakfast, he would probably get into worse trouble. He had stayed clear of the subject of religion since Christmas.

If only he could manage to finish the Koran. He had made several attempts on it. He had tried saying it out loud. He had tried reading it on trains, in bed at night, and even, on one occasion, in the bath. He had tried starting in the middle and working backwards. He had tried starting at the end and flicking to the beginning. He had tried reading isolated pages – reading three pages, skipping three, and then reading four. He had tried it drunk and he had tried it sober. He had even tried starting at page 1 and working his way through to the end. None of these methods had worked. After a page, his eyes would wander away. After two pages, he would find himself, without quite knowing why or how he got there, making a cup of tea or watching the television. After three or four pages, he found himself wandering the streets or pacing anxiously through some park he didn't even recognize, twitching and murmuring strangely to himself while mothers, at the sight of him, drew their children to them and stole softly away across the grass.

When he reached the bottom of the stairs, he turned and called up to Maisie. 'Coming!' she replied.

Hasan was sitting up at the table, eating a large slice of toast. The butter was dribbling across that huge mark on his cheek. Mrs Wilson was sitting on the sofa, smiling foolishly at him.

Immediately he heard Robert's footsteps, Hasan stopped. 'Hello, Mr Wilson,' he said, in his high, precise voice. 'I dreamed last night that Badger turned into a hedgehog. Would you see if there is a hedgehog on the lawn?'

Hasan was always having prophetic dreams. They were modest, small-scale affairs, usually about very mundane subjects. But the events described in them – the loss of some ornament, or the visit of some old family friend – quite often turned out to happen just as the little boy had predicted. There was something uncanny about him, his high forehead and his big, sightless eyes.

Robert went to the French windows and looked out to see if he could see anything. There, in the middle of the lawn, was a hedgehog. Robert whirled round on his mother, suspecting her of some collusion with the child, but, with the wistful fondness of a woman who has finished with childbearing, Mrs Wilson was still gazing at the Twenty-fourth Imam of the Wimbledon Dharjees.

'Is Badger around?' said Robert, trying to keep the panic out of his voice, 'because there's a hedgehog on –'

At this moment Badger skulked into the kitchen, loped over to the pedal bin, and stood gazing mournfully at a piece of orange peel, just visible over the edge of the plastic rim.

'Maisie!' called Mrs Wilson. *Le petit déjeuner est servi, ma chérie!*

There was a grunt from upstairs. Robert's father was awake.

Robert sat at a vacant space and put his head in his hands. His mother looked at him, briskly. 'What's the matter this morning?' she said, in the voice she had used when he asked her for an off-games note.

'Just the usual,' said Robert, with heavy sarcasm. 'I've been sentenced to death. Apart from that, everything is fine. Everything is a winner!'

Mrs Wilson snorted. 'I do not think, Robert,' she said, 'that anyone takes this man very seriously. All you said was that the Koran wasn't an easy read. Nobody kills anyone for saying something like that. It's fair comment. I personally think –'

Before his mother could get started on the Koran, Robert held up his hand. You never knew who might be listening. She looked, however, as if she was fairly determined to give her views on the matter, but before she could start on the *Why do they come over here if they don't like it?* speech or her *I believe in respecting people's religious feelings but would die to defend their right to disagree wth me* speech, Maisie came round the door.

She ate breakfast in a kind of compromise Islamic outfit. Just after her conversion – a moment of mystical submission she insisted on replaying several times a day – she had kept the veil on even at meals, and forked meat and potatoes in under her mask like a gamekeeper baiting a trap. She also stored food in there like a hamster, and sometimes, when least expected, her head would snake back inside her covering and the crunch of crisps or the slurp of a boiled sweet could be heard. But now her outfit, although loose and flowing, was slightly closer to the kind of garment you might expect in SW19. It was more like a giant caftan than anything else.

It was Mr Malik who had persuaded her to soften her approach. 'Even in Libya they don't carry on like that,' he had said. 'You look like something out of a pantomime. What are you supposed to be?'

Her friendship with the headmaster remained a close one. While Mr Malik hardly ever discussed religion with Robert, he spent many evenings in the La Paesana restaurant, Mitcham, going over the finer points of Islamic doctrine with Maisie. 'We always spend a lot of time with female converts, Wilson,' he said, giving him a broad wink. 'They are a lot more work, if you take my meaning!'

Robert was not exactly jealous of the headmaster – he could not remember meeting anyone less sexually threatening. But there were moments when he almost wished that what was happening between Maisie and Mr Malik did have a sexual con- notation. At least he would then have been able to understand it.

'Sports Day today!' said Maisie brightly.

No one, as usual, wanted to discuss the fact that he had been

127

sentenced to death. They were bored with it. At first, Robert's father had got quite excited. He had even gone to the Wimbledon police, but they had not seemed very interested. They had said a Detective Constable McCabe, a community policeman, would 'look in', which, after a couple of weeks, he did. He seemed mainly interested in whether there were any locks on the windows.

Robert's father appeared. His hair was matted and uncombed, and his face, as usual in the mornings, was a rather shocking blend of inflamed pink and seasick white. He was wearing a dressing-gown.

'What do you do for Sports Day?' he said. 'Stone one of the junior ticks to death?'

A lot of Mr Wilson senior's liberal attitudes had not stood the test of having two converted Muslims living in the house. He was often to be found slumped in front of the television, muttering about nig-nogs. At Christmas he had insisted on hanging up Robert's stocking on the end of his bed, and had suggested the two of them visit the Cranborne School carol service. He peered across at Maisie now, as he groped his way to the table, his face showing the strain of his forty-eight years in Wimbledon. 'You used to have nice legs, Maisie,' he said. 'What's wrong with our getting a look at them?'

Mrs Wilson had told him he should get out of the house more. This he achieved by getting along to the Frog and Ferret at about eleven each morning, where he spent hours in conversation with George 'This is My Coronary' Parker.

Maisie giggled. Underneath the Islamic garments she was still an English convent girl. With her veil pushed back and her black hood shading her face, she looked rather like a nun.

Mrs Wilson rose and, folding her hands together, bowed in an Oriental manner. 'Thank you,' she said, 'for our meal.' It was not clear whether this remark was addressed to Allah, Jehovah or the London Muffin Company. She had taken, this spring, to a sort of generalized reverence that looked as if it was planned to accommodate any new religion to which her son or his girl-friend might have become attached.

She had also given up all her domestic routines. She cleared the table as they were eating, following, as always now, her own weird domestic schedule. Sometimes she would start laying the table for breakfast at four in the afternoon; sometimes she would pursue Maisie and Robert out into the street with plates of hot food, begging them to eat more. And sometimes she would announce that she was doing no more in the house. 'There it is!' she would yell, pointing at the fridge. 'It's all in there! It's every man for himself from now on in!'

Perhaps, thought Robert, she was worried about him. It would be nice to think that someone was. He pushed back his chair, and, after one more careful look round the garden, went to look for Class 1's homework. At the top of the pile was a beautifully typed essay from Sheikh on the causes of the English Civil War. The little bastard, or his parents, or some hired professional historian, had written three thousand closely argued words. Robert had given him beta minus (query).

'There you are, Mr Wilson,' Maisie was saying, as she twirled her skirt above her legs like a cancan dancer – 'knees!'

He had to get out of the school. But how could he do it? How could he ever admit to Maisie that the very thing that had brought them together was, like so much else in his life, a lie? He was tied to her and to Mr Malik in exactly the way he was tied to his own parents. He was also, he realized, as he went through to the hall to get Hasan's coat, tied to the little boy in a way he could not have predicted. It wasn't simply that he felt protective towards him. It was that he was beginning to understand why Aziz the janitor and his friends might be convinced he was no ordinary child.

He took Hasan's hand and went out into the clear light of April.

'Did Badger turn into a hedgehog, Mr Wilson?' said the little boy. 'I have special powers and can foresee things!'

Robert squeezed his charge's hand. 'In a way he did, Hasan,' he said. 'In a way he did.'

He was starting to believe this stuff. As he and Hasan and Maisie started out down Wimbledon Park Road, he remembered something the headmaster had said to him, quite soon after he had started teaching the reception class. 'Islam means *surrender*, my dear Wilson. And so you must surrender. You may think you stand on your own, or have your own choices, or make your own fate, but you do not do so. You submit, and let your life take its course. The course that God has designed for it.'

The trees were out in Wimbledon Park. As the three of them started to climb the hill, Maisie, who no longer walked yards behind the men in her life, took Robert's arm and started to sing. At first he did not recognize the tune, and then he caught its cadences. It wasn't English. It had the swoop and the lilt of something one might have heard blaring out of a Turkish café. It was a song Mr Malik sang, and she was singing it to what must, surely, be his words.

> Come to me,
> My beautiful girl.
> Don't be shy now.
> Leave your mother,
> Leave your father,
> Leave your people.
> Don't be shy now.
> Come to me,
> My beautiful girl.
> You are one of mine now.
> You are one of ours now.
> Come to me, oh come to me,
> Beautiful,
> Beautiful,
> Girl.

14

From time to time he wondered whether he had made a mistake in sleeping with her. It was something he had been wanting to do for over ten years, but, now that he had done it, he had destroyed something that had been between them – a mysterious, almost exquisite, promise of delight. He was starting to tell the truth – that was what it was. It was hard to keep lying when you were alone in bed with someone. If this went on much longer, the real Robert Wilson might emerge – that awful, jelly-like creature that he had been hiding from the world for the last twenty-four years.

Perhaps they had taken too long to get together. If only he had moved earlier. If only he had pushed his advantage home the night the Dorking brothers gave their party ('The Night of the Hundred Cans', as it was still known in Wimbledon). If only he had made his move six years earlier, during the rehearsed reading of Martin Finkelstein's verse play *These Be Wasted Years, Brother!*

Except he hadn't. They were too like brother and sister, that was it.

If that was the case, incest had never been more fun. Sex with Maisie was about the most interesting thing Robert had ever done. It upstaged even Mr and Mrs Wilson, who had gone markedly quiet since Maisie entered the field. Maisie particularly enjoyed being spanked with a hairbrush, and liked to accompany this activity with a series of clear, confident expressions of her need to be disciplined. 'Oh my arse!' she would call in the still of the Wimbledon night. 'Oh my fat *arse*! Spank it! Spank it, you bastard!'

At the moment of climax she quite often addressed him as

Derek. Robert had not yet been able to fathom why this was the case. It was possible, of course, that she was referring, for purely symbolic reasons, to a specialized form of lifting gear.

Robert wasn't sure that their sexual relations were in line with Islamic thinking – at least as formulated by Marwan Ibrahim Al-Kaysi. They did not pray two *rak'ahs* before making love, or perform *wudu* after intercourse (perhaps because neither of them had the faintest idea what *wudu* might be), and they were woefully deficient in the sacrifice and dowry departments. Maisie was also guilty of one of Al-Kaysi's key errors, *leaving the house excessively* – a practice he quite clearly did not relish in women.

There were times when he thought Maisie was not much more of a Muslim than he was. The headmaster himself had accused her of only joining up for the uniform. But – and this was the real divide between them – she *thought* she was a Muslim. He knew he wasn't. However absurd her convictions might seem, at least they were convictions.

'Tell me,' said Robert, as they walked up the High Street, 'and I'm not going on about it, but exactly why did Ali sentence me to death?'

'Because you said Enid Blyton sold more copies than the Koran,' said Maisie, 'and said that pigs were terrific and Muslims had to learn to deal with them.'

'I did not say any of those things,' said Robert, 'and, even if I did, I don't think they merit the death penalty. I mean, this is a free country – isn't it?'

Maisie tightened her lips. 'You're not free to offend people,' she said. 'It's a very fine line!'

It was, thought Robert, a *very* fine line. You never knew these days when a casual remark was going to provide the justification for someone stalking you with an automatic rifle. He looked nervously over his shoulder, but saw nothing.

'Dr Ali said that you said bad things about Muhammad,' Maisie went on. 'Apparently he heard you.'

'When did he hear? Who was I talking to?'

'You were walking along muttering them to yourself. He said they were so shocking he couldn't even bear to repeat them.'

She seemed almost prepared to take the good doctor's part in this dispute, thought Robert. Why couldn't Ali forget the pig business? Why couldn't the guy loosen up? Robert had not even mentioned pigs in three months.

'The worse thing you can do to a Muslim is insult Muhammad.'

She was always showing off her superior knowledge these days, thought Robert. And the more she found out about Islam, the more she seemed to like it. His trouble was, he realized, that he was simply not able to grasp any religion, let alone a faith where his only spiritual mentor was a book from Wimbledon Public Library.

'I would never say anything bad about Muhammad,' said Robert. 'Even I know better than that.'

'Why would you want to?' said Maisie. 'You're a Muslim, aren't you?'

She had probably rumbled him. Even when he was being particularly careful not to offend, he seemed to manage to say the wrong thing. He had noticed, for example, that Dr Ali always accompanied the Prophet's name with the formula '*may God bless him and grant him peace!*' and, often, in the doctor's presence, Robert would work Muhammad's name into the conversation precisely so that he, too, could repeat the traditional blessing. He often went one better. 'Muhammad – *may God bless him and grant him peace* – who was, I don't need to remind you, quite a guy – once said – and what he said was, on the whole earth, listening to – on several occasions – not that he was a man given to repeating himself – once, anyway, said – and he had a beautiful speaking voice . . .* etc. etc. This cut no ice with the doctor. He watched Robert from under his hooded eyes, a slight smile playing around his lips.

'I have to get the bread for lunch,' said Maisie. 'Do you want to come in? You'll probably be safer in the shop. You could hide under the counter.'

'I don't see what's so funny,' said Robert, who was looking

nervously down the street. 'There are some funny things going on around here.'

As he said this, he caught sight of Mr Malik, who was walking towards the school. Robert held Hasan's hand tightly. The little boy showed no sign of rising vertically into the air or of summoning seven hundred fiery horsemen from out of the sky.

Robert was sweating. He wiped his brow. From the other side of the road, Aziz the janitor, on his way to school, a sinister smile on his face, started to wave his mop in greeting. For some reason Aziz always took his mop home with him. 'How is the boy?' he said, in his cracked voice.

'He's fine!' said Robert.

'I would like a cake please,' said Hasan, 'with some jam on it!'

Eager to get him away from Aziz, Robert handed him over to Maisie and peered, once more, carefully around him. He was seeing men with one shoe in his sleep these days. He had been sure one was following him round Sainsbury's the other day.

Apart from the headmaster, who had now gone into the school, the place seemed clear. Robert stayed on the pavement while Maisie went in to buy the school's bread. Suddenly a heavy hand whacked him in the shoulder blades. Robert wheeled round to see the beaming face of Mr Mafouz. Next to him, his round face straining towards the cakes in the shop window, was his favourite son.

'That's enough cakes, Anwar!' said Mr Mafouz, and, placing his broad hand on his son's backside, he propelled the boy towards the school.

'How's things?' said Mr Mafouz.

'Not too bad,' said Robert.

The sun picked up the colours of a girl's dress. It sparkled in her hair as she swayed past the grocer's opposite. Clasped into themselves like baby's fists, new shoots were hung along the branches of each tree in the High Street. It was spring. Spring and Wimbledon were still here, even if at times he felt he had landed in a foreign country. As he made the conventional response, Robert felt a curious exaltation, as if the phrase had

134

made such unpleasant things as Dr Ali melt away. He liked Mr Mafouz.

Perhaps, as Mr Malik had suggested, he was slowly learning to surrender, and, by surrendering, to enjoy the sun, the blue sky and the sweetness of having, at long last, a girl to share his bed.

'In fact,' said Robert, 'I feel great.'

'Malik declared the cricket season three months early,' said Mr Mafouz. 'Did you know one is not supposed to play cricket in April? We have been playing since February. He wishes us to get into training for thrashing Cranborne.'

On the other side of the road, Anwar was playing cricket strokes. Robert tried to remember whether the Egyptians had a cricket team and, if so, whether they were any good. Inside the baker's, Maisie had got involved in a complicated negotiation with the shopkeeper. Hasan had pressed his face to the glass in front of the cakes and was sniffing the fresh bread, a look of ecstasy on his face. Mr Mafouz and Robert idled along the pavement.

'How is Anwar's schoolwork?' said Mr Mafouz.

'He is a genius,' said Robert swiftly.

Mr Mafouz grinned. He put his right hand in his jacket pocket and produced a bulky envelope. Robert did not have to ask what it contained. Over the last months Mr Mafouz had given him two free tickets to Paris, a pineapple, six copies of the *Illutrated Tourist Guide to London* and a pair of bright green trousers. Recently, as the summer exams grew closer, he had started to offer money.

'I really couldn't, Mr Mafouz,' said Robert.

'Listen,' said Mr Mafouz, clapping Robert on the back, hard, 'there's more where that came from. If he passes his GCSEs, who knows what I might come up with?'

He leaned his face into Robert's. 'How does a week in Luxor grab you?' he said.

'Sounds fun!' said Robert.

Last week the ever amiable travel agent had asked him 'how

much' the Oxford entrance exam was 'compared with what they're asking in Sussex or Cambridge.'

The two men came level with the school gates. From the bakery, Maisie emerged with Hasan, carrying a pile of loaves, and walked into the road, narrowly avoiding an oncoming lorry.

'Tell me,' said Mr Mafouz, 'about "A" levels. Are those people reachable?'

It was impossible to refuse Mr Mafouz's gifts. Robert had done the decent thing and given Anwar alpha double plus for an essay entitled 'My Cat'. He shuddered now, as he recalled the essay: *'I have a cat. It was hit on the head with a spade by my brother. It was in agony . . .'*

From the Common came more parents. Mr Sheikh and Mr Akhtar walked slowly and seriously towards the gates. Mr Mafouz's face darkened. 'The Sheikh boy,' he said, 'is not up to much, I think.'

Robert thought of Sheikh's seventy-page project on 'Irrigation in the Third World,' his groundbreaking work in chemistry and physics, and the long short story, in French, he had recently submitted, successfully, to an avant-garde magazine. 'He is thin on the ground,' said Robert. 'There is something . . . shifty about the boy!'

Mr Mafouz grinned.

Mr and Mrs Mahmud joined the rest of the crowd at the gates. An elegant BMW drew up over the road and Fatimah Bankhead, the chain-smoking Islamic feminist, stepped out. She gave the assembled group of men a contemptuous sweep of her fine, grey eyes, and marched up the path. Another expensive car pulled in behind her, and Robert recognized Mr Shah, the man from whom they had collected Hasan last summer. He was still wearing the elegantly tailored suit he had worn on that occasion. His name was now inscribed above the door in the Great Hall, with the words OUR BENEFACTOR next to it.

'We'd better go through to the sports field,' said Robert.

He could hear the whoops of small boys from the garden. Up at the first-floor window, the curtains parted and Mr Malik peered out. Robert looked back at Maisie and Hasan. As they came up to the gates, Aziz sidled up to the little boy with his mop, an ingratiating smile on his face.

'Well, well, Hasan!' he began.

But before he could get any further, Mr Malik thrust his head out of the window. 'Clean!' he barked. 'This is Sports Day! I want everything sparkling clean!'

With a resentful grunt, Aziz shambled off into the school.

Mr Malik was wearing cricket whites and a large floppy hat; a dirty white jersey was folded about his neck. If what Robert had seen, to date, of the school's cricket was anything to go by, today was going to be an exhausting experience.

There was an Islamic doctrine, of which the headmaster had often spoken to Robert, known as *ijma*. It meant, as far as Robert could tell, a kind of consensus. It was rather like that strange spirit that hovered over the Wilson family when they were contemplating an evening out and told them where they ought to eat, and it had something in common with whatever it was that told the entire Liverpool football stadium to sing 'You'll Never Walk Alone' at the same moment. It was absent, however, during inter-house matches at the Islamic Boys' School (Day Independent Wimbledon). Every man was his own umpire. During the last match, the Husayn twins had nearly beaten the Bosnian refugee to death with the stumps after he had refused to accept a boundary decision. (In the absence of white lines, boundaries were hotly disputed.) As Robert rounded the school building, with Mr Mafouz by his side, he could hear Anwar Mafouz war-whooping his way round the lawn.

In the narrow passage that led through to the garden, they came upon Rafiq. He was standing with Dr Ali. When he saw Robert, he made what looked like a little, stunted bow and moved back towards the boys on the lawn. There was something decidedly odd about the engineering master; his manner was always friendly, but, in the six months he had been at the school, Robert had not exchanged more than a few words with the man.

Dr Ali smirked at Robert as Mr Mafouz went through to join

the other parents. 'Well, Wilson,' said the maths master, 'I see you are still with us.'

'Indeed,' said Robert. 'I'm still about the place.'

Robert looked at Dr Ali. There was nothing the matter with his features. The nose was roughly in the right place. The moustache was well groomed. The shape of the cheeks – if slightly too reminiscent of a cadaver – had a certain elegance. His eyes – full, black and watchful – were almost attractive. His hair was oiled, and arranged with obsessive neatness across his scalp, and his ears, the colour of raw tuna-fish, were big, intricate and well balanced. And yet about him there hung the indefinable air of ugliness.

The doctor smirked again. 'I wonder for how long!' he said, in a somewhat arch tone.

'It is,' said Robert, 'in the hands of Allah.'

The trouble was, of course, it might by now be in the hands of some high-spirited Islamic youth movement.

His earlier good spirits fading, Robert followed Dr Ali through to the back lawn, as, from a side entrance to the school, the headmaster emerged carrying a large white box. He held it aloft. 'New balls!' he said, and, swinging his arms like a sergeant-major, led his masters out towards the field of battle, in the bright April sunlight.

15

Robert took up a position on the boundary, fairly near to the maths master. As usual, he attempted to strike the correct tone with the man. You couldn't simply ignore the fact that he had sentenced you to death, but it was important to let him know that you weren't rattled. Except, of course, you were rattled. It was dangerous, too, to appear too over-confident, or to do anything that might provoke him into making his unofficial fatwa slightly more public than it was already. Ali was so mean that he was unlikely to buy advertising space, even for a religious edict, and, anyway, he had clearly found Robert's words so offensive that he had, so far, been incapable of repeating them to anyone. But you never knew . . .

Robert clasped his hands behind his back and tried for a light, bantering tone. 'Should I take out life insurance, Dr Ali?'

Ali looked at him. His expression did not alter. 'I do not think,' he said with some conviction, 'that you will find a company prepared to take the risk.'

Presumably the man expected him to add, in the section of the proposal form where you were supposed to talk about your passion for hang-gliding or free-fall parachute jumping, a brief paragraph along the lines of I HAVE ALSO BEEN SENTENCED TO DEATH BY AN ISLAMIC FUNDAMENTALIST.

'What I mean to say,' replied Robert, 'is that I feel I need to know where I stand.'

Mr Malik was fixing in the stumps. Rafiq was choosing the two teams. The Husayn twins wanted to be together. Nobody wanted the Bosnian refugee. Mafouz wanted to be captain. While all this went on, the parents sat around on the school's battered garden furniture, the mothers watching each other warily, the fathers armoured in a remote mildness that Robert recognized from his own parent. *We're the same really*, he thought. *What's the big difference?* Then he looked down at Dr Ali.

'You know where you stand, Yusuf,' said the doctor – 'you stand on slippery ground. *There are some who declare "We believe in Allah and the last day" yet they are not true believers. They seek to deceive Allah and those who believe in him. There is a sickness in their hearts which Allah has increased, and they shall be sternly punished for their hypocrisy.*'

Robert gulped. The man was on to him.

'That's the Koran, isn't it?' he guessed.

Dr Ali did not respond. Robert tried to compose his face into an expression of humble trust.

'It's an extraordinary book,' he went on. 'I'm going to take it away on holiday.'

'Are you a fool or are you pretending to be a fool?' said the maths master.

'A bit of both,' said Robert, trying to keep the tone light.

Dr Ali moved a few paces away from him. This approach was clearly not working. Perhaps, thought Robert, I should sentence *him* to death. Perhaps the gently gently approach only served to bolster Ali's confidence. He wandered over to the far wall.

As he did so, he saw Hasan walk out from the back kitchen. The little boy was wearing the same neat grey flannels that he had worn on the first day Robert had seen him, and, when the sun struck his face, he smiled up at it as if in gratitude. In his right hand was a large cake with jam on it. Robert wanted to go over to him, but judged it best to stay where he was.

Mafouz was bowling, urged on by his father. 'Smash them, Anwar!' Mr Mafouz yelled. 'Go for the bastards!'

Fatimah Bankhead gave him a mean look. Mafouz shuffled up to the bowling crease and started to wind his right arm backwards at high speed. 'I am good at cricket!' he yelled.

Sheikh, who was batting, stood crouched over his bat, patiently waiting for the moment when Mafouz would decide to let go of the ball. It was hard to tell, at the moment, whether it would be moving at or away from him, but Sheikh, a patient and methodical child, looked ready to run after it and beat it to death on the boundary should this prove necessary.

'Quiet, please!' called Mr Malik, crouching low over the stumps at the bowler's end. 'Please continue to bowl, Mafouz!'

Mafouz responded by altering the direction of his arm movement to a forward thrust. He also increased the speed. His face, red with the effort, wore a glazed, far-away expression. He started to bite his lip. 'Watch out, Sheikh!' he called – 'this is going to be a fast one!'

Mahmud, unable to restrain himself any longer, moved from his position in the slips to face Sheikh directly. 'Yeah, Sheikh,' he called – 'this will be punishment!'

Mr Malik lowered his nose until it almost touched the bails. 'You are directly in the flight path, Mahmud,' he said. 'Return to base!'

Mahmud stayed where he was. Eventually his father moved on to the pitch and, seizing his son by the right ear, dragged him back into a fielding position.

Still young Mafouz showed no sign of letting go of the ball. 'This is going to be an amazing one!' he yelled.

'Go, Anwar, go!' yelled his father.

Mr Malik did not seem anxious that Mafouz should let go of the ball until he was absolutely ready to do so. Perhaps, thought Robert, Mr Mafouz had bought his son into an unassailable position on the cricket team.

Anwar's arm revolved faster and faster, until it was no more than a blur above his shoulders. It looked very probable that the ball was not going to be the only thing to rise in the air – Mafouz himself, Robert felt, was about to climb up like a helicopter, clear of the grass, and hover over Wimbledon.

'You are dead meat, Sheikh!' Mafouz yelled.

Sheikh did not flinch. Holding his bat with the precision of a monk wielding a quill pen, he waited patiently for whatever Mafouz should deliver.

Finally the travel agent's son let go of the ball. It went neither forwards nor backwards but straight up in the air. Everyone, parents and boys, craned their necks back and stared into the cerulean blue above the Village. For what seemed an age, the dark speck hung above them, a piece of grit in the sky, and then, with languid slowness, started its descent.

'It's coming for you, Sheikh!' shouted Mafouz. 'It's on it's way, boy! Run and hide!'

For a moment, Robert thought that this was what Sheikh was going to do. He let the bat dangle from his fingers as he searched the horizon for the ball, like a fighter pilot seeking out his enemy above the clouds. The ball was headed for a spot almost equidistant between the two wickets. Suddenly Sheikh shouldered his bat and, letting out a kind of howl, set out for the middle of the pitch, elbowing a fielder out of the way. He looked like a man prepared to do battle.

When the ball finally reached him, the normally placid boy bared his teeth and, whirling the bat round his head, whacked the offending object back up to where it had just come from. It climbed vertically above the field, retracing its earlier journey, until it seemed to hang suspended at the precise point where it had rested a moment ago.

No one ran to catch it. It was more or less understood that this was something between Mafouz and Sheikh. Mafouz was flexing his hands and making crouching movements as the ball started its slow descent.

'It will destroy you utterly, Mafouz,' yelled Sheikh, brandishing his bat at him. 'You have minutes left to live.'

'Kill him,' yelled Mr Mafouz. 'Get it straight back at him!'

Indeed, Mafouz looked as if he was about to do something far more dramatic than simply catch the thing. He had made his right hand into a fist and was jabbing it up at the sky, feinting in the direction of the falling missile. Perhaps he was going to punch it straight back at the batsman.

The ball seemed to have acquired a life of its own. As Mafouz tacked one way, it would move in the other, and when he swerved round to get it once more in his sights it would sidle left or right until it was sure it was once again in his blind spot. It seemed to show a complete disregard for the laws of Galileo,

Newton and Einstein, moving through the atmosphere like an otter in pursuit of a fish. When it got within spitting distance of Mafouz, who was now standing, arms loosely apart, mouth open, as if hypnotized by the thing's movements, it did a sharp turn to the left, bounced along horizontally for a few yards, and then snarled up and down to land on the unfortunate boy's head.

Mafouz fell heavily to earth amidst sudden, devastating silence.

Robert was the only one among staff, parents and boys who was not looking at Mafouz. His eyes were on Hasan. The little boy was standing in the passage that led out towards the front garden. He was talking to Aziz the janitor. Aziz had lost his brown overalls. He was wearing the crumpled suit he had been wearing on the day Robert first saw him in the pub. He had his arms round Hasan. Robert started to make his way across the garden towards the two of them. Aziz, who had his back to the garden, did not see him.

Mr Malik was in the middle of a group crowded round Mafouz. Among them, Robert noticed, was Mr Shah. Mafouz's father was cradling the boy in his arms and saying, in a deep voice, 'Speak to me, Anwar! Speak to me!'

Robert kept his eyes on Hasan and Aziz from about ten yards away. It was only when Maisie emerged from the back kitchen, wearing her third headscarf of the morning (this one was in Liberty print and made her look as if she was about to go out to watch titled men shooting grouse), that he felt emboldened to get close enough to hear what they were saying.

'It is time!' Aziz was whispering.

'This morning,' said Hasan in conversational tones, 'a dog turned into a hedgehog!'

Aziz did not seem surprised by this information. He nodded gravely. 'I think so,' he said. 'It is time!'

Time for what?

'After my Occultation,' said Hasan, 'will I be able to see?'

'You will see with the inner eye!' said Aziz.

143

Mafouz was coming round in his father's arms. 'It is coming for you, Sheikh,' he murmured. 'You are dead meat!'

Mr Mafouz kissed his boy, first on the lips, then on the forehead, then on the whole of the upper body. 'We cannot afford to lose such a boy,' Robert heard Mr Malik say. 'He is a genius!' The travel agent was almost definitely slipping him something, thought Robert. Mind you, Mr Malik needed all the finance he could get. *'Spend generously and do not keep an account,'* ran his favourite *hadith* of the Prophet. *'God will keep an account for you. Put nothing to one side – God will put to one side for you!'* This was not a principle calculated to endear him to the Inland Revenue or the men from Customs & Excise. But, as he was fond of reminding Robert, one of the many good things about life in the Medina area in the seventh century after Christ was the complete absence of Customs & Excise men.

Maisie approached Robert. She too seemed uncomfortably aware of Hasan and Aziz. 'What's the matter?' she whispered.

'I think,' said Robert, 'it's Hasan's Occultation!'

Maisie put her hand to her mouth. 'My God!' she said. 'His Occultation!'

'What do you suppose he'll do?' said Robert.

Maisie seemed peeved by this question. '*I* don't know,' she said, 'what they do at the actual ceremony.'

Robert could not answer this question. Whatever it was, he felt it must be pretty nasty. It was not going to be a few bridge rolls and the odd glass of lemonade. These Twenty-fourthers were serious people. They wore weird slippers, they quoted the heavier bits of the Koran at you. What more did you want?

'I think Hasan sort of *turns into* the Twenty-fourth Imam,' said Robert. 'It's a bit like a presidential inauguration. But I imagine more basic. They probably sacrifice something. And, after it, he gets special powers.'

Hasan giggled. Aziz started to stroke his hair.

'He's probably a reincarnation of someone,' Robert went on – 'some Islamic character from the twelfth century. Didn't you say there was a Hasan in the Middle Ages?'

'Maybe they want his autograph,' said Maisie, with heavy

144

sarcasm. She was watching the couple very carefully, and, when they started out together down the passage towards the High Street, she followed them.

'What do you think you're doing?' hissed Robert.

'I'm following them!' said Maisie.

'They're dangerous!' whispered Robert.

'That's why you have to come too,' said Maisie. 'I'm only a woman. I need your strong Muslim arms.'

Robert did not try to contest the authenticity of either of these adjectives. Since her conversion, Maisie had been very assertive about her need to submit. 'I am low,' she would sometimes say, especially before breakfast. 'I am low, low on the ground next to you, Yusuf!' In these moods, she reminded Robert of his mother. She was particularly fond, especially when asked her opinion on some current controversy, of quoting the words of Muhammad to Abu Said al-Khudri: *'Isn't the testimony of a woman worth only half the testimony of a man? That is because of her inferior intelligence.'*

'These guys,' said Robert, 'are not messing about!'

They were now halfway down the passage. Rafiq stood in their way. His face wore that same enigmatic smile, but he did not speak. Maisie pushed past him, and, with a little sigh, the older man moved back against the wall.

'Mr Shah,' said the engineering master, 'is not such a nice man as you think!'

'No?'

Robert didn't want to talk to the engineering master, but neither did he want to go out after Aziz the janitor, who, in their first conversation in the Frog and Ferret, had made pretty clear not only his low opinion of infidels but also his readiness to use cutlery on other human beings with whom he disagreed.

Perhaps, he thought to himself, this was all part of a plot worked up by Dr Ali. Perhaps Twenty-fourthers hired themselves out on a contract basis to anyone wanting to lean heavily on un-Islamic behaviour.

Maisie had gone before him into the front garden. She turned to Robert and called. 'I need your strong arms!' she said. 'If Hasan is in danger . . .'

As Robert moved forward after her, Rafiq grabbed him, hard, round the waist. 'Do not do this,' growled the engineering master, 'or you will burn in everlasting fire, and hell shall be your couch! The ground will yawn open before you, and the trees will bend to strike at your face.' He had obviously not allowed his degree course to affect his view of what was and was not possible in the physical world. It was also depressing to realize that yet another member of the staffroom of the Islamic Boys' Independent Wimbledon Day School was barking mad.

Robert broke free of him.

'You do not know what goes on at this school,' said Rafiq. 'Who do you think watches you day and night? Is not this school damned? Who knows where the little boy is? Who knows what he is?'

'You tell me,' said Robert, as he moved after Maisie.

'His name is Thunder,' said Rafiq, 'and he brings curses. What do you know of any of this? What do you know of our secrets?'

The honest answer would have been to say *Fuck all*, but Robert did not feel inclined to do so. Pulling himself away from the older man, he ran after Maisie, who was now somewhere out in the road. Rafiq followed him, and for a moment Robert thought he was going to hit him, but, instead, he ran across the road and over towards the far side of the Common.

Maisie was screaming something, but he could not hear what it was. He ran, faster and faster, towards the sound of her voice, until the noise of the cricket game faded and the familiar world of traffic and aeroplanes and reassuring English faces crowded out the thought that had been started by Rafiq.

You're out of your depth, Wilson. You're in deep, deep trouble. Get out while there's still time!

16

When he got to the High Street, he saw Hasan and Aziz walking up to the Common. The janitor was still holding the little boy's hand.

Maisie rounded on Robert. She seemed to have decided that he was responsible for all this. 'Mr Malik put him in your care!' she hissed. 'Do something! Call him back!'

Robert started after the little boy. 'Hasan!' he called. 'I think you should come with me!'

Hasan turned to him, slowly. He reached out his hands towards the sound of Robert's voice. 'I must go, Mr Wilson,' he said. 'It is the time!'

With which he turned and trotted off beside the janitor.

When they got to the edge of the grass, Aziz turned and leered at Maisie and Robert. He looked, thought Robert, more than usually unappetising. 'Leave us!' he said. 'Go back to the blasphemer Malik! Crawl on your belly to the hypocrites! You are the vomit of the devil, Wilson!'

He was always saying things like this. Robert did not like to think of himself as a snob, but, had he been in charge of the Independent Wimbledon Day Islamic Boys' School, he would have expected a higher standard of civility from the cleaning staff.

'Listen – ' he began. But, before he had the chance to complete the sentence, a swarm of people came from out of the birch-trees and Aziz and Hasan disappeared into them. Most of them were wearing wellingtons. Many of the women had headscarves and, among the men, walking-sticks of the folksier kind were popular. Every single one of them – and there were upwards of seventy or eighty in the group – seemed to have brought at least one dog.

Robert recognized faces he had been trying to avoid for weeks. There was Ron 'Rescue Dog' Hitchens, with his three Rottweilers, one of which had recently eaten a Scotch terrier. 'He's only being friendly!' Ron had screamed as Mrs Coates's dog was consumed. There was the mad Irishman with Fang, his Alsatian, accompanied by Myrtle 'It's the Best Exercise' Freeman and her Dobermann. 'It's the Best Exercise!' was what she yelled at Robert every time the Dobermann came for Badger at about thirty miles an hour with the clearly expressed intention of biting his head off. There was 'Pooper Scooper' Watkins, a young woman who insisted not only on picking up her dog's faeces with a see-through plastic glove, but also on waving it in the faces of passers-by in order to emphasize her ecological soundness. There was Vera 'How Old is He?' Jackson, a woman who had told Robert the story of her dog's operation no less than seventeen times. There was the man from Maple Drive known as 'Is the Mitsubishi Scratched Yet?', dragging his Rhodesian ridgeback, known locally as 'He Just Wants to Play'. There was Mrs Quigley of the South Wimbledon Neighbourhood Church, with her pug, Martha. There was the German from Maple Drive known as 'The Nazi who Escaped Justice from Nuremberg', who, although he did not own any kind of pet, bared his teeth like an Alsatian . . . They were all there.

All of the people he had stopped and engaged in conversation over the last four years. People who had at first seemed so friendly and decent and open and neighbourly, but who, after two or three encounters, had turned into ravingly obsessive lunatics. People who had driven him further and further into the woods that slope down from the Common towards the main road to the south-west. People who had made him skulk behind trees until they had passed. People who had persuaded him that the only safe time to take out the dog was after the hours of darkness, when you were only likely to meet George 'Let's Get Rabbits' Grover.

They were carrying placards and posters. KEEP THE COMMON

FREE FOR DOGS! said one. OUR DOGS MUST NOT LIVE IN FEAR! said another. A third read I AM A DOG. I HAVE THE SAME RIGHTS AS YOU!

'It's the dog-murdering thing!' said Maisie. The Wimbledon Dog Murderer – already featured in several national newspapers – had already claimed the lives of six Labradors, eight poodles, a Border collie and fourteen Dobermanns. Although some claimed that his methods – shooting through the head at close range – were 'humane', most dog-lovers had lobbied their MP and campaigned vigorously in the local press under headlines such as STOP THIS DOG SERIAL KILLER.

There had been profiles of him that suggested that he was a jogger who had been bitten by one of Alex 'Down Sir' Snell's pit-bulls. There were some who said he was a man whose children had been savaged by a local hound. And there were some heartless people who maintained that he was a public-spirited individual who should be given as much help as possible in his self-appointed mission.

The dog lobby had clearly felt it was time to take action. Aziz and Hasan were caught up in a maze of stout shoes, Sherley's extendable dog-leads and sniffing, quivering red setters, corgis, Jack Russells, Old English Sheepdogs and pugs. Robert thought he saw Gwendolen 'Good for the Gardens' Mintoff trying to feed a Dogchoc to the Twenty-fourth Imam. And, when Maisie and he got into the crowd, he was, of course, stopped by almost every individual in it. 'I didn't recognize you without the dog!' some of them said. 'You're the chap with the Staffordshire terrier bitch, aren't you? How are the pups?' Some, with clearer memories, had long, detailed questions to ask. They remembered things about Badger that Robert had forgotten long ago. They asked about his speed and his fondness for Pedigree Chum Select Cuts, and all expressed interest in his bowel movements.

By the time Maisie and he got clear of the crowd, Aziz and Hasan were almost at the other side of the Common. Robert waved and shouted, but the little boy did not turn his head. He trotted obediently along beside Aziz. Even at this distance you could see that huge red mark across his cheek.

The two stopped outside a large house not unlike Mr Shah's. Aziz looked round, as if to check whether he was being followed. When he saw Robert, he picked up the little boy and ran towards the house. There was a high stone wall, a pair of wrought-iron gates and the kind of silence that suggested the sort of owners who could enforce their privacy.

The sky had darkened suddenly. Robert felt a drop of rain on his face. An April shower. 'What do we do now?' he said.

'We ring the doorbell,' said Maisie, 'and ask them what the hell they think they're doing with Hasan.'

'This isn't that easy, Maisie,' said Robert. 'We are talking about the Occultation of the Twenty-fourth Imam of the Wimbledon Dharjees! This is major-league stuff!'

'You talk as if you believe that rubbish!' said Maisie.

The two of them sat together on the damp grass. What had Mr Malik said the manuscript contained? A prophecy of some kind. And if Hasan was just an ordinary little boy, why did he have such an alarmingly high success rate in the prophetic-dreams department?

From behind, he heard a cough. Robert turned to see his mother and father peering down at him anxiously. What were they doing out here? Why didn't they have jobs like other people?

'Well, Yusuf,' said his mother, brightly, 'this is nice for you!'

Robert felt his mouth tighten. 'What's nice?'

Mrs Wilson flushed. 'Being out here,' she said – 'in the fresh air. With Ai'sha!'

She was almost the only person who regularly used their Islamic names. It wouldn't be long, thought Robert grimly, before she, too, was climbing into a large, black linen bag.

She tapped him, playfully, on the shoulder. 'Couple of love-birds!' she said.

Mr Wilson, anxious not to be left out of things, slapped Robert heartily on the back. 'I wish I had your faith,' he said – 'I really do!'

Maisie looked up at him, skilled, as ever, in the ways of dutiful daughters. 'You will believe, Mr Wilson,' she said. 'I know it. It must be!' She was always saying things like that these days.

Robert drew into himself and waited for his parents to go away. His mother was making small, agitated noises, while Mr Wilson senior was beginning to edge away across the grass. They were probably on their way to the pub.

'Don't you like me using your Islamic name?' said Mrs Wilson.

'It's not that,' said Robert. 'I think I don't like the Islamic name. I think I'm going to change it. I think I'm going to call myself Omar.'

Mrs Wilson kissed him, lightly, on the top of the head. 'Omar Bobkins Wilson,' she said – 'I like that!' And, with a nod and a wink to Maisie, she followed her husband.

When they had gone, Maisie started to pick at the grass with her fingers. She pulled out a stalk and wound it round her hand, watching it cut into her flesh.

'I sometimes wonder,' she went on, 'whether you're sincere about being a Muslim.'

Robert looked over his shoulder. There was, as far as he could see, no one else on the Common. 'I'm completely sincere about it,' he said.

Of course, the only way out of his troubles would be to confess to someone that he was passing himself off as a Muslim for the purposes of financial gain. That would be the sincere thing to do. Would they shake hands and agree to forget the whole thing were he to do so? He did not think so.

'I think,' Maisie said, 'you have to ask yourself some hard questions. Otherwise there's no future for us. What do you really hold dear, Robert? Are you Robert or are you Yusuf or are you Omar? What drives you forward?'

The desire to stay alive was what Robert wanted to say, but didn't. Staying alive seemed to be pretty low on the average Muslim's list of priorities.

He got to his feet. 'Let's go, then,' he said. 'We'll just bang on the door and see what happens.'

Maisie got up too. 'I'm changing, you see,' she said.

'Becoming a Muslim was a tremendous step for me. It's altered me in ways I can't even describe.'

'It's altered me too,' said Robert. 'Things have really sort of speeded up since I became a Muslim. It's very exciting.'

If you like being condemned to death and followed around by loonies with slippers on and becoming involved with weird prophecies from the dawn of time, it's a lot of fun!

Maisie pecked him on the cheek. 'I don't want us to lose each other,' she said. 'Mr Malik says that a harmonious relationship between man and woman is terribly important. At school, all I learned was that sex was wicked. In Islam it's different.'

Perhaps, thought Robert, as he trudged after her towards the iron gates, this was a signal for their lovemaking to become more decorous. Guilt was, after all, one of the things that made sex really interesting. One of the most positive things the Catholic Church had done for screwing was trying to stamp it out. She was living the part, he said to himself, and then: no, *it's me that's living the part. She actually believes this stuff.*

Maisie put her shoulder to the gates. They creaked open – one swinging wildly over to the left, while the other ground to a halt on the gravel after a few yards. He stopped, waiting for armed Twenty-fourthers to swarm out of every window, demanding to know why Robert was proposing to barge in on their most secret and important ceremony.

'Suppose he is an imam!' said Robert. 'Oughtn't we to at least consider whether these people have a right to *think* he is. I don't see what harm they're doing!'

'They're evil!' said Maisie. 'They are the scum of the earth! They're – ' her face reddened with fury – 'intolerant! Do you know why they wear one shoe? It's to shame the rest of the Dharjees, because they say that Dharjees flout Islamic law!'

She looked like Ronnie Gallagher, the pacifist organizer of the Wimbledon Peace Council, shortly before he put Derek 'Small Publisher With Big Problems' Elletson in hospital for suggesting that, under certain circumstances, war might be necessary.

'They have to be crushed, Bobkins!'

So saying, she marched off down the gravel path, making

the kind of crunching noise Robert had thought could only be produced by the BBC sound-effects department.

As they rounded the edge of the building, he could see that behind the house was a vast garden. There was a brick patio over on the left, studded with dwarf cypresses in terracotta tubs. Stretching up to and away from the patio was a vast lawn, smothered with spring flowers – yellow daffodils and a parade of brilliant hyacinths. In the middle of the lawn was a cedar-tree, and, attached to one of its branches by a knotted rope, was a child's swing, idling above the flowers as the rain guttered out and another squall of sunlight came in from the west. There was a terrible quiet about the place.

'I think,' said Robert, 'we should go and get reinforcements. We should go and ask Mr Malik.'

Maisie gave him a contemptuous look and marched up towards the patio. With a heavy heart, Robert followed her towards the smooth, mysterious features of the house, whose windows, on this side, he could now see, were blacked out from the inside.

17

When they got to the windows, Maisie put her ear to the glass. Robert, who was still looking nervously up and down the garden, stood a little away from the rear wall. But after a while it was clear that she could hear something, and he was unable to resist following her example.

The cloth inside muffled the noise, but when he got close to the window he could make out a human voice. At first he thought it was unfamiliar to him, but then, with a shock, he realized it was Rafiq's. But there was a quality to it he would not have expected. It was deep and assured.

'Say,' said the voice: 'Who is the Lord of the Heaven and the Earth? Say: Allah. Say: Why have you chosen other gods beside him, who, even to themselves, can do neither harm nor good? Say: Are the blind and seeing alike? Does darkness resemble the light?'

Other voices joined in, in a low growl, but Robert could not hear whether they were repeating what Rafiq had said, or, indeed, whether they were speaking English at all.

He pulled his ear away from the glass. 'I think we should ring on the doorbell,' he said, 'and just ask them, politely, what they're doing with Hasan. If they're worshipping him, could they guarantee to us that he . . . you know . . . enjoys being worshipped. Otherwise it may well be a form of child abuse. Worshipping someone without their permission . . .'

Maisie still had her ear pressed to the glass. From inside, the noise of the voices was getting louder. Someone was beating what sounded like a tambourine, and, high above all this, Robert thought he heard a flute. Then, slowly at first, but building to an almost military rhythm, the stamp of feet on wooden boards. Rafiq's voice was calling something, like a chant, and was answered by the other voices. Robert could not understand it at first, but, after he put his ear back to the window, it resolved itself into two syllables:

'Ha-san . . . Ha-san . . . Ha-san . . .'

Over and over again:

'Ha-san . . . Ha-san . . . Ha-san . . .'

And then, when the shouting had reached a climax, there was a ghastly scream from inside the room. At first Robert thought someone must have been hurt, but, a second later, the scream came again and he realized, with horror, that this was a cry of joy.

Maisie was waving at him wildly. She had found a gap in the blackout material and had fixed her eye to it. He wasn't at all sure that he wanted a good view of whatever was going on inside the house. It sounded a good deal more basic than, say, Holy Communion at Cranborne School. And that was bad enough. Were they committing human sacrifice? And if they were, shouldn't they get the police? Or might this be regarded as an intrusion on people's right to worship as they saw fit?

'You must look,' whispered Maisie, 'it's weird. You must look.'

Eventually, Robert looked.

The room was in almost total darkness. The only light came from a group of candles high in one corner. It smeared the faces of the men in the room, fighting a losing, fitful battle with the shadows. There might have been twenty or thirty figures in there, but it was too dark to distinguish anything more than their vague shapes. There didn't seem to be any furniture. All the figures, some of them cloaked like witches, were facing in the same direction – away from Maisie and Robert. But they were not looking at one point, as the worshippers did at the Wimbledon Islamic Boys' School (Day Independent): they were moving up and down, backwards and forwards, bumping into each other and generally carrying on like people at Victoria Station during the rush hour.

The only figure that stood out was Rafiq. He was standing on a kind of pedestal a little above the others, thrusting both arms up into the air. He seemed to be focused on the black space beyond the candlelight. The room, Robert felt, might go on for yards and yards. But, as he watched, even the sense that it was a room vanished. It was as if he was looking into a pinhole camera, as if the scene before him was a mirage.

'For nine hundred years!' called Rafiq.

'For nine hundred years!' answered the crowd.

'He was hidden!' called Rafiq.

'He was hidden!' answered the crowd.

'He is coming!' called Rafiq suddenly.

'He is coming!' called the crowd around him.

'What will he do,' yelled Rafiq, as if he had a good answer to this question, 'when he comes?'

'What will he do?' yelled the crowd in return. They seemed keen to find out.

'What will he do?' riposted Rafiq. He was not letting them get away with this easily.

'What will he do?' yelled the crowd.

Robert's eyes were starting to ache. But Rafiq was still not keen to put over the punch-line. He changed the topic, rather neatly, by howling, 'He is the Twenty-fourth Imam!'

The crowd liked this. They came back with, 'He is the Twenty-fourth Imam!'

'He has been hidden!' yelled Rafiq.

'He has been hidden!' yelled the crowd.

Robert wondered how this particular breakaway section of a breakaway section of the Nizari Ismailis had managed to carry on like this in Wimbledon for the last seventy years. Presumably, behind many of the net curtains in Wimbledon Park Road things as strange, or even stranger, were always going on. It was handy, anyway, that they celebrated their religion in English.

Back inside, Rafiq had gone back to the thousand-dollar question. 'What will he do when he returns?' he shouted.

Perhaps, thought Robert, he had simply been playing for time and had now come up with a credible answer.

'What will he do when he returns?' yelled the crowd.

It had better be good, thought Robert. *After a build-up like this, you can't afford to let them down.*

'He will destroy!' yelled Rafiq.

'He will destroy!' yelled the crowd.

'What will he destroy?' shouted Rafiq.

'What will he destroy?' answered the crowd.

The answer to this one was usually simple. *Everything apart from us, guys!* seemed to be the stock religious response. Imams or Christs, Mahdis or Messiahs were there to cancel all debts, atone for all insults. But, if this was the answer, Rafiq was not giving it all away at once. He clearly had something tasty up his sleeve.

Robert heard a cough behind him. He pulled his eye away from the pinhole and, turning, saw a near neighbour who had last year changed her name, by deed poll, to Cruella Baines. She was the lead singer in an all-girl rock group. She weighed fifteen stone.

'What's going on in there?' she said. 'Is it a party?'

Robert put his eye back to the pinhole. They had started dancing now. It was a fairly individualistic affair. Some of them were whirling round like dervishes. Others crouched on their haunches and kicked out their back legs behind them, like men carrying out a complex fitness programme. One man was lying on his back and cycling with his legs, rather like Badger, while a figure that Robert recognized as Aziz's friend from the Frog and Ferret was doing a lot of semaphore work with both arms.

Robert turned back to Cruella. 'There are naked people in there,' said Robert, 'having sex! Find a hole and have a look!'

Cruella Baines grunted and waddled off along the line of windows, her steel bangles rattling against her gigantic thighs. Eventually she seemed to find a gap in the blackout and, her enormous behind reared aloft, she glued her eye to the glass.

Inside, the lads were all enjoying themselves immensely. When the dancing had reached its climax, the whole crowd flung themselves on to the floor and further worked themselves up into what looked like a communal epileptic fit. *If this is Islam*, thought Robert, *give me more!* He hadn't seen anyone carry on like this since going to watch the World Wrestling Federation with Gilbert Lewis, the man next door's nephew, who had had a major seizure at the sight of a man called Hulk Hogan and had written to Robert afterwards to say that he 'had never expected to see anything like that in real life'. Perhaps Islam had developed differently in Wimbledon than in other parts of the world. Perhaps long exposure to tennis, bad public transport, English weather and the sight of miserable middle-aged people walking their dogs had driven this particular breakaway section of a breakaway section of the Nizari Ismailis right round the bend.

After a while they seemed to get bored with kicking their legs in the air. They wanted more. One by one they struggled to their feet. A man Robert recognized as the second man from the Frog and Ferret started to hop in circles, beating himself on the head and shouting something. Rafiq was doing a lot of waving into the darkness, as if he expected something to appear – a deputation from the Noise Abatement Society, thought Robert, if they all carried on like this for much longer.

'Oh!' he heard Maisie gasp, over to his left. 'Oh!'

Being a Twenty-fourther obviously called for high physical stamina, for the group showed no signs of slacking. They were now all waving in the direction indicated by Rafiq. But, although Robert strained his eyes against the glass, he could see nothing but impenetrable blackness beyond the hectic yellows and reds cast by the candles.

Rafiq started again. 'He is coming!' he shouted.

'He is coming!' shouted the lads in reply.

Suddenly the candles went out. Someone must have blown them or snuffed them, because the darkness was sudden and almost complete. Robert did not shift his eyes, waiting for another image to swarm out of the chamber in front of him, but all he could hear, now, was groaning.

'He was killed!' moaned Rafiq.

'He was killed!' wailed the support group.

'He was sent to hell-fire!' moaned Rafiq.

'He was sent to hell-fire!' his congregation replied. Some of them seemed to be actually sobbing.

Robert thought he could hear grinding teeth. With a start he realized they were his teeth and he was grinding them. Even looking at this stuff from behind a black screen was punishing. It wasn't surprising that some of them were cracking under the strain.

'He was the son of Hasan b. Namawar!' said Rafiq.

There was a slight pause. This was obviously not a name that tripped off the tongue, but the lads rose to it manfully, while managing to weep, groan and, from the sound of it, pull out lumps of each other's hair at the same time. 'He was the son of Hasan b. Namawar!' they yelled in the darkness.

'Of the Daylamis!' yelled Rafiq.

This was easier. 'Of the Daylamis!' they yelled back.

However long they had been in Wimbledon, the suburb had not yet managed to curb their enthusiasm. The sound from the room made your average Pentecostal church sound like a tea party given for a group of Radio 3 announcers. They were starting to thump the floor now, and the chorus that had played low, while they gave out the stuff of how he was the son of Hasan b. Namawar and had been sent to hell-fire, came back in loud and strong.

'He is coming to destroy!' yelled Rafiq, once more.

'He is coming to destroy!' they yelled back.

'What is he going to destroy?' yelled Rafiq.

'What is he going to destroy?' they answered.

If he doesn't give the answer to this one soon, thought Robert, he is in danger of losing his audience. But their patience seemed endless.

Instead of answering his own question, Rafiq let out a high-pitched wail, which was taken up by the rest of the men. The wail started high and went higher, until they were shrieking off the register. It was almost painful to listen to, and Robert was about to pull his face away from the window when, suddenly, high up in the far darkness, a tiny figure in white robes jumped into vision. He did not seem to be standing on anything. He seemed to hang suspended above the worshippers, his two tiny arms held out in front of him, and he was as still and quiet and calm as he had been when sitting at the Wilsons' table or resting, alone, at the back of Class 1.

'Oh, my God!' squawked Maisie. 'Oh, my *God!*' It was Hasan.

Robert took in the neatly combed hair, the frail shoulders, the exquisite cheekbones with the red blemish on one side, and the huge, sightless eyes that roamed the blackness below him like inverted searchlights, as if to soak up the shadows. He took in the way the little boy's hands stretched out over the crowd of distressed men as if to soothe them, and, for the first time in his life, he felt something that was not quite fear and not quite joy – an emptiness that longed to be filled. He heard Maisie's voice once more: *What* do *you believe in?* And, in spite of himself, he heard he was groaning quietly, like the men in the darkened room.

Next to him he heard Maisie gasp. He became aware that she was breaking away from the window. He hoped she wasn't proposing to make her presence known to the Twenty-fourthers. Robert had the strong impression that they viewed unwanted spectators in the same spirit in which the ancient Greeks received people barging in on the Eleusinian mysteries.

'I am Hasan!' said Hasan.

'You are Hasan!' shouted the crowd.

Behind him, Maisie had moved away from the window. Perhaps she had simply had enough. Hasan's voice had a chilling quietness to it. Robert had to put his ear closer to the glass to hear it. The crowd, too, had lowered their voices, but this had the effect of making the exchanges even more momentous.

'I am coming!' said the little boy.

'You are coming!' said the crowd.

How was he staying up there? thought Robert. And why was

his presence so disturbing? Even Maisie, who was now standing a few yards from the window, breathing heavily, seemed to have been paralysed by the sight of him.

'I am coming to destroy!' hissed Hasan.

'You are coming to destroy!' they whispered back.

'And what am I going to destroy?' murmured Hasan.

'What are you going to destroy?' muttered the crowd in answer.

Robert half-expected the whole cycle to start again, so long had he waited for an answer to this question. But this time the answer was forthcoming. The little boy leaned his face to one side as if he was listening to some signal inaudible to mere mortals, and he whispered, 'I am going to destroy Malik. I am going to destroy the seducer Malik and his friend Wilson,' hissed Hasan. 'They will both go to hell-fire!'

Robert felt something more than the natural peevishness of a betrayed parent or guardian. There was something so vivid and authentic about the little boy's face and voice that he had to look away. He lifted his face from the peephole, and in the glass in front of him he saw a face he thought he recognized. A round, plump, jolly, brown face that he remembered from back last summer, when all this business started. But, before he was able to put a name to it, something hit him on the back of the head, and for a long time he knew no more.

PART FOUR

18

'Stick close to me,' said Robert, 'and do not talk to strange men!'

'Can we talk to you, sir?' said Mafouz.

'Ha bloody ha!' said Robert.

His charges followed him. From time to time he would look back with a certain pride at them. Mafouz, Sheikh, Mahmud, Akhtar, and, at the back, their ears jutting out like radio antennae, the Husayn twins with Khan – or Famine, Pestilence and War, as Mr Malik called them.

He hoped the Museum had not left any priceless bits of Islamic art lying around the place. If it had, they were liable to end up in the Husayn twins' pockets.

He liked his class, though. In fact he liked the school. When it had beaten Cranborne Junior School by three hundred runs, two Saturdays ago, he had linked arms with the headmaster and sung three verses of 'We Are the Champions'. He had also, after five pints in the Frog and Ferret, referred to Malik as 'his Muslim brother' and said, publicly, that any lousy Christian cricket team could not, in his view, fart their way out of a swimming-pool.

The school was getting even bigger and even more successful. They had taken on extra teaching staff. There was a rather pleasant man, called Chaudhry, who showed worrying signs of having actually gone to Oxford. He was always saying to Robert, 'Do you remember old Jennings from Univ?' or 'Tell me, Wilson, did you use the Radcliffe Camera?' To which Robert replied that he had never been interested in photography. They had also hired a French teacher, whose name Robert was unable to remember from one day to the next.

A man from the local education authority, after being taken

over to the pub by Mr Malik, had announced his intention of sending his own son to the school. 'Let them all come!' said the headmaster to Robert. 'We send our little bastards to Cranborne – why shouldn't we take *their* money?' The school was, he had told Robert, officially in profit. Mr Shah, he said, had a return on his investment.

The more he enjoyed teaching, and the more Mr Malik's school seemed to prosper, the worse he felt about his original act of deception. As this summer, even hotter and drier than the last, worked its way up to August, Robert found he had developed a rich repertoire of twitches and guilty tics. He blinked. He snorted. He jerked his head backwards and forwards. He had even developed the beginnings of a stammer.

Maisie had told him he was 'getting more and more like a spaceman'. Now he was not only unable to remember the names of politicians, sportsmen and television personalities, he also found his memory was unable to supply the personal details of people he had known since he was a child. It was probably that blow on the head he had received at the end of the spring term. He had, Maisie had told him, been unconscious for nearly two minutes. She herself had had a bag placed over her head and had been left, trussed like a chicken, under the windows of the mysterious house on the Common. When they had recovered, the Dharjees had gone.

Had the shock affected Maisie too? Was that why she had moved out of the Wilson family home?

She had said she couldn't stand living in such close proximity to quite so many facial quirks, but there was something deeper in her decision to take a small flat near the school. He simply couldn't respond to the person she had become. He would only be able to find his way back to her when he managed, for once in his life, to be honest about what he really felt and believed.

He would be dead soon, anyway, he reflected, as he made his way up the Museum stairs. If some friend of Ali's didn't get him, then the Twenty-fourth Imam would probably grind him into little pieces. Hasan was waiting for him at the top of the stairs, and, as soon as he heard his guardian's tread, the little boy sat up, sniffed the air and stretched out his hands like a cat, waking after sleep.

Hasan had been unbearable ever since his Occultation. It can't, thought Robert, be good for the personality to have a load of middle-aged men prostrating themselves in front of you and sobbing every time you open your mouth. He wasn't yet quite in the Michael Jackson class, but for the last few months the little boy had been difficult in the extreme. He had refused to go to bed on time, insisted on watching *The Late Show* on television, and claimed that Badger was 'not worthy' to lick him. He had had a few more prophetic dreams. And one of them, Robert was almost sure, had foretold that something ghastly was going to happen in what sounded like the British Museum.

'I am not really me,' he had confided to Robert a few months ago, as the two were on a bus, on their way to the Megabowl in Kingston. 'I am a reincarnation of the true Twenty-fourth Imam of the Nizari Ismailis! My father was sent to hell-fire on the sixth of Rabi!'

'Is that right?' Robert had said, with a nervous glance around at the other passengers. 'Well, I hope it improves your bowling!'

Hasan giggled and put his hand in Robert's. On their last visit to the Megabowl he had hurled his projectile directly at the fruit machines. 'Sometimes you are so nice I do not want to kill you, Mr Wilson!' he said. 'And I know you do not really believe me. But you may look me up. I am in all the history books. I feature in *The Assassins*, by Bernard Lewis, a respectable work of scholarship.'

Robert had made the mistake of looking Hasan up in the work in question, at the end of which he had almost decided to call in an exorcist with some experience in the Islamic field.

'I will come into my kingdom on the Day of False Resurrection,' Hasan used to say, when Robert was trying to get him to brush his teeth, 'which is the eighth of August. The day when Hasan the Second betrayed The Law!'

As Bernard Lewis had put it:

On the 17th day of the month of Ramadan, the anniversary of

*the murder of Ali, in the year 559 (8th August 1164) under the
ascendancy of Virgo and when the sun was in Cancer, Hasan 2nd
ordered the erection of a pulpit in the courtyard of Alamut, facing
towards the west, with four great banners of four colours, white,
red, yellow and green, at the four corners. As the pulpit faced
west, the congregation had their backs towards Mecca.*

He wished he didn't know these things. He wished he'd stuck
to Marwan Ibrahim Al-Kaysi. You knew where you were with
Marwan. *'When putting on shoes they should be checked to make sure
no harmful insect has hidden in them during the night'.* That was fair
enough. But the true history of the Lord Hasan – Hasan the
Second, on his name be peace – was mind-boggling stuff.

If he had had any decency he would have talked to Mr Malik
about what was going to happen. He would have warned him.
He was the only one to know that today was the day when
Hasan was going to wreak his revenge. He was the only one to
know the whole story. But neither he nor Maisie, as far as he
knew, had spoken of what had happened at Hasan's Occultation.

'Come along, Wilson!' boomed Mr Malik's voice from the next
gallery – 'you'll miss the fun! Bring young Hasan along!'

The headmaster stepped out of the gallery with a couple of
the older boys. Beyond him, Robert could see Maisie and Rafiq.
Rafiq! The man Malik trusted! The man he thought of as his
oldest friend! Malik was simply too trusting. You simply could
not afford to trust anyone – especially where religion was concerned.

Robert had tried to open up the subject of Hasan several
times, but Mr Malik seemed far less concerned about him than
he had been. 'What people believe,' he had told Robert, 'is
their own affair. But I have ways of dealing with unbrotherly
conduct!'

He was whistling to keep up his spirits, that was all, Robert
said to himself as the boys clattered after him. He had been
nervous enough when the name of the Twenty-fourthers was
first mentioned. Down below, in the gallery below him and

Hasan, the Husayn twins and Khan were dancing round a case stuffed with priceless porcelain. *'Shake de belly!'* called Khan in a mock African accent. *'Break de glass and shake de belly!'* A man in a blue uniform was walking over towards them. Robert waved them on, and they scampered after the rest of the class.

'Do you know why we destroyed Hasan the Second?' said Hasan, in a conversational tone, as the two of them followed the headmaster and the rest of the school. Robert knew, but he wasn't going to give Hasan the satisfaction of knowing that he knew. The trouble with this Islamic history was that, like the Western version, you got involved in it.

'We destroyed him because he betrayed The Law!' said Hasan, in the kind of voice that suggested Hasan the Second, the Twenty-third Imam of the Nizari Ismailis, had only just popped out of the room for a cup of coffee instead of being stabbed nearly a thousand years ago.

The Twenty-fourther beliefs were not simply rumours from the dawn of time: they came, like the Dharjees themselves, out of real history. That was the frightening thing about them.

Towards noon, the Lord Hasan 2nd, on whose name be peace, wearing a white garment and a white turban, came down from the castle, approached the pulpit from the right side and in the most perfect manner ascended it. Addressing himself to the inhabitants of the world, jinn, men and angels, he said, 'The Imam of our time has sent you his blessing and his compassion and has called you to be his special, chosen servants. He has freed you from the burden of the rules of Holy Law.'

They had had a banquet in the middle of the fast. In the middle of Ramadan. And they had drunk wine on the very steps of the pulpit and its precincts. They had flouted the *shariah*, the fundamental law of Islam. That was what this argument was about, even now in the 1990s in Wimbledon. How closely should one follow The Law?

'Come and look at this!' shouted Malik. 'There's a bloke in here with nine arms! Can you beat that?' He indicated a large

Hindu carving, and the boys swarmed round it. The headmaster was clearly about to give one of his informal talks.

He had to get out, Robert thought. There was nothing else for it. He had to make a dignified and orderly retreat. Put himself out of the reach of Dr Ali, the Twenty-fourthers and everything else in the school. He was simply going to have to leave Islam, the way his father had left the Rotary club. You were allowed to leave, weren't you? It wasn't the British Army. He was going to ask nicely.

'And so,' Mr Malik was saying, 'we observe the *accumulation of gods*, very much as one saw in pre-Islamic Medina. The process of monotheistic religions can be seen as the beginning of the rational approach to the world!'

It wasn't going to be easy. He had already offered his resignation, twice, and Mr Malik had simply ignored it. When he had tried a third time, the headmaster had made some slightly menacing remarks about brotherhood and commitment.

'And yet,' went on Malik, 'the holistic nature of the Hindu world-picture still has much to teach us. Religions, like arts and sciences, must learn from each other, and toleration, which is an essential part of Islam, must be *studied*, *worked at*, not simply mentioned as a piety.'

This was well over the heads of his audience. Khan and the Husayn twins were making offensive gargling noises while dancing round a statue that looked to Robert as if it might be the Lord Vishnu; behind them, Mahmud did his Native American impression.

To his relief, the headmaster walked on. Maisie walked ahead, a little behind Rafiq. There was now almost nothing flagrantly alien about her, apart from her headscarf. And yet, paradoxically, she was, to Robert, more and more remote, more and more genuinely Islamic. Mr Malik had got to her in her most vulnerable area – the brain.

'I have a problem, Headmaster!' Robert said, as they walked through the gallery.

Malik clapped him on the back. Rafiq took Hasan by the hand, and, with a sly look at Robert, joined Maisie.

'You want money, my dear Wilson?' Malik said.

'It's not that,' said Robert. 'I don't think I . . . belong at the school any more.'

The headmaster stopped. He seemed distressed.

'Why on earth not?'

'I'm having . . . doubts!' said Robert.

Boys flowed past them and on into the next gallery. Malik seemed puzzled now, rather than distressed.

'Doubts about what, Wilson?'

'Doubts about . . . you know . . . Allah.'

Mr Malik chewed reflectively.

'What kind of doubts?'

'Well,' said Robert, 'I'm not sure if he's there.'

The headmaster started to move again. They were some way behind the rest of the school, but he did not seem in any hurry to catch them up. 'I think, Wilson,' he said at last, 'that you may rest assured that he is there. I don't think there is any doubt about that.'

'For you perhaps, headmaster,' said Robert, 'but, you see, while I'm sure he *may* be there, I'm not absolutely sure he is, if you see what I mean.'

They had somehow come into a gallery full of erotic Indian sculptures. In the far corner, the Husayn twins appeared to be trying to lift one of them off its pedestal. Mr Malik walked swiftly over to them and aimed a shrewd blow at their ears. They scuttled off after the other boys.

'You must simply ignore these doubts, Wilson!' said Malik.

'But I'm getting doubts about more and more things,' replied his junior master. 'I'm having doubts about Muhammad, for example.'

Mr Malik's eyes narrowed.

'What kind of doubts?'

'You know,' said Robert – 'did *he* exist?'

This seemed to puzzle the headmaster. 'I don't think there's much doubt about that,' said Mr Malik – 'the man conquered half the Near East!'

'Did he?' said Robert.

If the headmaster was surprised by Robert's vagueness on the most basic details of Islamic history, he did not show it.

'I mean,' went on Robert, 'we can't be *sure*, can we? I mean, we only have his word for it, don't we? And other people who were all friends of his. It could be a sort of . . . conspiracy.'

Mr Malik was giving him some very odd looks. He clasped both hands behind his back and wandered over to a bench. In the next gallery, Maisie was gathering the boys around her. Rafiq was nowhere to be seen. Robert was fairly sure he was making headway.

'And even if he *did* exist,' he went on, 'I'm not sure he was a terribly nice person.'

'What,' said Malik, 'has being nice got to do with anything? Who said Jesus was a nice person?'

'I'm not sure,' said Robert, deciding to get to the point, 'that I am a Muslim. I may be a Catholic.'

Mr Malik put his arm round Robert, as the two sat together on the bench. Was this the treatment he gave Maisie in the La Paesana restaurant, Mitcham?

'You cannot be a Muslim and a Catholic at the same time,' said the headmaster. 'It is just not possible. Although the principle of *taqiyah* – dissimulation – does make it perfectly possible for a Muslim to pretend to assume a religion to which he does not really belong. When faced by a Mongol horde, for example.'

This sounded promising. Was the converse also possible? Did it apply to agnostics faced by Islamic hordes? Robert was almost on the edge of confessing everything, when the headmaster gave him a brotherly squeeze.

'Hasan the Second,' said Robert, 'was a strange leader of the Nizari Ismailis in the twelfth century. And he was stabbed by his brother-in-law, Hasan b. Namawar, because he had said the Ismailis were no longer bound by Islamic law!'

Mr Malik grinned. 'And the Twenty-fourthers believe,' he said, 'that Hasan b. Namawar's son was hidden and is the true Twenty-fourth Imam of the Nizari Ismailis. And that he will return with hell-fire on the appointed day.'

'Which is,' said Robert, 'as it happens, today!'

'Indeed!' said Mr Malik, grinning.

He seemed positively cheerful about this. Perhaps the school was not the financial success that everyone seemed to think. It seemed impossible to convince him that anyone was in any danger. Robert would have to hit him with something a bit more serious than doubts. This situation called for a full-scale nervous breakdown.

'Actually, Headmaster,' he said, 'it's not just about Allah and Muhammad. I'm having doubts about everything. I'm having doubts about you.'

Malik grinned. 'I'm afraid I do exist,' he said, clapping Robert on the back. 'I am too, too solid flesh, my friend. There is a whole department of the Inland Revenue dedicated to proving that I exist.'

'What I mean,' said Robert, feeling a direct approach was required, 'is that I think I am having a nervous breakdown.'

The headmaster got up and started towards the next gallery. He did not seem very worried by this. 'I know,' he said, waving his arms expansively. 'I get nervous breakdowns. I get them all the time. All the damn time! I have nervous breakdowns every time I see the Husayn twins!'

They had come into a gallery at the centre of which was a large glass case, round which the boys – apart from Khan and the Husayns – were crowded. The Husayns seemed to have got hold of a piece of pottery and were trying to stuff it under Khan's coat. Malik ignored them.

'I mean,' said Robert, feeling he was not making the impression required, 'I think I may be Napoleon!'

19

Maisie overheard this remark. 'What do you mean,' she said, 'you think you're Napoleon?'

'I mean,' said Robert, 'I may be Napoleon.'

Rafiq grinned. He was standing a little away from the rest of the group, holding Hasan's hand in his. 'As opposed to Yusuf Khan!' he said. He was always being satirical about Robert's name.

'I don't know who I am,' said Robert – 'that's the point I'm making. Am I Robert Wilson? Am I Yusuf Khan? Am I Seamus O'Reilly? Am I Napoleon? You know?'

Rafiq folded his arms. He turned to Malik with a satisfied expression, as if to say *this is what comes of hiring infidels – even reformed ones*. 'And who are you now, Yusuf?' he said.

Robert looked him straight in the eyes. 'I really don't know who I am or what I'm doing here,' he said.

He managed to put a lot of conviction into this. It was probably the truest thing he had said so far that morning. Now might be the time to follow it up with a few troop directions in fluent French. He could dribble a bit. Even roll around on the floor. There was, he found, a tremendous sense of relief in being able to talk like this. Perhaps he could give them a bit of something Shakespearian. *'Faith my lords – how many crows may nest in a grocer's jerkin?'* And then, soon, an ambulance would come. It would take him away to a nice, warm mental hospital, where nice men would inject large quantities of Largactil up his bum. That was absolutely what he needed.

'Take it from me, Wilson,' said the headmaster, 'you are nothing like Napoleon. I have never met anyone less like Napoleon. You are Robert Wilson, a.k.a. Yusuf Khan, and you are a vital part of the creative team helming the Wimbledon Boys' Day Independent Islamic School.'

It was hopeless. The man would simply not take no for an answer. He was clearly prepared to continue employing Robert under almost any circumstances. What did he have to do to escape?

Malik walked over to the glass case. The boys parted, and Robert saw that it contained a villainous-looking man of about four foot in height. He was preserved in some kind of fluid, like an olive or a pickled onion, and had a baffled look about him. He looked more like an ape than a human.

'He was preserved in a bog, sir,' Sheikh was saying. 'Apparently he's a Druid!'

'He can't help that,' said Malik. 'We shall take lunch now. If an official representative of the Museum approaches, stuff your lunch under your jumper!'

Mahmud could be heard wondering whether they were going to have the Druid instead of packed lunch. Then, as one man, the boys produced plastic boxes, tinfoil and greaseproof paper, and the sound of small teeth munching bread, meat and fruit could be heard.

'This Druid,' said Malik, 'was ceremonially strangled many many years ago – which is what will happen to you, Husayn, unless you let go of Akhtar's ear.'

Robert wondered whether he should stage a more spectacular form of nervous breakdown. Thinking you were Napoleon was clearly not enough to get you out of the Wimbledon Islamic Boys' Independent Day School. Perhaps he could run back into the Romano-British Collection, gibbering.

'What does it all mean?' he said, in a loud, theatrical voice. 'What is it all for?'

Malik gave him a rapid glance, and then continued his lecture. 'He was strangled,' he said, 'because the Druids believed his death might avert a Roman victory. But the Romans, too, sacrificed. And irrationality is, I would argue, more firmly at the centre of Western, Christian, culture than it is at the centre of

175

Islam. Consensus is at the heart of the social contract the Faith makes.'

This, thought Robert, sounded like his cue. 'I am not a good Muslim, Headmaster!' he said. 'You must cast me out!'

Maisie grabbed his arm and steered him towards the next gallery. Behind him he could hear one of the boys mutter that Mr Wilson had gone mad, and another reply that he always had been. 'You are being *embarrassing*!' she hissed.

She was very big on Islamic *esprit de corps* these days. She talked of entering the Birmingham Islamic Women's Games. She had almost given up drink. Her manner had changed. She cultivated the kind of aloofness that Robert had observed in certain classes of minor official – he had the constant impression she was about to refuse him a visa. Her face had changed too. She had lost weight, giving her nose an alert, intelligent quality. She spent a lot of time looking at the floor, but her shoulders had become demonstrably assertive. She was a fully fledged Islamic woman.

She turned back to Mr Malik. 'I'll take him back to the school, Headmaster,' she said. 'He'll be all right for the pageant, I promise you.'

At the beginning of the summer term, shortly after the Koran Study Week at Lower Slaughter Manor, Gloucestershire, she had been made school secretary. She was now to be seen in a small cubby-hole next to Mr Malik's office, typing furiously, or on the phone to an organization called the Islamic World Unity Fund, which was said to be about to offer Mr Malik and Mr Shah a large sum in US dollars.

Malik grinned at her. Maisie pushed Robert towards the stairs, and the two of them moved down towards the crowded entrance hall. Outside, unbelievably, it was high summer.

Halfway down the steps, Robert sat down and put his head in his hands. Maisie sat next to him.

'Are you any closer to it?' she said.

'To what?'

'To whatever it is you want.'

'I don't know what I want,' said Robert. 'Do you?'

Another crowd of schoolchildren climbed the stairs towards them. Robert could see the brilliant light flooding the Bloomsbury street outside. Maisie put her hand on his.

'Are you having an affair with Malik?' he said.

'How do you mean "an affair"?' said Maisie.

'You know,' said Robert – 'you go out to the cinema, and he sticks his tongue down your throat, and then – '

Maisie sniffed. 'Please don't, Bobkins,' she said. 'Please don't. Don't be crude – I can't bear it.'

She patted his hand absently. 'We have slept together a few times,' she said, 'but we've never done it during school hours. You mustn't be jealous, darling. We're Muslims.'

Robert found he was snarling. 'What difference does that make?'

Maisie looked at him pityingly. 'The Prophet made it clear that you can have up to four wives,' she said.

'But I don't think,' said Robert, with heavy sarcasm, 'that he said anything about women having four husbands. I thought you were supposed to be low and submissive and made out of Adam's rib, and you weren't supposed to leave the house excessively. Marwan Ibrahim Al-Kaysi says – '

'Shut up about Marwan Ibrahim Al-Kaysi,' said Maisie crossly. 'He is a pedant from the University of Yarmouk. I *am* low and submissive, Bobkins. I'm a weak, silly creature at the mercy of my emotions and feelings. And I have rather strong feelings about the headmaster.'

So, to his surprise, did Robert. He had a strong feeling that he wanted to dash back to the Romano-British section and break a piece of statuary over the bastard's head.

Wearily, Robert got up and walked towards the street. Maisie followed him. 'We've all got to share,' she said, as they passed through the swing doors and found themselves looking down at the courtyard of the Museum. 'We've got to learn to live together and share and be at peace with the world. That's what Mr Malik says Islam is all about.'

Robert was aware of this. Mr Malik used those very words about three times every day.

'I think,' said Robert, 'that Islam is all about whatever Mr Malik wants it to be about on any particular day.'

'Well, in a way,' said Maisie, 'it is. He says once you've said these *suras* of the Koran and observed the obligations you *are* a Muslim. It's as simple as riding a bicycle. Once you've submitted, that's it. It's very simple.'

They walked across the courtyard towards a waiting line of taxis.

'What's he like in bed?' said Robert.

Maisie sighed. 'Why do men always want to know that?' she said. Then she grinned. 'He's better on the carpet.' She linked her arm through his. 'I'm so glad I told you,' she continued – 'I've been feeling terribly guilty while it's been going on.'

'How long has it been going on?'

'For about nine months,' said Maisie – 'apart from Ramadan, of course.'

The bastard, thought Robert. The snake! The lousy, double-crossing, deceitful . . . *Muslim!* There was nothing to tie him to the place now. He could go. He could walk away, down the street, go back home and try to start his life. Try to do something that was nothing to do with the ridiculous lie he had told the headmaster almost a year ago today.

Except he couldn't. This news, he realized, tied him to Malik and the school almost more than before. While he still had a chance of being near Maisie, he would take it. Submission! Surrender! They had come to the right guy! He was on his knees, begging to stay.

Maisie approached a taxi. As they got in, she said, 'I'm so glad we've got rid of that Christian guilt rubbish. I don't think this would be nearly so easy if we weren't Muslims.'

The taxi-driver did not seem keen on going to Wimbledon. Maisie took a ten-pound note from Robert's pocket and waved it at him through the glass.

'What does he think about me?' said Robert. He was curiously keen to know the answer to this question. Had Maisie said what a stud he was?

'He doesn't know we had an affair,' said Maisie. 'He thinks

it's just brother and sister. It is really brother and sister, isn't it, Bobkins?'

'Not to me it isn't,' said Robert mournfully.

She patted his hand and looked out at the sunlight glittering on London's rubbish. 'I'm sure we can manage it occasionally,' she said. 'I'd rather you didn't tell him about us! We don't really want trouble at the school, do we?'

From his jacket pocket Robert took out a grubby sheet of paper – the translation of the mysterious manuscript that had been given to him in the pub nearly a year ago today. He waved it at Maisie in a threatening manner. 'Do you realize,' he said, 'that the whole school is about to go up in flames today?'

Maisie smirked. She seemed as unworried as the headmaster at the fact that the place was due to be consumed in hell-fire. 'I know,' she said, 'that today is the day when the Twenty-fourthers believe Hasan will come into his own . . .'

'It's *serious*!' said Robert, 'and Rafiq and his boys won't stop at a few groans this time. They were prepared to hit me on the head, weren't they?'

'Quite a lot of people,' said Maisie acidly, 'are prepared to hit you on the head.'

Since she didn't seem willing to read the translation, Robert took on the job himself. Leaning forward in the seat, he started to intone, in a deep voice:

> Bow down,
> Bow down and listen to my words.
> On the sixth of Rabi
> I stabbed the seducer Hasan
> And was sent to hell-fire.
> But my son lived,
> My son Hasan.
> He is the Twenty-fourth Imam.
> He lives.
> He will return.

The taxi-driver turned his head slightly. 'I'm with you there,' he said.

This surprised Robert. Were there more Twenty-fourthers around than he had thought possible? Had they even penetrated the licensed taxicabs of London? He read on. Maisie turned her face away from him towards Green Park.

> He will come as a boy.
> As a little blind boy.
> From the West he will come.
> His face will be marked.
> His eyes will have no sight.
> And he will bear my name.
> Hasan—
> Hasan b. Namawar.
> He will destroy.
> He will destroy with fire.
> And you will show loyalty to me—
> You will show loyalty to The Law—
> And you will know my name,
> Which means companion,
> There is fire in my fingers.
> Bow down!'

The taxi-driver nodded. 'Sale or return,' he said, 'is a very good basis for a business deal. And business *has* gone down, no question about it!'

Maisie was still looking out of the window. If the prophecy worried her, she was managing to conceal the fact. Perhaps the headmaster had been able to reassure her in ways that were not open to Robert. As he thought of them actually screwing – of Maisie winding her arms round him, hitching her legs over his, pumping up and down, up and down – the blood rose to his face. Awful, racist thoughts and words rose in his throat like nausea, and then, moments later, a strange image of Mr Malik embracing him. *'You are my Muslim brother, Wilson!'*

He liked Mr Malik. That ought to make this situation easier to bear. But it didn't. He could not stop the clear physical image of their bodies together. He knew what Malik would say, how he would look when they were making love, how he would smile, beatifically, like a baby, when he was satisfied.

He wiped the sweat from his forehead. This wasn't getting him anywhere. He put down the paper. 'There's something weird going on,' he said. 'This man really *did* stab Hasan the Second. Because he broke The Law. And pushed Islam close to Christianity. And this manuscript describes our Hasan *to the letter*!'

She turned to him. 'So you really think,' she said, 'that that poor little chap is going to zoom in from the clouds and wipe us all out?'

'Is that any more barmy than believing that Muhammad went up a mountain and God spoke to him? Or that there'll be wine in heaven? Or that you're a duffer if you can't polish off a wall gecko in under two minutes?'

The taxi-driver nodded vigorously. 'This is it,' he said – 'two minutes! And we're given no warning, are we? We're just told to get on with it and hope the recession will go away!'

Maisie grabbed his hand. She looked suddenly nervous. 'You do believe that, though, don't you?' she said. 'Because you're a Muslim, aren't you? If you don't believe that, you aren't a Muslim. You're an impostor!'

'I don't know what I am,' said Robert. 'There are times when I think I'm a Twenty-fourther. They seem to have a lot of fun.'

'They do,' said the taxi-driver. 'They go to Spain twice a year. They have country cottages. They send their children to private schools. They pay no tax. They have it easy!'

They were crossing the river now. Even the summer sun could not take the grey away from the thick band of the Thames, sluggishly curving towards Wandsworth. As they sped back towards Wimbledon, Robert wondered why he still couldn't own up to the lie that had started all this. Why had it trapped him as neatly as she had done?

What did he believe? That was what she was always asking him. If he could say it, out loud, he might know what it was. It might even win him what he knew, in his heart, he wanted. Maisie. The spoilt, black-haired girl sitting beside him, staring out at the river. As they climbed West Hill, he started to sing, to Mr Malik's tune, words of his own.

> Beautiful girl,
> Beautiful girl,
> You don't go with them.
> You belong to your people.
> You are one of my people.
> You will stay mine.
> You are one of my people.
> Beautiful,
> Beautiful,
> Beautiful, beautiful girl.

20

The Great Hall of the school was hung with green drapery. A makeshift stage had been erected at the staircase end and, above it, Class 1 had hung a large, hand-painted Islamic crescent moon and star. Samples of their work were laid out on trestle-tables at the side. Mafouz's record-breaking account of the school journey to the Natural History Museum, for which he had been awarded alpha double plus, was in pride of place. '*My Cat*', it began, '*was in agony due to being hung upside down from our bedroom window by my brother, when I set off in the luxurious coach provided for us. I thought only about my beautiful cat as the huge engines purred and the round wheels revolved enabling us two-legged people to journey in comparative comfort through the streets of London town!*' It had been extensively rewritten by Robert, who was now so good at doing Mafouz's handwriting that it had affected his ability to reproduce his own signature convincingly. In the garden at the back, Sheikh had organised a chemistry exhibition. There was, he had told Mr Malik, a huge explosion planned for 16.00 hours.

It was the school's first Open Day. It was a shame, really, thought Robert as he lugged a crate of lemonade in through the front door, that it was also the day the whole place was due to be consumed in hell-fire. Would Mr and Mrs Husayn get a chance to study MY HOLIDAYS by M. and N. Husayn, a hundred-word masterpiece that it had taken three months to squeeze out of them? Would Mr Mafouz be able to glory in his son's seventeen straight alphas, or to admire his leading part in the headmaster's *The Bowl of Night*, a musical based on *The Rubáiyát of Omar Khayyám*? Would anyone be able to enjoy the first public performance of a pageant, devised and directed by Mr Malik, with the working title of *Islamic Wimbledon*?

'Put the buns on the far tables!' called Maisie. Robert picked up a large cellophane bag, and, with a resentful glance in her direction, pulled it across the polished floor. Outside he could hear the coach bringing Class 1 back from the Museum. There was a squeal of brakes, the sound of Mr Malik ('One at a time, please, gentlemen!') and then a noise as of wild horses galloping across a parquet floor.

Mahmud was the first through the door. He looked with interest and sympathy at Robert, who was setting out paper cups next to the pile of buns. 'Are you mentally ill, sir?' he said, in a small, polite voice.

'Yes!' said Robert.

This seemed to satisfy the boy's curiosity. Behind him came the Husayn twins. They were carrying the Bosnian refugee, feet first.

From the kitchens came the new master, carrying an armful of cardboard chain-mail. Nobody had wanted to play the Crusader, and so it was almost inevitable that the job should go to the Bosnian refugee. He had cheered up when told he was going to have a plastic sword, a cardboard helmet and the chance to run around the stage hitting the Husayn twins.

Mr Malik came into the hall. He gave Robert a brief, concerned glance and clapped his hands together. Next to him, his hand grasping the head's trouser leg, was Hasan.

'Keep an eye on Hasan, Wilson!' said Mr Malik. 'We want to avoid a major incident if we can possibly help it!' Then he turned to the other children and clapped his hands once more. 'Gymnastic boys,' he said, 'out to the garden!'

Behind him came Rafiq. He, too, gave Robert a glance. Then he went up the stairs towards Mr Malik's study. The headmaster caught his eye, and Rafiq turned, shiftily, towards him. 'I have to get some scripts, Headmaster!' he said.

Malik nodded and went to the back of the hall. He opened the door to the garden, and from Classes 2 and 3 a small group of boys in white running-shorts and T-shirts ran silently for the open air. As Rafiq disappeared out of sight at the top of the stairs, Maisie staggered in with a step-ladder and started to put up black drapes at the windows. They looked, from a distance, as if they might well be the remains of her first attempt at Islamic dress.

Mr Chaudhry started to dress the Bosnian refugee. He grinned at Robert. 'Doesn't it remind you of Cuppers?' he said.

Robert put on his Oxford face. 'Dear old Cuppers!' he said. 'How is he?'

Mr Chaudhry chuckled. 'Wilson,' he said, 'you are a joker! All Pembroke men are jokers!'

As Robert was trying to remember whether that was the college he had said he had attended, Mr Malik went over to the far wall and began to pin up the league table of exam results. Every boy in the school was placed, and next to his marks was a small graph illustrating his performance throughout the year. The x-axis was attitude and the y-axis achievement. Most of the graphs were set on a steep, ascending curve, apart from the Husayn twins'; they started in the top left hand corner and were headed, inexorably, for the far right end of the bottom line. Next to each graph was a Polaroid photograph of the boy concerned and his own brief reaction to his assessment. Mafouz had written, 'I have done brilliant. There is no stopping me in the Sports Department. We went on a skiing holiday.'

The Open Day, Robert thought to himself, was physical evidence of how far the school had come during the year. There was a running video of the television documentary about Sheikh, who had, at the beginning of June, gained entrance to Oxford and Cambridge and had published an article in an American scientific journal that an eminent German physicist had described as 'revelatory'. That had generated quite a bit of business.

Robert held on to Hasan's hand as Mr and Mrs Brown, the new parents, came through the now open front door of the school. 'Welcome, Brown!' called Mr Malik.

'The blessings of Allah upon you!' said Mr Brown, an assistant manager at the National Westminster Bank, Mitcham. He was a small, weaselly man of little charisma. It was a puzzle, really, how he had ever risen as high as assistant bank manager, although there were rumours that his immediate superior, Mr Quigley, had been confined to a lunatic asylum after claiming that aliens were about to take over South-West London. 'If he is a Muslim,' Mr Malik had confided to Robert, shortly after the Brown child joined the school, 'then I am the Duke of Edinburgh. He likes our record of academic achievement, that is all.'

Sheikh was not the school's only triumph. Mr Malik had a winning way with the press release. His coup in the *Wimbledon Guardian* was the headline ISLAMIC BOYS SCHOOL HEADS ACADEMIC LEAGUE TABLE. The story mentioned only in passing that the league table was one devised by Mr Malik for assessing Independent Islamic Schools in Wimbledon. A rather hard-line establishment in Southfields – the Islamic Academy of Learning – had been excluded as not being of 'sufficient weight'. He had also stolen Cranborne School's prize physicist, Khan, and had offered a free place to Simon Britton, a boy whose mother had had to take him away from Cranborne because of her financial circumstances.

The Browns started to browse along the wall, and, in ones and twos, other parents made their entrances. Mr Mafouz came in wearing his best blue suit, and dragging his six daughters behind him. Mr Husayn, wearing, as always, a bright floral shirt and smoking a large cigar, came in with a woman who was quite clearly not his wife.

Robert put Hasan on a chair in the corner. The little boy showed no sign of Messianic behaviour. He sat quite still, his delicate hands folded in his lap. Robert looked from Maisie to the headmaster. How had he been so stupid? That was easy to understand. Malik had such a generalized air of gravity that his manner to individuals never conveyed anything of what he might really be thinking. He was standing, now, with Fatimah Bankhead and Mr and Mrs Akhtar, talking of the school's future plans. 'The whole of the west wing,' he was saying, 'will be turned into an art and design complex, while we are starting an appeal for the boat-house! The rowing-team need somewhere to relax and "get their wind" after a damn good session on the river. And we also, obviously, need somewhere to keep the boats. I am fed up with having them in my kitchen!'

The boat-house was news to Robert. As was the fact that they had a west wing. Why did they need a boat-house? Was he planning to restage the battle of Lepanto? They did not even have a rowing-team, as far as he was aware. The man was a swindler. Robert could not stop these thoughts. Ever since he had heard about Maisie and the headmaster they had risen in swarms, like rats leaving a sewer.

There were quite a lot of parents that Robert did not recognize. Over in the corner, by the window, was an elderly man with a white beard, wearing what looked like a cut-down fez. Next to him was a middle-aged character in a suit. As he watched, the two men wandered over to the door that led through to the garden. One thing about them surprised him. Although they were both wearing neatly polished leather footwear, the laces on both of their right shoes were undone, trailing behind them as they walked.

'In ten minutes,' called Mr Malik, 'the pageant will begin!'

Robert crossed to Maisie. She was walking backwards and forwards over the makeshift stage shaking sand on to the boards from a small bucket, trying to evoke the desert sands of Saudi Arabia. In the opening section of the pageant, Mahmud, lying underneath the stage, was due to poke a flag decorated with a crescent moon up through a crack in the stage. The flag was tightly furled, but, at a signal from Mr Malik, three hair-dryers, manned by boys from Dr Ali's class, would be trained on it and, in the headmaster's words, it would 'symbolically flutter across the stage'.

'You're right,' said Robert, 'I am a mess. I need to stop lying. I need to face up to what I am.'

'I shouldn't be too quick to do that,' said Maisie – 'you might not like what you are. I might not like what you are.'

'You can't go on lying to yourself,' said Robert. 'How can you expect people to take you seriously, if you don't have any convictions about anything?'

'Why do you want people to take you seriously?' said Maisie. 'One of the things I like about you is that you're so ridiculous.'

This was not quite how Robert had planned the conversation. Conversations with Maisie had a habit of going astray like this. You would go in there planning to discuss, say, her habit of ogling men in restaurants or her inability to repay money she had borrowed, or her ability to disseminate confidences throughout the whole of Wimbledon about five minutes after they had been imparted to her, and you would end up discussing the state of affairs in Europe, the merits of Beethoven, or, more usually, your own deficiencies.

'What I mean is,' said Robert, 'if I could be . . . you know . . . *me* . . . do you think you could, you . . . sort of . . .'

Maisie kissed him lightly on the cheek. 'I don't think there is a real you, Bobkins,' she said. 'I think you're just wonderfully insubstantial. That's why I love you.'

As opposed to the Islamic loony now prancing around on the other side of the room, thought Robert bitterly. Maybe he could report Malik to some high-up official in the Islamic world. During the summer term the man had consumed about twenty pints of Young's Special a week. Did he ever give to the poor? Not really. He seemed far more concerned to take money off the rich – especially if they happened to be Muslim. Did he believe any more than Robert did? Wasn't religion simply a pose with him, as it was for so many so-called Christians?

And yet – and yet . . . there was something glorious about him. Watching him now, as he shepherded parents in from the garden for the start of the pageant, listening to his deep, authoritative voice, he seemed, to Robert, more English than he himself could ever be. He seemed to summon up an England of green lawns, elegant teas and beautiful women in long dresses, trailing parasols. An England that, these days, existed only in Merchant–Ivory films. There was nothing squalidly European about him. He was imperial in scope.

'Ladies and gentlemen,' called the headmaster, 'we are ready to begin our pageant, to which we have given the lighthearted title *Islamic Wimbledon!*'

There was laughter, and a smattering of applause.

From the stairs came Rafiq, with the two strangers Robert had noticed earlier. If Mr Malik noticed them, he showed no sign of it. They kept to the back of the crowd, hugging the wall in an almost furtive way. Opposite them were two or three other characters Robert could not remember seeing before at the school. One – a round, jolly, brown man of about fifty – was vaguely familiar. He kept shifting from foot to foot, as if in pain. Mr Malik was guiding parents to their chairs.

There had been much discussion about the music. Mr Malik had been keen for it to 'bridge the gap between the musical traditions of East and West', and the result was something that sounded suspiciously like the soundtrack from a commercial advertising Singapore Airlines.

As the lights started to fade, Mr Malik gave the signal to the school's new music master, Mr Kureishi – a small, fat, serious man – who started to belabour an upright piano at the edge of the stage. Class 1 started to sing the opening chorus.

> A few hundred years ago
> In Saudi Arabia
> A man was born—
> A remarkable man,
> With remarkable behaviour!

Mr Malik had tried a number of rhymes for the opening number. He had been unable to find one for 'Mecca', and had rejected a stanza that rhymed 'keener' with 'Medina'. He himself was still not sure about 'Arabia' and 'behaviour', and he coughed loudly when the chorus reached this point in the song.

> He was the seal of the prophets—
> He really was an incredible guy.
> He still has a great deal to teach us,
> And if you listen I'll tell you why.
> Muhammad went up the mountain—
> He was up there for more than an hour—

But when he came down he was different,
He had been through the Night of Power.
He received a Divine Revelation,
Which we still read to this day.
And if you read it regularly,
you'll probably be OK.

At this point, Mahmud started to poke up the flag through the floorboards, and the offstage chorus went into the big number – the words of which were, mercifully, inaudible, but of a general philosophical nature.

As the flag waved around, to tentative applause, Mr Malik stepped into a spotlight and began. 'People have come to Britain from many lands,' he boomed, 'and today the country is a melting-pot! We are an integral ingredient of that pot!'

The audience were no surer of this than they had been of the song. The Islamic world, even in Wimbledon, thought Robert, was not quite ready for the fusion of styles unleashed on it by Mr Malik.

'We must adapt,' he went on, 'and become one with the UK while remaining ourselves. This is the message conveyed to you by the Independent Islamic Wimbledon Day Boys' School!'

As he spoke, various boys in various kinds of national costume trooped from the left and right of the stage; at the same moment, from beneath the stage, Mahmud started to poke a second flag up through the floorboards. It was, Robert noted with a mixture of horror and relief, the Union Jack. Some members of the audience applauded it.

Mr Malik raised his right arm. 'The conflict between Islam and Christianity,' he said, 'is an old battle. And one that no longer needs fighting!'

At this point the Bosnian refugee leaped on to the stage on a small wooden horse, designed and built for him by his mother. From the other side of the acting-space came the Husayn twins, tied together with a cardboard chain. 'Confess your sins, Muslim dogs,' said the Bosnian refugee, in slightly cautious tones, 'and become Christians, or we slash you up!' With these words he ran at the Husayn twins and started to belabour them with his plastic sword.

The boys stood this for as long as was decent, and then, after a particularly heavy blow to the head, the brothers grabbed the Bosnian refugee by both feet and up-ended him over the sand. 'Die, Christian!' said the fatter of the two twins.

This was not, as far as Robert remembered, in the script, but it seemed to be going down rather well with the audience. Mr Mafouz was clapping loudly.

But Robert's eye was no longer seriously drawn to the stage. The fat man over to his right had leaned down to the floor. When he straightened up again, Robert saw that he was carrying something. It was impossible, from this distance, to see what he was wearing on his feet, but it seemed likely that he was one short of a full complement of shoes, because in his right hand he was holding a large, brown, elastic-sided boot. Robert recognized him now: it was the restaurant-owner he had met on the day he had brought home Hasan – Mr Khan. Not only that: his was the round, jolly face he had seen in the window the day he had been hit on the head outside the room where he had been watching the Occultation of the Twenty-fourth Imam of the Wimbledon Dharjees.

21

Now, as he looked around the hall, Robert could see that the whole place was full of single men wearing one shoe. When had they come in? Presumably during the opening sequence of Mr Malik's pageant. It would not have been difficult to have removed the chairs from under the parents watching the curtain-raiser of Mr Malik's production – their attention was concentrated on the stage with what looked like some degree of permanence. Macbeth spotting a character he had recently bumped off could not have showed more interest.

Dr Ali, over by the kitchen door, in the darkness, was rocking backwards and forwards on his haunches, muttering something to himself. It was possible, thought Robert with some satisfaction, that he had finally got around to sentencing his employer to death. Serve the bastard right.

Robert looked around for Hasan. The little boy was no longer on his chair. Nor, as far as Robert could see, was he anywhere in the room. How had he managed to get out on his own?

Mr Malik, apparently unaware that his school was full of Twenty-fourthers, or that the Twenty-fourth Imam himself had started to display some of the talents referred to in Aziz's manuscript ('He shall come and go as he chooses, shall vanish and appear again'), was warming to his theme. 'This,' he said, indicating the Husayn twins, who were now beating the Crusader with his own sword, 'is what happens when religious bigotry rules a nation. We see it in Northern Ireland. We see it in Tehran. We see it in Wimbledon!'

The audience did not like the direction this was taking. Mr Husayn started to mutter something to his neighbour. Two or three of the ladies present clicked their tongues loudly.

Mr Malik went for safe ground. '*Those who believe and do good*,' he went on – '*the merciful will endow them with loving kindness!*'

Fatimah Bankhead was nodding in the gloom, and Mr Mafouz, too, was looking appreciative. Something told Robert that the headmaster had managed to find another line in the Koran that wasn't about chucking people into hell-fire and making them chew dust for the foreseeable future. Malik had got them on his side once again.

'If this school is to survive,' he went on, 'and if the things it stands for are to survive, then it must adapt! We must learn to live in peace with our neighbours!'

The Husayns had now got the Bosnian refugee up against the far wall and were thwacking him in the kidneys with a piece of wood. Malik turned towards them, managing to give the impression that all this was part of a carefully arranged plan, and said, 'Look! Look where hatred and bigotry leads!'

Robert could still not see where Hasan had gone, but he did see the janitor. Aziz was leering, wickedly. In his right hand he held a rather grubby trainer, and he was shaking it at the oblivious headmaster as Malik continued his speech. He looked pleased to have got it off, thought Robert. It must be torment for these guys to have to lace up a whole pair of feet every time they wished to pass themselves off as normal people.

'We are making our own rules,' went on Malik, 'and we must not allow others to dictate them to us. Our prosperity, and the prosperity of our children, depends on it!'

The Bosnian refugee was having trouble breathing. He had collapsed on the ground, and the Husayn twins, having appropriated his horse, were busy riding it round the stage, waving at the audience.

'Let us see them!' called Malik. 'Let us see the children of many lands!'

At this point the plan was for the entire school to process across the stage, carrying flags of many nations and waving their exam certificates. They were then to turn to the audience, waving lengths of green silk and go into a non-representational routine, devised by Mr Malik, entitled *The Dawn of Islam in*

Wimbledon. But, as the first wave of boys hit the side of the stage, the Twenty-fourther over to Robert's right – the fat man, restaurant-owning Mr Khan – raised his elastic-sided boot and yelled, 'The Prophet said, "Do not go with only one shoe!" '

Heads in the audience turned. They wore the polite expression of people who assumed that this was part of the show.

The Twenty-fourther was answered from across the hall and all along the stairs – quite a few more of the sect seemed to have crept in during the blackout that had preceded Mr Malik's speech. 'We go with one shoe to show the shame of breaking Islamic law!' they yelled.

Mr Mafouz, who was obviously still convinced that this was part of the pageant, started to applaud vigorously. The boys, who were supposed to file off the stage in order, stopped to peer out past the lights at this interruption, with the result that the next wave of boys collided with those milling around on the sand.

At this moment, Mr Khan the restaurant-owner yelled, 'Down with Malik! Down with Shah! Down with the Wimbledon Independent Boys' Islamic Day School!'

The other Twenty-fourthers, waving their right shoes above their heads, answered with the skill born of long practice, 'Down with Malik! Down with Shah! Down with the Independent Boys' Islamic Day School (Wimbledon)!'

The audience were now definitely convinced this was part of the headmaster's grand design. Mr Mahmud could be heard telling his wife that these people represented narrowness and intolerance in the Islamic world, and that they would shortly be vanquished by the rightly guided headmaster.

Before this happened, however, Rafiq, who had up to this point been seated with the staff and parents, leaped to his feet and, in full sight of the assembly, yanked off his right shoe. He seemed to be wearing wellington boots, and he had clearly not changed his socks for some days, because the people near him started to scrape their chairs across the floor in an effort to escape. 'Mr Khan here has been betrayed by the man who bears the name of Shah!' he yelled. 'That Shah is a hypocrite Muslim! He has not given his promised support to The Taste of Empire tandoori restaurant. Especially on Wednesdays!'

He pointed at the school's principal benefactor, the tall man in the elegantly cut suit who still bore an uncanny resemblance to the Duke of Edinburgh. This Mr Shah was looking at Mr Khan in a hurt and puzzled manner. 'My dear man,' he began to say – 'if this is part of our business disagreement – '

But, before he could finish, Rafiq heaved his wellington boot at the members of the school now threshing around on the stage under the lights. His example was followed by many of his companions. A hail of plimsolls, trainers, leather shoes, mountain boots and sandals rose up in the air and rained down on boys, parents and teachers.

Robert could see that Mr Malik, who still seemed remarkably unworried by all this, was signalling to someone at the back of the hall, behind him. And then the lights went out.

For a moment everything was quiet. *This is it*, thought Robert, *Molotov cocktails!* Next to him a woman was whispering something, although he could not hear what it was or what language she was speaking. Suddenly, high up above the stage, as high as that afternoon on the other side of the Common, a light flicked on and Hasan stood before them. At first Robert thought he was hovering above the blacked-out room; then he saw that he had been slipped over the banisters of the stairs and was perched, perilously, on the edge of one of the steps.

He was dressed all in white, in a long, flowing garment of bright silk. On his left foot was a golden sandal. His right foot was naked. He stretched out his hands over the faces of the crowd and began to speak. 'Bow down,' he began:

> Bow down and listen to my words!
> You are led by the wicked!
> You are led by transgressors!
> We wear one shoe
> To show your leaders have lied to you.

Bow down.
Bow down and listen to my words!

Quite a few people actually did start to bow down. Robert
himself, now fairly well trained in the act of Islamic prayer, felt a
strong urge to make, head first, for the parquet floor. The little
boy's voice was so eerily still! His face so withdrawn and delicate! His shoulders seemed to beg some invisible presence for
mercy!

> My father stabbed the seducer Hasan.
> I am the son of Hasan b. Namawar.
> I am the rightful Twenty-fourth Imam,
> And I return to punish.
> Bow down.
> There is fire in my fingers.
> Bow down!

Rafiq, observing the early success of this performance, joined
in well. 'Bow down!' he yelled. 'Bow down! Do not serve the
hypocrites! Bow down!'

Behind Robert a woman started to hiss. Whether it was fear or
anger or pleasure that made her do so was impossible to tell. All
over the hall, people were murmuring and hissing and breathing in sharply. This, thought Robert, was entirely reasonable.
As apparitions go, Hasan was certainly in the Angel Gabriel
class. At a school Open Day he was a guaranteed sensation.

Hasan's fingers quivered as he stretched out his hands over
the audience, but whether it was in a blessing or a curse was
impossible to tell. His sightless eyes sought the light as he went
on:

> Do not listen to the seducer.
> Do not listen to those who would lead you.
> Do not listen to those who betray the Law.
> I am the Twenty-fourth Imam.
> I come to destroy all this.
> I come to destroy this school!

People were getting quite emotional. Apart from Mr Mafouz, who was heard to announce that this was the best damn show he had seen since *The Bodyguard*, most of the parents seemed entirely convinced by Hasan's performance. One or two were openly crying. As the little boy's voice rose to a shriek the Twenty-fourthers came in, like Elvis Presley's backing group, perfectly on cue.

> Destroy this school!
> Bow down!
> Destroy this man!
> Destroy the seducer Malik!
> Bow down!
> There is fire in his fingers!
> Bow down!

In the gloom, Robert could see that Rafiq was fumbling with something underneath his jacket. Aziz the janitor, now up on the stairs, seemed to be holding something, and, with a shock, Robert realized it was a lighted match. *They really are*, he thought – *they really are going to burn the place to the ground*.

It was then that the lights came on – not just a single lamp, but a whole battery of arc lights ranged along the stage. It seemed, at first, like a deliberate theatrical effect, which indeed it probably was. And, if the Twenty-fourthers had a developed sense of theatre, they were mere amateurs compared to the man who now strode to the centre of the stage – Mr Malik, the one and only headmaster of the Boys' Independent Day Islamic Wimbledon School. His voice rose over Hasan's as he stretched his huge hands up towards the boy. 'Who has done this evil thing to you?' he said.

It was fairly obvious, to Robert anyway, who had done this evil thing to the little boy, but that didn't deprive the head-master's rhetorical question of any of its power.

'Who has filled your head with lies?' went on Malik. 'Who is the real seducer here? Who are the real seducers?'

The audience were now thoroughly enjoying this. They had not been sure about the song; the flags of many nations had left them decidedly cold; but this, their faces seemed to say, was worth leaving the shop to see.

'I will tell you,' went on Malik. 'This man Rafiq, who has claimed to be my friend, has sought to get his hands on a profitable enterprise. As has this fat swine Khan – a man who has the business ethics of a stoat!'

Hasan knew when he was outclassed. Anyway, in the rehearsal process to which he had been undoubtedly subjected by Rafiq and his friends, presumably no allowance had been made for an Oscar-award-winning interruption from the head-master.

Malik was now waving something above his head, and the Twenty-fourthers were looking at it with some interest. Robert recognized it as the manuscript that had been given him, along with the locket, last summer.

'This,' Malik shrieked, 'is the "document" that tells the story of the Twenty-fourth Imam. This is the "document" that gave substance to what, in previous times, were only whispers and rumours – a secret as closely guarded as the Golden Calf of the Druze. This is the "prophecy" with which my so-called friend has deceived you and deceived this child!'

Here he rounded on Rafiq, who, Robert now saw, was busy stuffing what looked like an oiled rag into a milk bottle.

'It is a forgery!' shouted Malik. 'I can prove it is a forgery! This gentleman here – this Khan – is the manager of The Taste of Empire restaurant, Balham, and owes our benefactor a consider-able sum of money. He has exploited the credulity of a section of the Wimbledon Dharjees in an attempt to wreck a business rival!'

Rafiq, the bottle in one hand, was now snarling at his employer. But his one-shoed companions, like the rest of the audience, were giving signs of enjoying the show.

Robert was more confused than ever. What was this religion, where what looked like theology turned out to be politics? Where loyalties and friendships seemed to acquire the force of a mystical belief? Where God was not a remote, almost human presence but a chord struck in the communal mind, echoing into every corner of life, facing you when you argued or made love or fought for money or power? He had no place here. He did not – could not – belong.

'The Twenty-third Imam – ' began Rafiq.

'There is no hidden imam among the Nizari Ismailis,' said Mr Malik. 'The Twenty-third Imam was, as you quite rightly say, stabbed by Hasan b. Namawar, but there is no record of the assassin having issue. You have taken a piece of true history and doctored it, gentlemen!'

The parents and staff gave this a round of well-deserved applause. Mr Akhtar was heard to say that the opening part of the pageant had been a total let-down, but this was 'world class' and gave evidence of 'money well spent'. People could be heard muttering that Malik was a man to watch.

And then the headmaster reached down, pulled off one of his expensive brown brogues, and waved it above his head. 'See!' he yelled. 'See! I go with one shoe!'

Everyone leaned forward in their seats. Robert, wondering whether he was about to witness a spectacular conversion, held his breath.

'I go with one shoe, my people,' went on Mr Malik, 'as my so-called "friend" asks you to do! And do you know what will happen if I go with one shoe?'

'What will happen?' asked a Twenty-fourther, who was clearly expert at this kind of dialogue. 'Tell us – what will happen?'

22

By way of reply, Mr Malik ran around the stage gobbling like a chicken for some seconds. He not only gobbled, he brandished the shoe and twitched, and did a fair impression of a man who has taken complete leave of his senses. Then he stopped and rounded on Rafiq. 'I will get my feet wet!' he yelled. 'I will carry on like a lunatic and be of no use to anyone!'

Then he turned to face the audience. He drew himself up to his full height and said, 'We must learn to fight for what is rightfully ours and also *to live in peace with our neighbours*. Do we wish our sons to go to war?'

There were shouts of 'No No!' and 'We do not wish this!' Robert was not aware of any immediate plans for conscription in the Wimbledon area, but the assembled crowd, who were showing as much volatility as the Roman plebeians after the death of Caesar, pressed in on the stage, shouting, crying, and waving their hands in the air.

'I put on my shoe!' screamed the headmaster. 'And I advise you to do the same!'

All over the darkened hall, men started to struggle back into their footwear – those, that is, who had not hurled it on to the stage. Those who had done so were openly weeping and grabbing hold of their neighbours' laces. Even Aziz the janitor was, in a highly emotional manner, trying to get his right toe into a canvas boot, although where he had got this from was unclear.

'Put on your shoes,' yelled the headmaster, 'and keep them on your feet always!'

Several people were trying to persuade Rafiq to put on his shoe, though whether this was for religious or hygienic reasons was not obvious. He did not seem keen to do so. Mr Mafouz had got hold of him and was beating his head against the back wall.

'Put on your shoes,' cried Malik again, 'I beg you! I beseech you! I implore you to do so! In the words of the Prophet to Abu Hurayra, *"Don't walk with only one shoe. Either go barefoot or wear shoes on both feet!"* '

This seemed to decide matters once and for all. Quite a few people took off both shoes, and those who didn't borrowed other people's until almost everyone in the room, apart from the engineering master, was equipped with a pair of properly Islamic feet. This generated a welcome and often jolly spirit of conviviality about the place. People were laughing and joking, clapping each other on the back and helping each other find some way of getting properly attired below the ankles.

Truth, Robert's old history master was fond of saying, *is whatever is confidently asserted and plausibly maintained*. The world of Islam seemed more purely about society than he had ever supposed possible. Islam, he saw clearly as if for the first time, was a nation, a nation on the march. It was only now that he finally understood a favourite phrase of the headmaster's: *Belief, my dear Wilson, is for us an intimate part of the social contract. It was Ayatollah Khomeini who pointed out that 'Islam is politics!'*

And Mr Malik was no ordinary politician. No one even seemed bothered about testing his claim that the document was a forgery. He was a strong man, and his word – like the Prophet's – was law.

Robert thought, bitterly, about Malik. Why should the man find everything so easy when Robert found it so hard? Why could *he* sway a room with a few well-chosen sentences, when on one of the few occasions when Robert had opened his mouth to express his real feelings he had been sentenced to death by a deranged mathematics master? Why was life so unfair? Was the reason the man was so complacent to do with the fact that his religion was *right*? That fate, destiny, whatever you liked to call it, was now on his side and the world was slowly turning his way, so that soon the power and the glory would all come from a long way east of Wimbledon?

Whatever the reason, something in Robert Wilson snapped. 'Who gives a toss how many shoes you wear?' he heard himself shout into a sudden silence. 'Who gives a toss? And who gives a monkeys how many blows it takes you to polish off a wall gecko, frankly? I mean, why is it that *all* you people construct your lives around the not very reliably reported table talk of a man whose chief claim to fame would seem to be his talent for carving up his immediate neighbours in some God-forsaken chunk of desert?'

The silence that had preceded his remarks seemed to lengthen miraculously.

'All I'm saying,' said Robert, 'is that when I joined this school I knew absolutely nothing about the Muslim faith, and that, after teaching here for a year, I really feel that ignorance is bliss, frankly!'

Up on the stage the colour was draining from the head-master's face. He moved towards Robert, and his voice had the throaty intensity of a cello in the slow movement of the Elgar concerto. 'Wilson,' he said, reaching out towards his first recruit. 'Wilson! Do you know what you are saying? You are a Muslim, Wilson, are you not?'

'No,' said Robert, with some satisfaction – 'I am not. I have never been a Muslim. I do not wish to be a Muslim. I have no plans to be a Muslim. I would, frankly, rather swim the Helles-pont in November than be a Muslim.'

This did not go down well with the punters. Many of them looked as if they might well be breaking into tears in the near future.

Mr Malik held out his arms to Robert. 'Wilson –' he began.

'Oh, stop calling me "Wilson", can't you?' said Robert – 'as if we were both at some non-existent public school. You live in a fantasy world. And you don't know anything about me. You don't know who I am, or what I think, or what I feel about anything.'

Mr Malik looked utterly devastated. 'Wilson,' he began, in a trembling voice. 'You are a Muslim. And, as a Muslim – '

'I am not a Muslim,' said Robert. 'I only said I was because I needed a job. I am not – repeat, not – Muslim. Do I look like a Muslim?'

The crowd fastened on this new act with enthusiasm. Mr Akhtar could be heard to say that Robert did not look like a Muslim. Indeed, he had always thought there was something funny about Wilson. Mr Mafouz, his thick, black eyebrows well down in his face, was fighting his way through the crowd towards his son's form master.

Robert started to walk up to the stage, and, like the Red Sea, parents, staff and pupils parted to let him pass.

Mr Malik had recovered well. He was managing some kind of transition, from deeply wounded to sad but hopeful. 'I suppose,' he said, 'someone who lies out of fear of or respect for the truth is to be helped and not scorned. I liked you, Wilson, because I saw your weakness. Like you, I feel, I am not a very good Muslim!'

The house was divided on this. Some people thought the headmaster was an absolutely first-class Muslim, while Dr Ali declared him to be a blasphemer, a hypocrite and no better than the vomit of a dog.

'It's not a question of not being a *good* Muslim,' yelled Robert, as he climbed up on to the stage – 'I just am not a Muslim at all. I am an imitation Muslim, ladies and gentlemen. How many times do I have to say this to get it into your head?'

Fatimah Bankhead told her immediate neighbour that she viewed this as an encouraging sign. Imitation, she said, was the sincerest form of flattery.

Up on the stage, Mr Malik spread his hands in a gesture of endless tolerance. 'Perhaps,' he said, 'you will come to understand that – '

'I will never come to understand,' said Robert, 'because your religion is, to me, completely and utterly incomprehensible. I believe – '

Malik brightened a little at this remark. 'What do you believe, Wilson?'

Robert looked down from the stage at the faces of the crowd. He saw Mahmud, his eyes wide with horror at what was happening. He saw Dr Ali, his nose quivering with excitement, tensing himself like a man about to burst into song. And he saw Maisie. She was by the door to the front garden. Her big, black eyes looked reproachfully up at him from the white oval of her face. What did he believe? The question she was always asking him.

'Oh,' he said, 'I believe in something really sensible. Of course. I believe that Jesus Christ came down from heaven and was born of a Virgin, turned water into wine, walked on the water, and then was crucified and whizzed back up to heaven!'

Mr Malik stretched out his arms to him. 'There is no need to caricature your beliefs, Wilson,' he said. 'If you have lied to us, you have lied for a reason. The great religions of the world have more in common than you might think. And if we worship one God –'

'Oh, then that's fine, isn't it?' said Robert. 'I'll swap you the Garden of Gethsemane for the Night of Power, you know? You'll let us believe something clearly insane, and we can allow you to do the same.'

Mr Malik's brow wrinkled. He seemed upset again. 'What are you saying, Wilson? I do not understand. You are a Christian? You are a Muslim? What are you?'

Robert strode across the sand towards his headmaster. Between them lay the cardboard chain-mail and the plastic sword that had belonged to the Bosnian refugee, who was now being given mouth-to-mouth resuscitation by Mr Husayn. Robert picked up the imitation Crusader armour and held it aloft, facing out to the audience. 'I'm nothing,' he said. 'Don't you understand? England is full of people who are nothing. You're living in a country that doesn't exist. A country where people go to church, and try and help their neighbours, and bicycle to work down country lanes, and believe in . . . ' Here he brandished the armour and its painted cross in the faces of the crowd. ' . . . all this!'

The Bosnian refugee, coming round in the arms of Mr Husayn, was heard to order his men to slay the Saracen dogs.

Robert rounded on Mr Malik. He had always thought, somehow, that Malik had seen through him. That the headmaster was keeping him on for his own private amusement. And it was this knowledge that allowed him to suspect that, at last, someone had really understood quite how empty he was inside. What finally broke him was the realization that here was yet another person who, like his parents, thought him a stronger, nobler person than he actually was. Why did the world assume that you must be interested in any kind of truth, let alone the fundamental variety? Why did people always want you to have aspirations?

'England,' went on Robert, 'is no longer anything to *do* with the country that carved up India or shipped out whole generations of Africans as slaves. It's a squalid little place, full of people who don't believe in anything. Am I making that clear? I don't believe in *anything*. I think it's all a load of toss really. That is my considered opinion.'

Mr Malik looked at his first member of staff. There was infinite sadness in his eyes. 'You believe in something, Wilson,' he said. 'You must believe in something. Everyone must believe in something.'

Robert looked across at Maisie. He felt suddenly tired. As if all these people were a dream. As if he had been asleep for a whole year. He would say what he had to say, and then he would leave. He would get out – not only of the school, but of the suburb. He would find somewhere a long way away from Mr Malik, from his parents, and from everyone else who wished him well.

'Maybe I do,' he said eventually. 'Maybe I do.'

Then, with the cardboard armour in one hand and the plastic sword in the other, he stepped slowly down from the stage and walked through the assembly to where Maisie was waiting.

'Look,' he said, 'you're the only person who understands.

We're . . . well, we're . . . Wimbledon, aren't we? What are you doing here? You know you don't belong here, don't you?'

Maisie looked back at him steadily.

'I'm going!' he said. 'Will you come with me?'

Maisie looked at him. She sighed. Then she looked up at the headmaster, standing on the shabby stage in his crumpled green suit. Malik mopped his forehead, glowing under the lights.

'No,' she said – 'I won't!'

23

Robert had not expected her to say this.

'Why not?' he said.

She looked impatient. 'Because, Bobkins,' she said, 'I love him.'

'Love who?' said Robert.

'Mr Malik!' said Maisie.

This created a sensation in the audience. If they had ever had doubts about their headmaster, they were dispelled instantly. The general feeling seemed to be that not only was Mr Malik a good public speaker and a man of learning and conviction, he had also performed well in the Islamic virility stakes.

Up on the platform, Mr Malik was positively preening himself. He smoothed his hair back over his ears and gave a little smile at a mother in the front row.

'You *love* him?'

'I'm afraid I do, Bobkins!' said Maisie, with a sigh. 'I'm afraid he means more to me than anything else.' She shook her head, and her thick, black hair trembled under her scarf. One of the spotlights caught her face.

'Why?' said Robert.

'I don't know,' replied Maisie. 'Maybe it's Muslim men. They have something you just don't have!'

Robert did not like the way this conversation was going, but there seemed no easy way to get control either over it or over its alarmingly public nature.

'What,' said Robert with heavy irony, 'do Muslim men have that I don't?'

He recalled, with some bitterness, that it was only after he had publicly announced his conversion that she had become interested in him. Was she just kinky for Muslims, the way some people were kinky for football-players or trombonists? Perhaps he should reconsider his position.

'They're virile,' said Maisie. 'They're strong! They're decisive! They're proud and certain and noble!'

This went down incredibly well with the male members of the audience. Even Rafiq could be heard to say that this was fair comment. Mr Mafouz, who had been looking deeply depressed during Robert's altercation with the headmaster, straightened himself up and threw out his chest. Mr Akhtar was seen to stroke his moustache.

'They're gentle, too,' went on Maisie, 'and loyal and straight-forward and kind and clever and respectful and good with children and God-fearing!'

This brought a smattering of applause. Robert looked up at the headmaster, who was stretching out his hands to Maisie. 'Come to me, my daughter!' said Malik, in deep, resonant tones. Maisie squared her shoulders and, with a toss of her head, prepared to come to him. She looked, thought Robert grimly, as if she was prepared to get on the floor and kiss his feet should this prove necessary.

'I wonder why this should be!' shrieked Robert. 'What is it makes them so amazingly wonderful? Is it that they don't drink except behind closed doors? Is it halal meat – is that it? Is it that they have devised an unusually energetic form of prayer?'

Mr Malik, his eyes big with grief, was still holding out his hands to Maisie. 'Maisie,' he said, 'come to me! And, Wilson, go! Go in peace. Without curses or recrimination.' He put his head to one side. 'If you have been foolish,' he said, 'God will forgive you. He forgives the ignorant.'

Maisie started towards the stage. As she walked, women touched her dress, murmuring words of encouragement, and men, with wistful smiles on their faces, stepped back to let her pass.

'I suppose,' yelled Robert, 'it's their role model! I suppose it's because Muhammad was such a terrific guy! Is that it?'

No one answered this question, but there was suddenly a dangerous silence in the room.

'I mean,' went on Robert, shaking his long, lank, blond hair across his face, 'it may just be that I'm an ignorant Brit and don't know anything about anything, but the thing that really puzzles me about your religion is the endless respect you're supposed to pay to this guy. What is it all in aid of, may I ask? I mean, who was he? What makes him such a big cheese?'

Mr Malik glanced down at the audience. He looked worried. 'Please, Wilson,' he said, 'go now. Go back into Wimbledon, and we will forget that we ever met. Do not – '

'I'm only asking,' said Robert, 'because I have picked up a little gen about Islam over the course of the last year and I have formulated my view of your top man which, if you like, I will be happy to give to you!'

Mr Malik, and several others in the audience, winced visibly. 'I really would not do that if I was you, Wilson!' said the headmaster.

But Robert did it.

He went on to give detailed, and not always accurate, criticisms of the *hadiths* of the Prophet. He questioned their relevance to modern society, their internal logic, and their implications for women, infidels and anyone not prepared to accept the central tenets of Islam. He quoted several at length, and laughed, mockingly, during his rendition of them.

After he had questioned the Prophet's reported views, he went on to denigrate his character in sometimes offensive terms. He went on to criticize, in an uninformed way, the Prophet's skill as a military tactician, and made several spectacularly ill-informed remarks about the history of Islam.

At this point, Mr Malik, who like almost everyone else in the room had his hands over his ears, begged him to stop. He explained that one of the missions of the Wimbledon Islamic Independent Boys' Day School was to make peace between religions and communities, and that he, personally, along with the Wimbledon Dharjee businessman Mr Shah, had worked hard over the last year to create an institution that would 'build bridges' between Muslims and Christians and, indeed, any other decent, civilized individuals who were prepared to let others live with their faith without insult or abuse. He wept at this point.

He explained how Mr Shah's rival, the restaurant-owning Mr Khan, had been trying to destroy the unity of the Muslim community, and said that their unity was only an aspect of the wider union that peace-loving and civilized Muslim men and women sought with the country to which they had come.

He went on to beg Robert not to say any more. He said that, unlike certain people he could mention in the hall – here he looked narrowly at Rafiq and Dr Ali – he was a reasonable man, and that some in his community had said he was 'a hypocrite' because he went too far in accommodating others' beliefs and opinions. He said he was not a hypocrite. He repeated that he was a sincere, if not always scrupulous, Muslim, and he repeated several *hadiths* of the Prophet – to whom, in this context, he gave the traditional blessing – to support his view that Islam was a tolerant, generous and beautifully constructed faith.

But, he said, there was a limit. Many people in the hall agreed, and said, loudly, that Robert Wilson had already passed it. Dr Ali made reference to his earlier sentence on the reception-class teacher, and several parents said that this was 'too good' for the young man who was now standing by the door, open to the summer day, waving a plastic sword and cardboard armour decorated with a crucifix at pupils, teachers and parents associated with the Wimbledon Islamic Independent Boys' Day School.

'Why do you all think you're *right*?' Robert was yelling. 'What makes you so *certain*?'

Mr Malik begged for silence, and got it. He appealed to Robert Wilson as an English gentleman. He appealed to his sense of honour and fair play. He mentioned the British royal family and the ancient universities of Oxford and Cambridge, to which, he reminded him, he belonged, and he spoke, movingly, of the game of cricket. 'Try and play a straight bat, Wilson!' he said.

Robert said he was not an English gentleman and he was

incapable of playing a straight bat. He said that he had only played cricket once or twice, and that throughout his schooldays he had persuaded his mother to 'write him a note'. He said he had lied about a great deal more than being or not being a Muslim. He told Mr Chaudhry, whom he referred to as 'the Nabob', that he had never been to Oxford or Cambridge, that he had no academic qualifications whatsoever apart from a GCE in woodwork, and that if Mr Malik had not been such a 'gullible idiot' he would never have employed someone so obviously fraudulent as he, Robert Wilson. He maintained, also, that he felt no loyalty to his family, describing his father as 'the kind of guy you would not want to get stuck in a lift with' and his mother as 'Wimbledon's answer to Jackie Onassis'.

He went on to talk about Wimbledon. He put forward the view that almost everyone in Wimbledon was, like him, completely lacking in convictions, principles or indeed anything that makes human beings tolerable. He said Wimbledon was 'an armpit'. 'Why did the Bhajjis, or whatever they call themselves, bother to cross the world to *Wimbledon*?' he asked. He foamed at the mouth at this point, and started to bang his plastic sword on the front door.

He then went on to make several spectacularly insulting, ill-thought-out remarks about the Koran. He added that *Morals and Manners in Islam* by Marwan Ibrahim Al-Kaysi was the most boring book he had ever read.

At this point he returned, once again, to the subject of Muhammad, saying that he had 'one or two home truths to put across'. He began, once again, to make wildly inaccurate and distorted remarks about the Prophet. It was at this point – and it is not necessary here to mention even the general drift of his remarks, except to say that they were offensive in the extreme – that several members of the school, both parents and staff, started towards him in an urgent and often openly angry manner. They pulled at his clothes, and he responded by beating them around the head with his plastic sword.

The headmaster appealed for calm. He did not get it. Robert ran for the street.

He was followed by Mr Mafouz, Mr and Mrs Akhtar, Mr and Mrs Mahmud, Mr Sheikh, Mr Shah, running side by side with the restaurant-owning Mr Khan, Mr and Mrs Husayn, Fatimah Bankhead, the parents of the Bosnian refugee (whose name no one could pronounce), Mr and Mrs Khan, Mr Malik, Dr Ali, Rafiq (who was now wearing two left-footed wellington boots) and Maisie. Behind them came other parents and every single child in the school – people united not only by a common faith and a common confidence and belief in their school but also by a deep desire to beat Robert Wilson to a pulp.

He ran fast. People who saw him pass – and there were people in the High Street on that summer afternoon who had known him since he was a boy – agreed that he had never run so fast in his life. His lank, blond hair bounced off his temples, and his long, thin legs pounded the pavement as, behind him, over a hundred very angry British Muslims screamed, shook their fists, and spat at his heels.

They did not catch him. Robert ran down the High Street towards Wimbledon Hill. By the time he reached the round-about at the top of the hill and swerved right along the Ridge-way, they were spread out in a long line behind him. But none of them gave up the pursuit. Several women, who joined in enthusiastically, were in tears. The men at the head of the chase – Mr Mafouz and Mr Sheikh – were starting to gain on him as he panted his way past trim suburban houses, his face purple with effort, his neck damp with sweat.

Only one person did not seek to follow Robert Wilson, 'the fraudulent Muslim, the apostate and the blasphemer', as he later became known inside the community. He was left behind on the stairs above the makeshift stage in the Great Hall. Hasan tilted his fragile little face up at the lights as the crowd screamed and jostled out of the school, but he made no sound himself. He put his big, ungainly head to one side, like a bird listening for worms.

He gave no sign of hearing the commotion. Or of the lorry that roared past the school, turned right at the roundabout, and thundered down the Ridgeway. Or of the wild squeal of its brakes as Robert, too frightened and exhausted to look, darted out into its path. Or of the noise of the ambulance siren, wailing like a call to prayer, as it sped up the hill to take Robert away. The only thing to which Hasan seemed to be listening was silence. The silence that had been there before all these little, local noises. The silence that he had seemed to hear behind the cries and shouts in the hall and that was there, once more, stretching endlessly away, after they, like the ambulance, had departed.

24

The Wimbledon Islamic Independent Day School for Boys is still there. And, in case there should be any doubt about the word order of the title, Mr Malik has erected a large, handsome notice-board in the front garden. You may see the buildings as you pass down the High Street going south. The school has now bought two buildings on either side and is negotiating for a large playing-field in Raynes Park.

Maisie and Mr Malik were married in the autumn term that followed Robert's accident. They started to have children almost immediately. Maisie gave the headmaster two boys – Yusuf and Ahmed – causing several people to remark, openly, that he 'had very strong seed' – and, subsequently, a girl whom Maisie insisted on calling Roberta. The children are all polite, hard-working and well-behaved Muslims.

The school has prospered too. It now has a total staff of twelve, including Dr Ali, who has not sentenced anyone to death for years, and Rafiq, who has sworn eternal allegiance to Mr Malik and frequently describes him as 'a genius'. Mr Malik himself has not touched alcohol for four years, and, while observing his duties as a Muslim most carefully, is still fond of quoting *hadiths* that emphasize the Prophet's tolerance and good sense.

The pupils, too, are doing well (although Anwar Mafouz failed all his GCSEs and now works with his father in the travel agency). Sheikh took up his Oxford place at the age of fifteen, and one of the Husayn twins, to the surprise of his father, gained a place at Exeter University (although his brother is now serving a short sentence at an open prison near Winchester). The school is often spoken of as a model for others in the neighbourhood, and last year it defeated Cranborne at cricket, rugby, cross-country running and chess. There is even talk of admitting some non-Muslim children and for them to be allowed to form a Christian Circle when the others are at daily prayers.

Hasan was sent back to live with Mr Shah. He is a big boy now and helps out at the school. Mr Malik has taught him Braille, and he compiles mailing-lists of prospective parents. He never mentions his Occultation, although once or twice he has been heard telling the school cat that he is someone rather important.

Aziz, too, is a reformed character. He cleans the whole school, from top to bottom, three times a week. 'Say what you like,' he can be heard to say with a grin – 'Dharjee, Ismaili, we are all Muslim and we all must be brothers and not surrender or oppress!'

Robert Wilson recovered from his encounter with the lorry; it was generally agreed he got off more lightly than he would have done had he fallen into the hands of the local Muslim population. He has never really been the same since, although his mother told a neighbour recently that 'he was always as hopeless as this really'. He has a set of symptoms – listlessness, lack of interest in the world, and a tendency to sleep more than twelve to fifteen hours out of the twenty-four – that make him unfit for any kind of regular employment, but at least now he has a doctor's note to explain the fact to the authorities.

He still lives at home. He spends most of his days walking Badger across the Common. He always takes the same route. He follows the golf course, past Caesar's Camp, up to the Windmill and then returns to Wimbledon Park Road via one of the streets that slope down from Parkside, past quiet, ordered suburban houses, protected by English trees and English lawns. He never walks on the same side of the road as the Wimbledon Islamic Independent Day School for Boys, and if he happens to pass the place he turns his eyes away.

As he walks, he mutters to himself, though no one has ever heard what he is saying or understood why he sometimes gets angry or agitated. If a passer-by stops to talk to him – which few do, since his moods can be unpredictable – he will stand and chat for hours. Sometimes he is to be found in the Frog and Ferret, with the dog by his side, and there he usually spends hours talking to Mr Purkiss of the Wimbledon Interplanetary Society. People keep away from them. Unlike Mr Shah, who has opened two new shops in the High Street, or plump Mr Kureishi, who gives recitals in the public library, they are not really part of the community of Wimbledon.

AUTHOR'S NOTE

The Wimbledon Dharjees are, of course, an entirely fictitious Islamic sect, but the group from which they are alleged to come, the Nizari Ismailis, are a real and well-documented group of Shiite Muslims. A full account of the true, and incredible, story of Hasan the Second, the Twenty-third Imam of the Nizari Ismailis, is to be found in Bernard Lewis's *The Assassins* (Weidenfeld & Nicolson, 1967). Robert's one guide to his assumed religion, *Morals and Manners in Islam, a Guide to Islamic Adab*, by Marwan Ibrahim Al-Kaysi, was published by the Islamic Foundation in 1986.